ALEX

— VS —

AXEL
The Impossible Quests

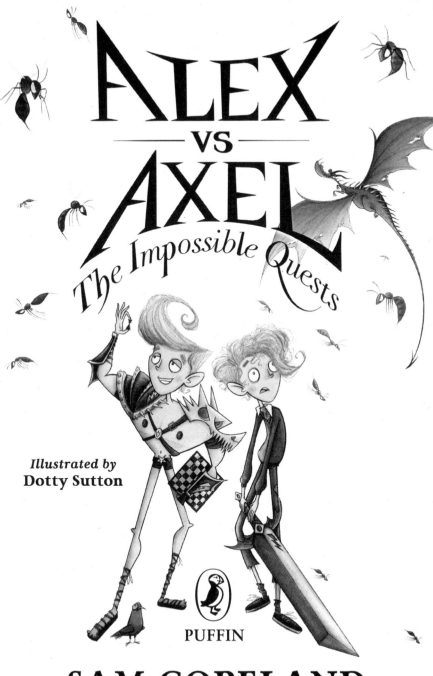

Alex
vs
Axel
The Impossible Quests

Illustrated by
Dotty Sutton

PUFFIN

SAM COPELAND

PUFFIN BOOKS

UK | USA | Canada | Ireland | Australia
India | New Zealand | South Africa

Puffin Books is part of the Penguin Random House group of companies
whose addresses can be found at global.penguinrandomhouse.com

www.penguin.co.uk
www.puffin.co.uk
www.ladybird.co.uk

First published 2024

001

Set in 10.5/18pt Kudryashev
Typeset by Jouve (UK), Milton Keynes
Printed and bound in Great Britain by Clays Ltd, Elcograf S.p.A.

The authorized representative in the EEA is Penguin Random House Ireland,
Morrison Chambers, 32 Nassau Street, Dublin D02 YH68

A CIP catalogue record for this book is available from the British Library

ISBN: 978-0-241-57313-6

All correspondence to:
Puffin Books
Penguin Random House Children's
One Embassy Gardens, 8 Viaduct Gardens, London SW11 7BW

MIX
Paper | Supporting
responsible forestry
FSC® C018179
www.fsc.org

Penguin Random House is committed to a
sustainable future for our business, our readers
and our planet. This book is made from Forest
Stewardship Council® certified paper.

To my brother and sister, Ray and Liz.

CONTENTS

The fates are sealed, cannot be fled,
A world of wonder lies ahead ...

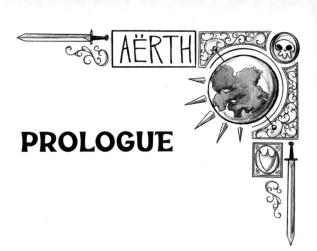

PROLOGUE

The story had to end.

The old man stilled his trembling hands and dipped his quill in the pot of ink, his heart pounding as hard as the fists on the front door.

A flash of lightning lit the room as he scribbled feverishly on the page before him, rain lashing the study window. With a crack, it burst open, wind whipping at his white beard and what little wispy hair remained on his head. The candles on his desk sputtered and died.

They hadn't been slowed down by the storm that the old man had written into their way, and now time had almost run out. He had to finish before they took the Book from him and an endless emptiness swallowed everything.

The door split with a crack of wood. Faster he wrote, the ink smudging as his hand raced across the page.

The exchange had to be made. A soul for a soul. One boy in place of another. A last hope from another world.

The door splintered open, followed by the thunder of footsteps on the stairs. Then they were in the room. One of the intruders pressed a knife against the old man's neck and whispered in his ear.

'Put the quill down.'

'You're too late, Tarka Screed,' the old man said.

'I think not. We have you. We have the Book. We have everything we need. So put it down, Narrator,' repeated Screed, her voice as cold as the blade she was holding. 'Now.'

The tip of the knife pressed harder against the old man's throat. He gently set the quill down on his desk, his face crinkling into a soft smile of relief.

Just in time, the last full stop had been placed. He had finished.

One last tale before the end of the world.

CHAPTER ONE

THE EXCHANGE

'It's not the end of the world, Alex,' said Mr Grimes.

Alex Always looked down at his trousers.

'It's not the end of my legs either. They're halfway up my shins. I *cannot* wear these. I just can't.'

'You look . . . fine,' the PE teacher said, doing very little to stifle the grin matched by half the children in the changing room. 'I mean, if you hadn't managed to lose your own clothes in the first place, you wouldn't have to wear stuff from lost property.'

'I didn't lose them!'

Alex glared at the four kids laughing behind their hands: Nathan, Simone, Willard and Sniper. They'd stolen his clothes. He knew it, but he'd be in even more trouble if he said anything.

'Whatever. You'll just have to ask your mum to replace them,' Mr Grimes said and sauntered out before Alex could remind him that he didn't *have* a mum but lived with his gran, and there was no way she could afford to buy him new clothes anyway.

5

'Why did you take them?' Alex asked Nathan.

'Serves you right for being a nerd!' Nathan brayed.

'I'm not a nerd!'

'Then how come you pass every single test with full marks? Nerd.'

Alex looked down at his feet. 'I just have a good memory, that's all.' And then he looked up. 'Now let me have them back!' he demanded, trying to fake the bravery he didn't feel.

'Yeah, so kneel down in front of me and I might take pity on you,' Nathan said, grinning from ear to ear. The class fell silent, watching.

Alex glanced at his too-short trousers and the tiny shoes that were already rubbing his toes into blisters. Wasn't this humiliating enough? But the thought of having to tell Gran was worse; he had no choice. Cheeks burning, he knelt.

'Now say, "please",' Nathan sneered.

Wanting the ground to swallow him, Alex whispered, 'Please.'

'Say it loudly so everyone can hear, yeah? "Please give me my clothes back, *sir*."'

'Please give me my clothes back, sir,' Alex said, tears pricking at his eyes.

'Oh, sorry!' Nathan gave a barking laugh. 'I chucked them on the roof, bro.'

Alex stood up, his heart pounding with humiliation, and before the tears spilled, before the silence could erupt into laughter, he charged out of the changing room and through the school gates towards home.

How could he tell Gran what had happened? It was the last thing they needed right now. The kitchen counter was already awash with overdue bills. Alex sighed. There was only one thing for it. It was a faint hope, but *anything* was better than asking Gran to fork out for new clothes.

Pulling out his phone, Alex texted her that he was going to Sienna's house. But instead he hopped on the bus. As it pulled away, Alex stared out of the window, trying to ignore the shame crawling up his neck.

It was time to visit his father.

As Alex slipped through the gate and up the drive of his father's house, he reflected again on how hopeless an idea this was.

Alex hadn't seen his father in nearly a year. Had only met him for the first time eighteen months ago. His father had never been part of his life; he'd never taught him how to ride a bike, never played football with him, never given him so much as a birthday card. Would he really help now? Only one way to find out.

Alex rang the doorbell. There was a pause, then the door swung open, and there was his father.

His face fell at the sight of Alex. 'What do *you* want?'

'Hi, Dad, so I –'

'I've told you before – don't call me that.'

'Yes, sorry, Mr Abiss.' Alex swallowed his shame again. 'So . . . I know you told me not to come here again but, well, I need a new uniform and Gran's really short of –'

Mr Abiss's lip curled. 'Ah, so it's money you're after.'

'No, um, yes, I –'

'Well, I don't have any.'

Alex couldn't help but let out a sharp laugh; the vast house in front of him told a different story.

'Not for you, anyway,' Alex's father continued. 'You are not *my* responsibility. You were an *accident*. And an expensive one, might I add. I already pay your grandmother the *generous* allowance my lawyers agreed with her. I'm not a charity.'

'But Da–'

'Don't call me that!'

Alex's face fell. He knew his trip had been a waste.

'Oh, don't look so pathetic,' Mr Abiss snapped. 'Stand up for yourself for once and don't be such a . . . disappointment.'

The door slammed in Alex's face, leaving him standing alone, his father's words reverberating in his soul.

Pathetic. Disappointment.

They were like daggers.

Alex boarded the bus home. His heart was deflated, a limp balloon.

'I mean, how do you even go about losing your clothes anyway?' Gran asked next morning, after Alex had appeared in the kitchen in his too-short lost property trousers and told her what had happened. 'You never forget *anything*. Not like your old gran.'

Alex sniffed and said, 'You're not *that* forgetful, Gran.'

Gran flashed a smile at him, but it didn't last long.

'Look, I'm sorry, love,' she continued. 'I'll get you new trousers, soon as I can afford it. It's payday in a couple of weeks. Until then you'll just have to make do. No one will notice.'

Alex had very serious doubts about *that*.

He turned away, glancing over the kitchen counter.

Another letter had appeared on the pile. He picked it up, stomach churning.

'Gran!' Alex gasped, staring at the bill. 'This is for twenty thousand pounds! And it says if we don't pay it in two weeks we'll get evicted. This is serious!'

Gran gave him a pained smile. 'Don't worry, love. Something'll turn up.'

'Like what? Where are we going to find that kind of money?'

'I've got my jewellery. That'll get us a bit.'

Alex didn't know much about jewellery, but he knew a couple of gold bands and an engagement ring with one tiny diamond wouldn't fetch anywhere near the sort of money they needed.

'But that won't be enough!'

'Well, it'll buy us some time until I think of summat else,' Gran said, brow furrowed.

Before Alex could protest any further, the doorbell rang. Through the frosted glass he could spy the twig-legged frame of his best friend, Sienna. The thought of her seeing him in these trousers made him cringe, but there was nothing that could be done.

Even though she was short for her age, Sienna always made the flat feel somehow smaller. It wasn't her fault; Alex just felt uncomfortable having her see where he and Gran lived. It was a damp one-bedroom flat (he had the bedroom and his gran slept in the sitting room). Sienna had a nice, warm flat with two bedrooms, two sofas and two parents.

'You think I care where you live?' she'd asked once when Alex had muttered something about being embarrassed. 'I don't. So stop talking nonsense.'

He *had* stopped talking at the time, but Sienna's words didn't stop Alex from thinking it, or from seeing the black mould that bloomed across the walls no matter what they scrubbed it with, or the cigarette burn on the threadbare, second-hand sofa and the chipped, non-matching mugs on the sideboard. They didn't stop Gran's face crumpling with worry every time she wrote a shopping list, or stop the bills piling up on the kitchen counter, even though Gran worked two jobs. And it hadn't stopped the latest bill. Twenty thousand pounds . . . Where could they get that kind of money in two weeks?

'Hey, Alex. A'right, Mrs A,' Sienna said, as Alex opened the door.

'A'right, chuck?' Gran replied, sipping a cup of tea. Their cat, a wiry ginger tom called Mr Sunshine, all spiteful claws and menacing hisses, slunk between her legs. 'Don't forget your sandwich, Alex. And message us if you're going to be late home!'

A moment later, Alex and Sienna were out in the biting November morning. Standing by the door, stamping his feet to keep warm, was Irving, Alex's other best friend. Irving, round of frame, coal-haired and snow-pale, was never seen out of black clothes if he could help it, so their school uniform suited him a treat.

'All right, Irving?' Alex asked.

'Obviously not,' Irving replied. 'The thought of school weighs heavy upon my soul, like a void of misery.'

'Ah, come on, it's not so bad!' Sienna protested.

'It is! My spirit craves poetry! Art! Mournful music!'

Sienna rolled her eyes.

'It'll be fine,' Alex sniffed.

'Fine for you!' Irving groaned. 'Not all of us have a photographic memory! Some of us have brains more focused on the beauty of petals falling from a dying flower.'

'Look, there are worse things than school, you know!' snapped Alex. Immediately, he saw the look of surprise and hurt on Irving's face. 'I'm sorry, Irv. I'm just a bit stressed. Gran got a bill. From debt collectors. We have to find twenty grand in two weeks or we get kicked out.'

Sienna and Irving gasped in horror.

'What you going to do?' Sienna asked.

'Dunno,' Alex replied flatly.

The three walked in silence until Alex broke it, with a grim smile.

'Neither of you going to comment on the obvious?'

'Obvious what?' Irving asked.

'The obvious state of my trousers.' Alex lifted his leg to demonstrate his point.

'What about them?' Irving asked shiftily.

'Don't pretend you haven't noticed.'

'They *are* a bit on the short side,' Sienna said, giving a tiny shrug.

'Above-ankle length is fashionable now,' Irving said.

'Irving, no offence,' Alex replied. 'But you have the fashion sense of a Victorian funeral director.'

Irving nodded. 'No offence taken.'

'No one'll notice, though,' Sienna added.

Less than two minutes later, Sienna was proved wrong.

'Still in your lost property costume, bro?' Nathan Jones laughed, trying to trip Alex up as he walked through the school gates.

'Shut up, Nathan,' Alex muttered.

'Yeah, try and make me.' Nathan sneered.

'Just leave it,' Sienna said to Nathan, and gave Alex a smile that lay somewhere between encouragement and sympathy and made him want to crawl into a hole somewhere.

The rest of the morning was no better, and by the time the bell rang for lunch Alex still wanted to crawl into his hole, but this time never get out.

'Hey,' Sienna said, catching him up between the playing fields. 'You didn't wait for me.'

'Hey,' Alex replied, glumly. 'Sorry, I just had to . . .' The rest of the sentence never made it out of his mouth. 'You know, I should just punch Nathan straight in his stupid nose.'

'Yeah. But, Alex, that's not you,' Sienna replied, kicking through a pile of leaves.

'Yeah, because I'm a coward.'

Over the last year, Alex had concocted countless fantasies of squaring up to his bullies. But he never did. Every time he was confronted by them – their cold-eyed leader, Nathan; the vast meat-slab twins, Willard and Sniper; clever, cruel Simone – fear gripped his heart, squeezed the dignity out of him and crumbled his courage to dust. And he hated himself for it.

It was behind the eyes, whatever it took to be strong – they had it, Nathan and his mates, and Alex didn't.

Peeping out from skin the colour of cheap mayonnaise were watery blue eyes that filled up far too easily with tears, and behind them, a brain that remembered every insult, every humiliation, in perfect detail.

Sometimes Alex wished he could make himself forget, but he couldn't. The memory of the day before, kneeling in front of Nathan, made him die a tiny bit inside and he swore to himself: never again.

Never again would he kneel to anybody.

'No. It's just not you – and that's why I like you,' Sienna said. 'Serious. You aren't one of them wastemen.'

'No, instead I'm weak.'

'You're not weak, you're brilliant. They're just jealous.'

'Oh yeah, of what?'

'Of that brain of yours.'

Alex grimaced. Having perfect recall was handy in the classroom, but of no use when he was being given a wedgie for the umpteenth time of his school career.

Alex was miserable all the way to last period. A never-ending science lesson nearly sent him to sleep; for a short while, he was able to forget just how grim everything was. He battled drooping eyes as the teacher droned on about the discovery of conductivity and explained how to avoid getting electrocuted.

On and on they went until finally the lesson ended and everybody ran out of class, chattering. But not Alex. The misery followed him all the way home, as he walked with Sienna, and was still there as they ate sausage sandwiches for tea. It even hung around while they played chess in his room afterwards, ruining his favourite game.

Finally, Alex did his usual twenty press-ups (Mr Sunshine looking at him with his usual disdain), then stood in front of the mirror, examining himself for improvements on the muscle situation. He couldn't see much.

'Any change?' he asked Sienna.

Sienna nodded a little too vigorously. 'Yeah, I can deffo see more definition,' she said, not quite hitting the convincing tone she was going for.

Alex sighed. 'Turn around,' he said quietly. 'I need to change out of this uniform.'

Sienna turned round, fiddling with her phone, and Alex started struggling to pull off his overly tight trousers.

Things, thought Alex, *couldn't be any worse.*

Things, he realized a few moments later, *actually could be a lot worse.*

A lot worse indeed.

It started with a crackling, as if the whole room was suddenly filled with static. Alex shook his head and rubbed his eyes. Was this a migraine? But no – by the look on Sienna's face, she could feel it as well.

'What's that?' she asked, turning back round.

'I don't know,' Alex replied, completely forgetting he was standing there in only his underpants.

The crackling got louder. Alex had the strange feeling his brain – or the world – was glitching. Then a silent flash and a thumping shockwave rippled through the room, knocking Alex and Sienna backwards. For a heart-pounding moment Alex thought there had been an explosion. He rubbed his eyes and blinked.

It was no explosion.

Hovering in the middle of his bedroom was a shimmering, iridescent circle – a ring of rippling, liquid colours, taller than he was.

Alex's knees went to jelly, his mind not accepting what he was seeing. He stared at the ring, open-mouthed. Sienna stammered but no noise came out.

Then the colours parted to reveal a hole. No, not a hole – it was a *doorway*. And on the other side, there was a somebody.

A somebody who was staring back at Alex, as open-mouthed as he was.

A somebody who looked very much like Alex – the same wavy, blonde hair and thick eyebrows – and yet slightly different. The other boy was wearing more clothes, for a start. But aside from that, he looked stronger somehow, more confident.

And before Alex had any more time to consider what was going on, he felt a great force pulling him towards the doorway, as if the whole world was being drawn into it, like water down a plughole. Sienna grabbed hold of a wardrobe with a scream of panic. Alex staggered forward and slipped to the floor.

Just in time, he clutched on to his headboard. The force became stronger, though, and his legs left the ground.

'Sienna!' he screamed. 'It's pulling me in!'

Sienna stretched out an arm to grab him, but it was too late.

His hands slipped and he flew through the air, through the liquid ring of light towards the other boy. They each stared into the other's eyes, panic mirroring panic, and then, as easy as a hand through smoke, they passed through one another. On Alex flew, into a tunnel of light stretching through the universe, inside time itself, and out the other side.

And everything – *everything* – changed.

CHAPTER TWO

OF WITCHES AND HEROES

The first sensation Alex felt was a wooziness that swirled up through his whole body and muddled the thoughts in his head. Thoughts which told him he must be dead.

He didn't *feel* dead, though.

There was light. A bright light shining through his closed eyelids. He wasn't sure if seeing a light was a good or bad thing, so he stretched out his fingers. He could feel blades of . . . grass. He was lying on his back on grass. How . . . ?

He felt warmth on his skin too, across his face and over his body. And heard the sound of trilling birdsong. Alex plucked up the courage to slowly open his eyes . . .

And saw eyeballs. Three pairs of them, goggling down at him. Belonging to three of the strangest people he had ever seen.

There were two men and a girl. One of the men was scrawny and scraggly, like a chewed piece of stringy gristle, with a patchy, ill-tended lawn of grey hair on his head. The other man was young and round, his tongue hanging out of his smiling mouth like a hungry dog that knew it was about to be handed a particularly juicy lamb chop. The girl was about the same age as Alex, with long, brown hair and a broad, open face. She had leather straps wound all the way up her arms and looked rather fierce. All three were wearing the oddest clothes Alex had seen in his life – threadbare smocks and battered sandals – and seemed to be examining him closely.

The older man sneered, revealing a mouth almost devoid of teeth, the odd blackened stump all that remained to tell a tale of terrible dental neglect. Slowly he lifted a long, crooked, bony finger and pointed it at Alex.

'Witch!' he shouted.

Alex sat bolt upright.

'Pardon?'

'You're a witch!' shouted the man again.

'I'm a w-w-what?' Alex stammered.

'You're a witch . . . with bad hearing!'

The younger man prodded Alex with his foot. 'You sure it's a witch?'

'Course I'm sure! I knows a witch when I sees one!'

'I am not a witch,' Alex protested, struggling to his feet. 'I'm a boy!'

The older man hooted. 'Well, if you're not a witch, how comes you appeared out of nowhere, fell out the sky and landed here in this very field? I seed you do it with me own eyes.'

'I . . . er . . .'

Alex found he didn't have an answer to that question. In fact, he didn't have answers to *any* questions at that moment. He wasn't even sure what the right questions were.

'I says you're a witch and you're a witch!'

Alex had had just about enough of this and, though his heart was thrumming with fear, he held his hand up. 'I am not a witch!' he shouted, then more quietly added, 'I am a twelve-year-old boy – and I don't know where I am.'

The old man eyed him suspiciously. 'That's exactly what a witch might say. And what do we do with witches round here, Shrude?'

'We . . . burn 'em?' answered the younger man, uncertainly.

'Tha's right! Burn the witch!' the old man shouted.

'No!' Alex protested. 'You can't –'

'Right,' snapped the girl. 'That's enough. You pair

of brainless bumpkins need to leave him alone. This –'
she pointed at Alex – 'is not a witch.'

'But –'

'Grimbald,' the girl interrupted. 'Remember my
poor pig with the black marking in the shape of the
moon? You said *that* was a witch who had magically
changed themselves into a pig. We watched that pig for
three days and nights and it did nothing but eat, squeal
and do its business all over the kitchen floor. It was
nowt but a plain, ordinary pig. And I don't remember
you being too bothered about eating chops from it after
it was slaughtered, neither.'

Grimbald shifted from one foot to the other,
clearly a little embarrassed. 'So, mayhaps I was wrong
about tha' pig. But this boy . . . there's summat not
right about him. I still say we burns him. Jus' to be on
the safe side.'

'Grimbald! We don't burn witches here.' The girl
gave Alex a proud smile. 'We are a more accepting
society. We don't even call them witches any more. The
preferred term nowadays is "hags". Now –' she nodded
in Alex's direction – 'does that look like a hag to you?'

Both men shook their heads and looked at the
ground, shamefaced. Shrude in particular was clearly a
man well used to looking at the ground, shamefaced.

'So, Lorca Stonearm, you're *certain* he's not a witch?' asked Grimbald.

'Absolutely.' Lorca nodded firmly. 'Because I know exactly who he is.'

'You *do*?' asked Grimbald in disbelief.

'You do?!' asked Alex in even more disbelief.

Lorca nodded solemnly and pointed at Alex. '*This* is Axel Stormward. First son of the Sorcerer-Queen of Aërth, mighty scourge of the unrighteous, flayer of evil and slayer of wolves.'

There was a long pause.

'Ermmm,' said Alex. 'I'm not. In fact, I quite like wolves. I mean, not to pet them, but I certainly wouldn't go around *slaying* them.'

'Yes, you are,' Lorca said, putting her hands on her hips. 'I'm *completely* certain of it. And I'm never wrong. Except when I thought I could teach my dog Bessie to fly. Poor Bessie. I still miss her.'

'Look, I'm sorry about your dog, but my name isn't Axel. It's *Alex*. Alex Always. I think you might have mistaken me for somebody else.'

'Rubbish,' said Lorca. 'I'd recognize you anywhere. I watched you at the Young Hero of the Year Trials!'

'You really didn't.'

'I did! You autographed my smock!' She thrust her

arm out, and Alex could indeed see a faded, scrawled signature upon the worn fabric. 'You're the *greatest*,' she added, with the hint of a swoon. 'You inspire me in my own hero training! I'm only a Grade Three but one day I'll be a Grade Nine, like you. I watched you win the Seven Kingdoms Under-Sixteen Battle Royale! The way you bludgeoned Rosie Gladfoot, the Under-Thirteens champion, was a wonderous thing! Brutal, yet beautiful . . .' Lorca sighed.

'I've never bludgeoned anybody!'

'And we still sing of how bravely you fought against the Maggot King of Murkin Wood.'

And before anybody could stop her, Lorca broke into song.

Oh, brave Axel hero
Facing up to the maggoty foe!
Oh, proud Axel hero
Showed that king some maggoty woe!
With a fa-la-la and a rinky-dink-dum
Kicked him right up his maggoty b–

'I'm not him!' shouted Alex. 'And maggots creep me out!'

'He don't looks much like a hero.' Grimbald slowly

eyed Alex up and down. 'Standin' there in his fancy undergarments.'

Alex's hand's shot between his legs, trying to hide his underpants.

'An' look upon his skinny arms! Like twigs on a one-winter sapling.'

'Hang on, there's no need to get personal!'

'And those bandy legs!' Grimbald pointed and roared with laughter. 'Them legs couldn't stop a pig in an alley!'

'Why would I even *want* to stop a pig in an alley?' asked Alex, exasperated.

'Well, if you don't knows that, then you's dopier than you looks!' roared Grimbald.

Lorca folded her arms and shook her head slowly.

'Hmm. You might be on to something, Grimbald. It is clear that a foul and terrible curse must have caused him to lose all his strength and heroic nobility.'

'Now, look here,' Alex snapped. 'You're all being very rude.' His voice began to waver. 'My name is not Axel, it's *Alex*. I'm not a hero and I don't kill wolves. A minute ago I was in my bedroom and now I'm here, wherever *here* is, and I don't want to be. All I want is to go home. And some clothes, so I'm not stood here in my underpants!'

Silence fell upon the group – until it was broken by Shrude. 'Does you know what he's on about, Lorca Stonearm?'

Lorca frowned. 'No, but I know who might.'

'Who?' asked Grimbald.

'The Old Hag of the Hill.'

Grimbald and Shrude gasped in fear.

'Did you just gasp in fear?' Alex asked.

'No,' Grimbald said. They shook their heads in unison. 'We was just . . . breathin' dramatically.'

'Look, I only need to borrow a phone. I'll be sorted then.'

'I do not know what this "foan" you speak of might be,' Lorca said. 'But the Old Hag might.'

Grimbald and Shrude gasped again, but were met with an eyeroll from Lorca.

'Perhaps my *mother* might,' she clarified. 'Now come. We have far to travel before night falls. And you look like you might be a slow walker with a timid stride.'

With no alternative and no clothes, Alex knew that he had no choice but to follow. As they trudged through the countryside, the two men nibbled at him with questions for which he had no answers.

'Was your mother a witch?'

'When were the las' time you ate a full roasted sheep with a flagon of ale?'

'Did you steal your undergarments from a dainty princess?'

The questions were only halted when they walked past a man, lying on the ground, utterly still and silent. Grimbald and Shrude eyed him nervously. The man's eyes were blank, staring into the sky. He was still breathing but his skin was so pale he looked as if he was disappearing. The man's eyes fixed on Alex and he lifted his arm.

'Help . . . me . . .' he stammered.

'Stay away from him,' Lorca warned, nervously edging past. 'You can't do anything.'

Alex didn't need to be told twice. He gave the man a wide berth.

He decided it was safest to believe he was experiencing a very, very vivid dream. He tried to ignore the jabbing of twigs and stones under his feet, the warm breeze on his skin, the sound of the river that gurgled crisply next to the path and the sharp smell of Grimbald. But it was all too horribly *real*.

Lorca turned back to Alex. 'Stop dragging your heels! Timid stride – I knew it. Hurry up, we need to get you some clothes before winter comes.'

Alex gave a nervous laugh. 'Before winter comes? When will that be?'

'This afternoon.'

'Excuse me?'

'There's a season-changer approaching.' Lorca nodded at a large cloud ahead.

'A what?'

'You'll see,' Lorca said.

And sure enough, he did. It was the temperature Alex noticed first; a drop so sudden and sharp his breath puffed out in clouds of disbelief. He began to shiver, clasping his arms round his chest. But then he saw something that chilled him more than the weather-change. The leaves were turning brown and dropping from the trees.

Alex picked one up and stared in wonder – it was already crisp and dry, and it crumbled in his hand. An hour before, the trees had been lush and green and full of life. Now they were bare. The flowers which dotted the embankments were curling up and dying in front of Alex's eyes. Winter had arrived.

Alex shook his head. 'Impossible,' he said to himself and shivered again, an icy, disorientating fear spreading through him.

'You must know we get season-changers round

these parts,' Lorca said. 'You lost your memory as well as your muscles?'

'There's *nothing* wrong with my memory,' Alex retorted.

'Well, we'll get you something to wear in Gnarly Botton,' Lorca said.

'I'm sorry?'

'It's the next village,' Lorca said, rolling her eyes.

'Oh, great.'

When they walked into Gnarly Botton, though, it was less than great. The stares of the villagers, slack-jawed and wide-eyed, made Alex feel even more naked. A couple of small, grubby children stopped their game and stood rooted to the spot, goggling with astonishment. Even the scraggly chickens that were pecking all around seemed to have a good stare as he walked past.

A nervous child of about seven sidled up to him. 'Hey, Mister Stormward, can I have your autograph?'

'No!' snapped Alex. 'I mean, I'm sorry. I'm not him. I just look like him.'

The child eyed him up and down. 'I did wonder why a great hero would be wearing no clothes. Axel Stormward would *never* be caught trouser-less. Unless there was an excellent, heroic reason.'

Alex had never wanted something to wear more in his life. He regretted ever complaining about his too-short trousers. He turned away and considered his predicament.

He had three theories:

1. **He really *was* dreaming.** This was looking more and more unlikely, as he had tested it by pinching himself and hadn't woken up.
2. **He had lost his mind.** This was possible, but as he had never experienced it before, he didn't know what to expect.
3. **He was part of some elaborate prank.** Perhaps it was for a new TV show and his reactions were being recorded, but he couldn't see any cameras anywhere.

'Wait here,' Lorca said, ducking into a small cottage.

Shrude turned to Grimbald and whispered, 'There's no need for us to go to see the Old Hag – I mean, Lorca's mother – is there?'

Grimbald shook his head. 'I don't reckons there is, no. This skinny-ma-jimmy'll be perfectly fine without us. What says you and I goes and warms ourselves by the fire in tha' pub?'

And with a parting shout of 'Good day, lanky long legs!' they scuttled off towards a stone building with a sign swinging outside, leaving Alex with just the gawping villagers for company.

Alex swallowed and took stock of the situation. There were no cars. No street lights. No telephone or electricity wires overhead. No pavements, no street signs, no adverts, no concrete. Where *was* he?

A moment later Lorca popped back out of the cottage. 'Here. Stick this on.'

Alex gratefully snatched at the piece of clothing she passed to him and pulled it over his head. His gratitude quickly disappeared, though. It felt rough, smelled of smoke and was tied round the waist with a belt made of rope, which made it feel a little like a dress.

'I don't mean to be rude,' he said. 'But is this a sack with holes cut in it?'

Lorca glared. 'You were expecting the latest fashion in Gnarly Botton?'

'OK, no. Thanks, this is great. You wouldn't have any, um, *trousers*, though, would you?'

Lorca ignored his question and look around sharply. 'Hang on – where did Grimbald and Shrude go?'

'I don't think they wanted to meet your mother,' Alex said.

'Pah! The great pair of lolloping chickens! You aren't frightened, are you?' Lorca eyeballed Alex. 'And don't lie to me. I can *always* spot a lie!'

'I'm absolutely not frightened,' Alex lied. 'I'm looking forward to meeting her,' he lied again.

'Excellent!' Lorca clapped her hands. 'That was *definitely* the truth. Now, let's go find some answers.'

'And a phone,' reminded Alex hopefully.

But the hope was slowly draining from him.

For several miles they followed a muddy path in the direction of the slowly setting sun, which hung low on the horizon, pink, fat and lazy, until they approached what looked like a larger settlement.

'What's that smell?' Alex said, holding his nose.

'The great town of Howden Leeth,' Lorca replied. 'Biggest supplier of frog-rot in the Seven Kingdoms.'

'Frog-rot? Why would anybody want *that*?'

'Says someone who clearly hasn't ever tasted frog-rot soup.'

Alex wanted to reply, *And will not ever*, but he was too busy being shoved hither and thither by the crowds milling into the town. The higgledy-piggledy wooden houses clustered on either side of the main street were piled high, each new storey thrown precipitously on top of the previous one so that it projected over the thoroughfare. Each house leaned so far out that it nearly touched the building opposite, blocking out much of the fading daylight in the alleys and streets below.

They had to battle for space as they walked, dodging between people, the open drains that ran along the gutters and all manner of foul-smelling excrement. Alex couldn't tell which type of animal had produced it, but it urgently needed to see a vet.

Lorca suddenly grabbed Alex and pulled him back. Where he had been stood, an enormous wash of yellow liquid splashed to the ground. The stench hit him immediately.

'Is that wee? Did someone just throw their wee out of a window?' he asked, disgusted. 'Look,' he said, holding up a splattered leg. 'I'm covered!'

But Lorca wasn't listening. Her attention was on a person lying on the ground a short way ahead of them – a woman, with a man kneeling next to her, stroking her hair. The woman's eyes were blank, staring lifelessly into the sky. She was still breathing, so she wasn't dead, but just like the man they had seen earlier that day, she was so pale she almost looked as if she was disappearing.

'Keep your distance,' Lorca warned, nervously edging past. 'There's no helping her.'

But as Alex sidled by, the man looked up and spoke in a choked voice. 'Please, can you help? She's going. I can't stop it.'

The woman's face was even paler than Alex had thought. In fact – Alex squinted – was she actually *transparent*? Was that the gravel of the street he could see through her body?

'I'm sorry,' muttered Lorca. 'There's nothing we can do.'

She grabbed Alex by the arm and pulled him past the unfortunate pair. 'What was wrong with her?' Alex asked.

'An illness,' replied Lorca. 'The White Death.'

She lifted her hand and showed Alex a pale patch on her palm. 'This here's the Mortmark. That's how it starts. One day last week we woke up and we all had them. They don't hurt, but eventually the mark begins to grow. Nobody knows when it'll happen, but once it starts it spreads across the whole body. The victim becomes paler and paler until eventually they just ... disappear.'

Alex gulped, and Lorca continued, 'I dunno any more than that. Nobody does. Apart from my uncle. He reckons it's caused by people's clothes being too tight and squeezing their lifeforce out of them. But then he

also said that eating flies makes you grow wings and I'm not sure if that's true.'

'And what happened to him?'

'He got arrested for walking naked through the town square.'

Alex didn't know what to say to that, so he said nothing.

On they walked through the town, flurries of snow eddying around them, until they reached the main square. In the centre, about a dozen women, hooded and robed in white, stood in a circle around more victims of the White Death, who all seemed to be at different stages of fading. Alex shuddered – how widespread *was* this White Death? An illness, Lorca had called it. It seemed more like a plague.

The women raised their arms aloft, crying out to the skies.

'The Bann Sí,' Lorca whispered. 'They're keening. Watch the sky . . .'

Alex looked up in wonder. Above the Bann Sí, a perfectly round gap appeared in the clouds and a single, golden ray of sunshine fell on the women and the victims.

'They're trying to light-heal them. Mum says that won't do any good, though. Nothing seems to work.' Lorca shrugged. 'Come on, let's go.'

They skirted round the square and trudged down a long road until they reached a steep hill. Lying at the bottom of the hill like a dead sheep was a low hut that looked as if it had survived all manner of natural disasters, without any of the necessary repair work. Tied to a post outside the hut, a mean-looking goat eyed Alex warily while chewing on some hay.

'Here we are!' Lorca beamed. 'Hovel sweet hovel.'

'It's not a hovel. It looks ... homely,' said Alex, thinking of threadbare second-hand sofas and feeling a pang of miserable homesickness.

'Of course it's a hovel. Now, shall we go in and see the Old Hag of the Hill?'

Alex shook his head. 'Look, I *really* don't think it's polite to call your mother an old hag.'

'Rubbish!' said Lorca. 'She likes it.'

'I'm sure she doesn't.'

'If you don't believe me, ask the goat,' said Lorca.

'Very funny.' Alex laughed. 'I wasn't born yester–'

'Mabel, does my mum like being called the Old Hag of the Hill?'

The goat spat out its mouthful of hay.

'Of course she does,' it replied, sharply. 'Now stop bothering me with your inane questions.'

Alex, who was naturally rather surprised by this, staggered backwards.

'The ... the ... goat! It c-c-can talk,' he stammered.

'Of course I can talk!' the goat said. 'Now be off! I don't wish to waste any more of my time conversing with you pair of witless dizzards.'

A few hours ago, Alex had been happily playing chess in his bedroom. Since then, he had hiked across a strange country in his underpants, seen the seasons change in a matter of minutes, been dressed in a sack and seen people fading out of existence before his very eyes.

Now, faced with a talking goat, his brain had finally had enough. There was only one sensible course of action and Alex's brain took it.

He fainted.

CHAPTER THREE

THE
BROKEN CAT

Impossibly near to Alex and yet also impossibly far away, Axel Stormward – first son of the Sorcerer-Queen of Aërth, mighty scourge of the unrighteous, flayer of evil and slayer of wolves – crashed to the floor of Alex's bedroom.

'What foul magic has brought me to this place?' he bellowed, springing to his feet, sword drawn.

Mr Sunshine, now a puffed-up ball of fur and claws in the corner, hissed furiously.

'You there, Cat! Tell me! Was it you? Is this part of my quest?'

Mr Sunshine hissed again.

Axel sheathed his sword, strode over to the cat and picked him up by the scruff of the neck.

'Speak, Cat! Who has summoned me here?'

Mr Sunshine hissed even more and did his best to scratch Axel's face off.

'Talk to me!' Axel shouted, shaking Mr Sunshine.

It was at that moment that Sienna slowly rose

from her hiding place behind the wardrobe door, her arms up.

Axel thrust Mr Sunshine towards her.

'Your cat is broken!' he snapped. 'Who are you, wench?'

'W-w-who are *you*?' stammered Sienna. 'What happened to Alex? Why do you look like him? And *what* are you wearing?'

'Stop asking questions!' replied Axel. '*I* ask the questions! Now, why is this cat refusing to talk?'

Sienna collapsed on to the bed. 'I must be dreaming . . .'

'I fear this is no dream,' Axel said. 'Some evil spell has cast me down here. The last thing I remember was preparing for my next quest. I had just been handed my instructions –' Axel pulled a small scroll from his belt – 'and then *bang*! I am transported to this lowly abode.'

Before Sienna could reply, Gran burst into the bedroom, rubbing her eyes.

'What's all this bloomin' racket? You woke me up from me nap. Alex, stop flinging Mr Sunshine about the place, for God's sake.'

'Who are you, crone?' Axel glared, dropping the cat, who shot out of the room like a bolt of ginger lightning.

'Call me crone again, I'll have your guts for garters, you cheeky so-and-so.'

Axel blinked in surprise. 'What are you, then? A hag?'

'Alex Always, don't you dare speak to your grandmother like that!'

'Mrs A,' stammered Sienna, pointing at Axel. 'That's not –'

'My grandmother! Ha!' Axel laughed. 'You are not my grandmother. My grandmother is the picture of elegance and grace and wisdom. You are . . .' He looked her up and down. 'Well, you are not.'

'I'm going to pretend I didn't hear that,' snapped Gran. 'Now, Sienna, love, you'd best be getting off. Your folks'll be worried and it's past Alex's bedtime.'

'But-but . . .' stuttered Sienna. 'But that's not Al–'

'Go on!' Gran ushered a gobsmacked Sienna out of the room and down the hall. 'Give my love to your mam,' she added, as she closed the front door behind her.

Gran turned and pointed a finger at Axel. 'Right, you! Bed. Now.'

'No! Tell me, witch, are you the one responsible for bringing me to this foul and miserable hole?'

'I'll be responsible for slapping you round the earhole if you don't stop messing about and get into your pyjamas this minute. Actually, what *is* that you're wearing?'

'It is the latest in leather armour technology. Maximum manoeuvrability, minimum muscle coverage,' Axel said, flexing his impressive pecs. 'With engraved silver wrist guards, bronze shoulder trim and dragonskin nipple protectors.'

'Where did you get it from? Down the market?'

Axel's eyes bulged indignantly. 'This is no market-bought armour! It was fashioned by a master-craftsman. He tanned it by the light of the first full moon of the year, then sewed it for the next seven days and nights without rest.'

Gran shrugged. 'Sounds like the market. Anyway, Alex love, maybe it's time for bed, eh? You're sounding a bit . . . odd.'

'Of course I am sounding odd!' Axel gestured around the bedroom. 'I have been dragged through space and time by some infernal sorcery and dumped in this . . . dungeon, with only a broken cat for company, and you expect me to sound normal? And why do you keep calling me Alex?'

'Because that's your name. Now –'

'My name is not Alex. It is *Axel*. Axel Stormward. First son of the Sorcerer-Queen of Aërth, mighty scourge of the unrighteous, flayer of evil and slayer of wolves.'

'Of course it is,' Gran said, putting the back of her hand on Axel's forehead, her brow furrowed. 'Come on, hop into bed and get some sleep.'

'Never! Now is not the time for sleeping!'

'Now *is* the time for sleeping, so get into bed or there'll be trouble.'

Axel eyed Gran warily. 'You have a shrivelled weak body but a voice of strength and power. I fear there is something dangerous about you.'

'Too bloomin' right there is! Bed. NOW!'

'You win for now, crone. I shall get into bed and gather my strength. But on my oath, on the morrow you shall release me from this dungeon or feel the cold steel of my sword!'

'That's right, love. You'll be released from the dungeon tomorrow,' Gran said, putting a tender hand on his shoulder. 'Now, come on.'

'A final warning,' Axel growled. 'I shall not sleep! For even the briefest moment. If you *or* the broken cat dare to try anything to – Holy of Holies, what witchery is this?! This bed is unnaturally soft! Never have I felt something so demonically comfortable. I cannot resist . . . my eyes close . . .'

'OK, sweetie. You get a good night's sleep then,' Gran said, giving Axel a kiss on his forehead. 'You'll feel better tomorrow.'

'Gah!'

Axel jumped out of bed, sunlight streaming through the thin curtains. 'Unnatural sleeping magic! Hag or cat, whoever is responsible shall pay for this.'

But Mr Sunshine was nowhere to be seen. 'I'll find you later, treacherous creature,' Axel growled.

He picked up his sword and tried the door. It opened and Axel's eyes widened in surprise. 'The crone did not lock the dungeon!' he muttered.

He edged silently down the corridor, paused at the sitting-room door, then burst in, brandishing his sword – to find Gran eating her breakfast.

'WHERE THE HELL DID YOU GET THAT THING?' she yelled, dropping her spoon.

'This,' said Axel, holding the blade aloft, 'is Aëthelmrir the Spirit-Slayer. Forged at the dawning of the Third Age atop the Ninth Peak of the Mountains of Ice and –'

'What are you banging on about? Just stop bloomin' waving it around – you'll have someone's eye out!'

'I shall lower Aëthelmrir out of respect,' Axel said. 'You have been true to your word, hag, and indeed released me from my dungeon.'

'Ohhh . . .' Gran said, her face dawning with realization. 'Are you back to doing your live action role-playing again? You should have said.'

Axel gave her a mystified look. 'I have no clue what you are talking about, shrew. Anyway, what manner of hovel is this?'

'Pardon?'

'It is a squalid, tiny home, of a size fit only for a peasant.'

'How dare you, you cheeky –'

'But,' continued Axel, looking around him, 'it is filled with strange and magical wonders. Moving tapestries.' He nodded at the television. 'And lights without flame.' He pointed at the light bulb above his head. 'Clearly you are no mere hag. I can only conclude you are a powerful sorceress. But why then are you wearing such a drab garment? Surely a sorceress would not allow herself to be seen in the dowdy clothes of a peasant.'

'You mean my dressing gown? You bought me this two Christmases ago!'

'But these mysteries can wait. For now, I must eat.'

Axel sat down at the table. 'Fetch me my breakfast. Some fried boar's head. Or ox's innards.'

Gran gave him a withering look.

'We're all out of ox's innards, so Weetabix will have to do. And you can get off your backside and get it yourself.'

The early-morning sun crept across the ancient roof, bright light sliding across dark grey stone. The castle clung to the side of a cliff, waves crashing and seething on the jagged rocks below. Over many years it had held fast, the howling winds that whipped in from the sea shaping its stone walls, smoothing their edges into rippling striations, until it looked like a vast bulbous growth on the cliff face.

Inside, a man, tall and gaunt, climbed the spiral staircase which formed the spine of the building. His long legs allowed him to take the steps two at a time in a steady, striding rhythm. Thin shafts of sunlight lit his bald head, the skin stretched so taut across his skull it looked as if it might tear if the slightest emotion disturbed his pale, waxen features. It was an uncanny visage, as if put together by somebody who had never seen a face but had only heard tell of them. When he reached the room at the top, his breathing was as sure and even as it had been at the bottom of the two hundred stone steps.

In front of him was a wooden door, from which a low hum emanated.

The man pulled a large, rusty key from one of his deep pockets and slid it with a firm hand into the keyhole. He closed his eyes and turned it. His long, bony fingers enclosed the handle, and he slowly pushed the door open. The droning became immediately louder, a chaotic static of buzzing.

In front of him, twenty swollen nests, thick with crawling flies, hung from the wooden beams. The flies were huge; finger-length, with needle-like stingers. Sunlight flooded in from the many carved holes in each wall. Countless flies, warmed by the morning sun, swarmed and buzzed around the room. The noise was ferocious and constant.

The man closed the door behind him, walked to the centre of the room and stood, bathed in the white light, oblivious to the flies around him. He closed his eyes, arms outstretched, and then his lips peeled back into a grin, revealing large, pale gums.

A single fly landed on his face. And then another.

He remained motionless. More flies landed. One crawled over his mouth. The humming intensified as the flies whispered their secrets. More and more settled on him, on his outstretched arms, his chest, his neck.

Soon, every centimetre of his skin was alive with bristling insects.

There came a knock on the door.

As quickly as the swarming flies had alighted upon the man, they left, and the air was suddenly thick with them. Some flew out of the holes, some returned to their nests. A moment later there was not a fly to be seen on him.

'Come.'

The door opened a crack and a woman's voice slid through, cold as the blade of a knife.

'Master, I bring news.'

'What is it, Screed?' the man replied.

'The Narrator refuses to speak.'

The man gave a short sigh.

'Very well. I shall deal with him myself . . .'

CHAPTER FOUR

QUESTIONS AND ANSWERS

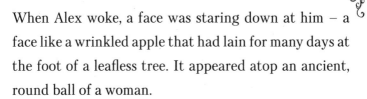

When Alex woke, a face was staring down at him – a face like a wrinkled apple that had lain for many days at the foot of a leafless tree. It appeared atop an ancient, round ball of a woman.

'Get up!' she said. 'Before you freeze to death.'

More snow was falling, feather-like, and settling around Alex, and he realized he was numb with cold. He sat up, rubbing his eyes. 'Are you the Old Hag of the Hill?'

'Rude!' the woman snapped.

'Oh,' said Alex, mortified. 'I was told that you liked being called that!'

'Who said so?'

'Well . . . the goat.'

'Pah!' The woman flapped a hand at him, her wrinkled face scrunching in disgust. 'Everyone knows goats can't be trusted! And that one least of all.'

'How dare you? I'm outraged!' said the goat, clearly un-outraged, then it went straight back to chewing a bush.

'Anyway,' continued the woman. 'I do have a name, you know.'

'What is it?'

'Chelsee.'

'Chelsea?'

'Yes. Chelsee. With two e's.'

'Your name is *Chelsee*?'

The woman scowled. 'Yes. Do you have a problem with that?'

'No! Not at all.'

'Good! Well, don't just sit there with a face like spilled porridge. Follow me into my hovel . . .'

Chelsee gave him a sharp kick on his shin, and Alex jumped up, rubbing his leg. 'Come on then, daughter!' she said, putting her arm around Lorca. 'Get some tea on.'

Chelsee and Lorca disappeared inside through a front door that hung off its hinges. Alex had no choice but to follow.

He blinked, trying to let his eyes grow accustomed to the dark, then wished he hadn't. The hovel was – there was no other word for it – *filthy*. Animal skins hung off the ceiling. Animal skins lay in a pile in the corner. And there were animal skins in a bucket.

'What a l-l-lovely house you have,' Alex stammered politely.

''S not a house, it's a hovel!' snapped Chelsee.

'Told you,' said Lorca.

'Well, what a l-l-lovely hovel you have,' Alex said, correcting himself.

'Nonsense!' replied Chelsee. 'It's a foul hovel and you are a terrible liar – the polite stammering gives it away. Now, boy, you came here for answers, did you not?'

'How did you know?'

'Because that's why everyone comes here. They sure don't come for the company and the luxury ... Now, sit!'

Alex looked around for a chair. Seeing none, he plumped himself down on a pile of skins.

Which growled.

Alex jumped up again.

The pile of skins shook itself and two small, black eyes appeared. Alex realized that what he'd just sat on was actually a dog: a large, long-legged, floppy-eared dog with brown-and-white fur in dire need of a brush.

'Watch where you're sitting, you great oaf!' the dog growled.

'You can talk too?' Alex gasped.

'Of course I can! And next time you sit on me, I'll bite you so hard you won't be sitting down for a year!'

'I-I-I'm sorry!' Alex stammered.

'Hmm,' growled the dog. 'You'd best be.'

'Sit!' ordered the old woman, and the dog sat down immediately.

'Not you, Fetlock.' Chelsee sighed. 'The boy!'

'Sorry,' Fetlock said, holding up an apologetic paw. 'Basic training.'

'Look, do you have a phone, by any chance?' Alex said, clutching a gossamer-thin sliver of hope. He had never seen anyone or been anywhere less likely to have a phone.

'A what?'

'A phone.'

Chelsee's face stayed blank. She turned to Lorca and shrugged, and Lorca shrugged back. Alex's heart sank even further. He let out a groan of misery.

'Ah, do not fall into despair, young man! I may not have this *foan* you seek, but answers might be easier to come by. Questions ye have, telleth me now!'

'Pardon?'

'It's her Old Hag act.' Fetlock yawned. 'She thinks swapping around the order of words makes her sound mysterious. She means, tell her what questions you have.'

'Oh.' Alex took a breath. 'I need to know where I

am, why I'm here and how I got here.' He looked down, his voice soft. 'And how to get home.'

'Questions big these are indeed.'

'These are indeed big questions,' Fetlock translated, absent-mindedly chewing on a claw.

'*Questions big these are indeed,*' Chelsee repeated, glaring at the dog. 'But fortunately, where to find the answers, I know.' She sprang up, sprightlier than she looked, and began rummaging in a cupboard.

'Hey,' Alex whispered to Lorca. 'Is that really your mum? She looks quite . . .'

'Old?' Lorca whispered back. 'She uses ageing cream.'

'You mean anti-ageing?'

'No, ageing.'

'But why?'

'Cos nobody's going to trust the wisdom of a *young* hag, are they?' snapped Chelsee, without turning around. 'And there's nothing wrong with my hearing neither, young man. Now, where is it?' she muttered to herself. 'Ah! Here we go!'

From under some skins she pulled a large ball wrapped in a blue silk cloth.

'Behold!' she said, pulling the cloth off the ball and holding it aloft. 'The Orb of Exposition!'

'What?' Fetlock gasped. 'The Orb of Exposition? How long have you had that lying about?'

'Ages.' Chelsee shrugged. 'I forgot it was here.'

'What does it do?' asked Alex.

'It sees everything,' Chelsee whispered darkly. 'Knows everything. And even better still – it *explains* everything.'

'Everything?' asked Alex.

Chelsee nodded. 'Yup.'

'Well, that's . . . convenient. How does it work?'

'No idea.'

'You've no idea how it works?' asked Alex incredulously.

'None at all,' said Chelsee. 'It's just magic. Don't you have things from where you come from that just work without you knowing how?'

Alex thought of his mobile phone. It could video call people instantly on the other side of the world. It put the sum of human knowledge at his fingertips. It had a map and a camera and a thousand other things. And he had absolutely no idea how *any* of it worked. A magical orb with all the answers suddenly seemed less unbelievable.

Alex stared at the orb, which Chelsee had placed on the floor between them, a perfect crystal sphere.

'So, what do I do?'

'*You* don't do anything, boy,' growled Fetlock. 'It takes a lifetime to learn the magic to –'

'Actually,' interrupted Chelsee. 'It's quite easy. You put your hand on it, and it just sort of knows what to say. But one thing, know you must –'

'One thing you must know,' interrupted Fetlock.

'That fur of yours is looking mighty soft,' muttered Chelsee, glaring at the dog. 'Be a shame if you ... lost it.'

Fetlock said nothing, but Alex could swear he heard a gulp.

Chelsee nodded and continued, 'But one thing, *know you must*, to argue with the Orb of Exposition is pointless. 'Tis like arguing against the flow of a river. And you best be polite!'

Chelsee gently placed her hand on the orb and immediately a silvery cloud seemed to escape through her fingers. It hung above them, softly glowing from inside. When it spoke, it was as if the words glided around the room on wisps of unseen air.

You come for knowledge ...

'Go on, then,' Chelsee urged Alex. 'Speak!'

'Me?'

'Yes!'

Alex gulped nervously. 'Oh . . . Great Orb of Exposition . . . I need to know how to get home.'

That is the end of the story, and no one can see the end, not even I. But to get there, you must know many things.

'Yes! Show me!'

I do not show. Only tell. Tell, don't show. That is the rule for the Orb of Exposition.

'OK, tell me then.'

A new tale has been written and many tales have been broken, began the Orb of Exposition. *A great sickness spreads through the world.*

'But what world? Where am I?' Alex blurted out.

You are on Aërth.

'Earth?'

*No, **Aërth**. A world in great peril. The Narrator – who writes the story of every living creature in his Book of Lifetales – has been kidnapped.*

Everyone but Alex gasped.

'What?' he said, confused.

'I thought the Narrator was a myth!' exclaimed Fetlock.

The Narrator is very much real, continued the Orb. *And has been kidnapped by the man who calls himself the Father of Flies.*

'No!' Lorca said. 'Anyway, who's hungry?'

'Now is not the time for snacks!' Fetlock said, shooting a glare at Lorca. 'Orb, please continue.'

I mean, the Orb said haughtily, *if your stomachs are more important than my wisdom ...*

'No, they're not. Please, Orb, carry on.'

As I was saying, the Father of Flies has stolen the Book of Lifetales. Without it, the Narrator can no longer tell the story of the people of Aërth.

A heavy silence fell upon the room.

'I have literally no idea what you are talking about,' said Alex.

Fetlock gave an annoyed sigh. 'Tell us, O Orb, what this boy is doing here?'

'That's exactly what I'd like to know,' said Alex. 'How does any of this involve me?'

Before he was kidnapped, the Orb continued, *the Narrator wrote one last tale. He exchanged you with a boy. A boy named Axel –*

'Oh, yes, I think I saw him!'

'Aha! So, you *aren't* Axel Stormward!' Lorca cried triumphantly.

'I told you I wasn't!' protested Alex.

'I mean, I was beginning to suspect. He's ... not like you.'

That boy you saw – Axel Stormward – is your cosmic twin. A stronger, braver version of you. Trained to be a great warrior. Groomed to be a hero. He is everything you are not.

'Excuse me?!'

It should have been Axel Stormward's quest to defeat the Father of Flies and recover the Book of Lifetales, continued the Orb of Exposition. *Sadly, that terrible task must now fall . . . to you, Alex Always.*

Alex's eyes boggled. 'Let me get this straight. You want me to defeat some super-powerful evil dude called the Father of *Flies*? Yeah, that's not really my area of expertise.'

'You surprise me,' said Fetlock flatly.

'Well, anyway, if this other kid is such a big-shot hero, why did the Narrator swap us in the first place?'

Because you are not of this world, the Father of Flies cannot harm you, for your tale was written elsewhere, the Orb replied. *But you must succeed. For now the Father of Flies has the Book, the lifetales of Aërth's people are no longer being written. One by one, until the Book of Lifetales is recovered, they will fade and vanish until soon none remain.*

Fetlock grimaced. 'How soon is soon?'

In fourteen days, all life on Aërth shall be extinguished.

'So that's why I am here?' Alex said.

Unless you have some other hidden power which might explain it. Very well hidden. So hidden that even I cannot see it.

'But how does this help me get back home?' Alex asked, once again turning to despair.

To earn your return, you must fulfil the quest Axel Stormward was destined to undertake. By the first light of the sunrise two weeks from today, you must defeat the Father of Flies and rescue the Book of Lifetales. But know this – as cosmic twins, you and Axel are two sides of the same coin, two souls linked across two worlds. Your spirits are intertwined. Together you must find strength or together you shall fall. Fail, and the world is doomed.

'This is a joke, right?' Alex demanded.

The Orb of Exposition does not joke. It merely gives out information in a really helpful and convenient way.

'You want me to go on some ludicrous quest –'

It is not a ludicrous quest, hissed the Orb, a shiver of anger rippling through its words. *It is an impossible one.*

'Wonderful,' said Alex. 'You want me to go on some really dangerous quest —'

*I said **impossible**. The levels of quest are: Peasy, Tricksy, Ticklish, Dangerous, Very Dangerous, Really Dangerous, Really **Really** Dangerous, Desperately Dangerous, Ludicrously Dangerous and, finally, Impossible. Your quest will have the highest amount of danger and life-imperilment.*

'Oh fantastic,' groaned Alex.

Do not despair, though, continued the Orb. *For you shall not travel alone. It is fated that two allies must join you on this quest. To guide you . . . Fetlock!*

'Great,' growled Fetlock, putting his hairy head in his paws.

And to protect you . . . Lorca Stonearm!

'No!' Chelsee gasped.

'Yesss!' Lorca whooped, pumping her fist. 'Impossible Quest time!'

'Absolutely not, young lady,' Chelsee said. 'You're not ready.'

'Too late! It's fated. The Orb said so!' Lorca crowed.

'No!' cried Chelsee. 'You've only just passed your Ticklish Quest. On your eighth try, I might add. You are NOT gallivanting off on some Impossible —'

DO NOT ARGUE WITH THE ORB OF EXPOSITION! roared the Orb. Then it continued in a low, chanting voice:

> *The fates are sealed, cannot be fled,*
> *A world of wonder lies ahead.*
> *A past life gone, now dare behold*
> *Stories new and terrors old.*
>
> *Three shall set out but some shall fall,*
> *A sacrifice gives hope for all.*
> *Two realms are crossed, two quests unfurled –*
> *Defeat the father, save the world.*

And, with that, the cloud was sucked back into the Orb and silence fell upon the room.

CHAPTER FIVE

A WEAK AND FEEBLE BOY

'Well,' said Lorca, with a bright smile. 'That was a nice poem to finish on, I must say.'

'I mean, let's just take a moment here,' said Alex. 'Do we have to go just because some crystal ball says so? Couldn't we call the police or –'

Chelsee hobbled up to him and spoke gently. 'I do not wish my daughter to go on an Impossible Quest either, but she is correct – it is fated.'

'Nobody cares about me, I see,' muttered Fetlock. 'Maximum peril, big chance of dying and nobody checks to see how the dog is feeling. Typical.'

'Well, I'm a human and nobody cares about me either!' Alex complained.

'Don't be daft,' said Chelsee. 'I'm sure somebody cares if you live or die.'

Alex's mind filled with thoughts of Gran, Sienna and Irving. Yes, some people did care. But would he ever see them again? To get home, he had to complete an Impossible Quest. He could barely climb the rope in the gym.

'I don't even know which way to go!' moaned Alex.

'Don't worry,' Chelsee said, with a warm smile. 'Leave this place with hope in your heart, go to the very end of the last lane you find, follow the song of the wind and then turn left at the end of time.'

'*That*,' Alex said, 'is without doubt the most ridiculous set of directions I have ever heard.' He shook his head. 'You really want to send a child out into the middle of nowhere with *those* directions? So irresponsible. You're going to need to come up with something a lot better, or – and you can trust me on this – I am going to end up totally lost. And almost certainly die.'

The one time he had been orienteering, he had got so lost the school had to send out a search party. They had found him two days later, starving, dehydrated, mud smeared over his face, half a mile from an Asda car park.

'You won't get lost,' said Fetlock quietly. 'In my youth, I travelled the length and breadth of Aërth. I will guide you, as the Orb has fated. First we will go to the Infinite Palace. There, we will consult the Finding Engine, a magical machine that knows the location of all things. It will be able to tell us where to find the Father of Flies.'

'Well, I'm still going to die!' exclaimed Alex. 'And never get home to see my gran.'

'Shush now,' said Chelsee. 'You aren't going to die.'

'But the Orb said some shall fall –'

'I know what the Orb said. But there is a prophecy . . .'

'A prophecy?' Alex asked, sitting up.

'Yes,' Chelsee said, her eyes shining bright in the gloom. 'An ancient prophecy that foretells of the coming of a boy from another world.' Alex's eyes widened in wonder, and Chelsee continued. 'A boy who saves two worlds and lives happily ever after. A boy with thick eyebrows whose name rhymes with . . . um . . . falex.'

'You're making this up!' Alex fell back and slapped his forehead.

'OK, fine!' said Chelsee, holding her hands up. 'I lied. There is no prophecy.'

'I knew it!' shouted Alex. 'Unbelievable.'

'Well, pardon me for trying to give you a little bit of confidence before your inevitable and painful death. But the important thing is that you do your best. It's the taking part that counts.'

'No, it's not! That's what you tell kids when they are about to play in a big football match, not when they are about to die on some really dangerous quest!'

'Impossible Quest,' corrected Lorca.

'Whatever!' Alex flung his arms in the air. He wanted to run away, far from these strange people and their quests. But in the back of his mind an image of Gran appeared. And bills from debt collectors. And Irving and Sienna. He had to try to get back to them. 'Fine! I'll do it!'

'That's the spirit!' Chelsee beamed. 'You may have the body of a weak and feeble boy, but you have the heart and stomach of a reasonably brave warrior – or at least a warrior too stupid to realize quite how deadly the dangers he is facing really are.'

Alex had heard enough. He stormed out of the hovel, blinking in the sudden light. To his shock, he felt the warmth of the evening sun and saw that all the snow that had fallen earlier had melted.

Alex looked at the trees, amazed. 'The leaves! They're growing back!'

And sure enough, they were – each tree sprouting buds before his eyes, green leaves unfurling, glowing anew.

Fetlock stepped outside. He sniffed the air deeply, his fur rustling in the gentle breeze.

'Ah,' said Fetlock. 'Summer's back, I see. What's the matter? You look like you've never seen a tree before.'

'Not like these I haven't.' Alex shook his head. 'It's all . . . just . . . I don't even know where to begin. I mean, for a start I'm talking to a dog.'

Fetlock turned to Alex, but before he could say anything there was a huge clatter from the hovel, followed by a shout of pain.

They ran inside to find Lorca staggering around, crashing into walls and furniture. For a moment, Alex thought she was wearing some sort of war helmet. Then he realized she had her head stuck in a bucket.

'Not *again*,' sighed Fetlock.

'Sorry!' Lorca's voice echoed from the bucket. 'I was just trying to lick up the last drops of milk.'

'Oh, Lorca!' Chelsee said. 'I've warned you about that a hundred times!'

'I know. I'm sorry, Mum.'

Chelsee took a pat of butter from the larder and began smearing it up under the bucket. After much pulling and tugging, Lorca's head finally popped free.

'And *she* is supposed to protect me?' said Alex.

'Indeed! From any danger!' Lorca cried. She drew a sword from a sheath at her side, but it flew out of her grip and nearly struck Alex in the face. 'Sorry!' she said. 'Buttery fingers.'

71

She wiped her hands on her sides, then picked up the sword, knelt before Alex and pressed it against her forehead. 'I swear I shall do all I can to keep you from harm.'

'Err ... thanks?' Alex replied, thinking that the thing he most needed protection from was probably Lorca herself. 'Does *everybody* round here carry swords? It doesn't seem very safe.'

'Only the most pathetic weaklings do not carry swords,' Lorca declared. She cast a suspicious eye over Alex. 'Did you leave yours at home?'

'Ah, well, yes, so –'

'Oh, that's a relief!' Lorca said. 'So you know how to fight with courage and bravery?'

'Well, err –'

'Excellent!' Lorca jumped up, ran to a great wooden chest in the corner of the room and pulled out another sword. 'Then we must spar!' she declared.

She threw the sword to Alex. The sword clattered to the ground.

'Did you just yelp in fear?' Lorca asked, eyeing him.

'No! It was a . . . shout of delight,' Alex said, unconvincingly.

'Sounded more like a squeal to me,' Fetlock added. 'And I'm pretty sure I saw a flinch before he squealed.'

'I did not flinch,' Alex protested. 'I was . . . closing my eyes in excitement!'

'Great! Then now we spar!' Lorca said, brandishing her sword.

'Now?' stammered Alex. 'As in *now*-now? I mean –'

Without warning, Lorca swung at Alex, who snatched up his sword to protect himself. The blades clashed against each other and his hands shook with the vibration. She swung at him again, this time knocking his sword out of his hands.

Lorca eyeballed him. 'Have you *really* used a sword before?'

'Yes! Lots!' Alex lied. 'It's just . . . my arms are really tired.'

'Enough!' barked Chelsee, holding a hand up. 'You all need rest –'

'Exactly,' Alex nodded.

'For tomorrow your quest begins. An Impossible Quest where danger is certain and death is fated for some of you.'

'Thanks for the reminder,' Alex said. 'That will really help me getting to sleep.'

'Now,' said Chelsee. 'Who's for a spot of frog-rot pie?'

After dinner (which for Alex consisted of a leathery pie-crust with most of the frog-rot scraped off), Chelsee went off to bed, leaving blankets for Alex, Lorca and Fetlock in front of the fire. Within moments, Lorca was snoring gently, but as the fire glowed low, crackling softly, sleep evaded Alex. His mind was burning with questions. In particular, a question about a name.

'Fetlock?'

'Mmm?' Fetlock lifted a sleepy head.

'This Father of Flies I'm supposed to defeat. Who is he?'

Fetlock gave a quiet sigh. 'He is everything that is wrong with this world.'

'Could you tell me a little more?'

'Some call him the Father of Flies. Some call him the Engineer of Fear. But his real name is Felonious Gloam. He comes from a lowly background, but he has climbed and climbed, seeking more and more power, crushing all who stand in his way.'

'And I am supposed to defeat *him* to save the world?' Alex asked, incredulous.

Fetlock nodded. 'Each year his reach grows and spreads like mould. And anybody who dares even disagree with him is murdered. Or worse.'

'What's worse than being murdered?'

Fetlock leaned forward and whispered, 'I pray you never find out.'

Alex shuddered and decided that it would probably be for the best not to ask any more questions. Fetlock curled himself back up and was soon snoring. It took sleep much longer to take Alex, though. He lay awake for many hours until exhaustion finally consumed his whirling thoughts.

Alex woke to the smell of sizzling meat. He had never been so hungry in his life. He wolfed down the bacon and sausages that Chelsee presented to him but spat out the foul-tasting drink.

'What is that?'

'It's ale, of course,' Lorca replied.

'Ale? As in *beer*? You give beer to *children*? For *breakfast*?'

Chelsee shrugged and poured Lorca another mugful.

'What's your problem?' Fetlock asked, his eyes glinting as he lapped his from a stone bowl. 'You not big enough to drink ale?'

'Yes! Of course I am! I – erm – drink it all the time,'

Alex lied, and to prove his point he took a great swig. It was the foulest thing he had tasted in his life. He tried to hide his grimace and forced out a satisfied sigh. 'Delicious,' he squeaked, wiping his mouth.

Fetlock finished his last sausage and went back to his place by the fire, hobbling slightly. Spotting Alex watching, he answered the question before Alex could ask it. 'I just get a little stiff in the mornings, OK? It's nothing.'

Breakfast was cleared away, although the ale still gurgled ferociously in Alex's belly and his head felt a little light. While Lorca was busy packing a gigantic backpack with dozens of assorted weapons, Chelsee approached Alex and handed him the sword from the previous night.

'You will need to learn how to use it,' she said. 'My daughter will teach you. She is a great fighter.'

Fetlock spluttered. 'Errr . . . would we say *great*?'

'OK, she is a very good fighter!'

Fetlock tilted his head. 'What about that time she was tasked to rid the North Country of the Slightly Grumpy Badger?'

'All right, she is a significantly above-average fighter –'

'And the battle with the Gentle Granny of Glossop

Green? She didn't come off well there either, as I recall.'

'That granny was not gentle,' protested Chelsee. 'She had a knuckle-duster.'

'She was ninety-two years old.'

'Fine! She is a slightly above-average fighter, most of the time.'

'I am very reassured,' Alex said, very un-reassured.

'The thing is, Alex, Lorca has the biceps, and she has the bravery, but she has not been overly burdened with brains. My daughter is as loyal as the day is long but not blessed with wisdom. Please, promise me you'll look after her.'

Alex nodded uncertainly. 'I'm not your usual go-to guy for looking after things. I mean, the school hamster lasted less than a day with me. Who knew hoovers could be so . . . sucky?' Alex was surprised to see Chelsee's eyes suddenly well with tears. 'Oh, I think it was a quick death.'

'I'm not worried about your hamster. I'm worried about *her*!' Chelsee choked, nodding at her daughter. 'She's all I have.'

'I'll try, but –'

'You were brought to Aërth for a purpose, Alex Always! You will find strength. So, please, take care of her.'

And, for some reason that Alex felt was knitted in his bones, he suddenly knew that he would. He *would* look after Lorca – or do his best, anyway. He nodded solemnly. 'I promise I will look after her. And keep her well away from hoovers.'

'And buckets.' Chelsee sniffed. 'She doesn't do well with buckets, neither.'

'And buckets as well.'

'Thank you.' Chelsee gave him a warm smile. 'Now, here. Take this.' She passed him a small metal disc, burnished with a deep engraving of whorls of leaves. 'Be careful with it. It has been passed down this family for generations. It's incredibly precious.'

'It's a . . . errr . . . mirror?' Alex asked, opening it.

'Not just an ordinary mirror – it's an All-Seeing-I.'

'What's an All-Seeing-I?'

'A magical object! When you look into it, it shows you the person you need to see most.'

'It can see anyone I want?' Alex grinned. 'Cool!'

'No,' explained Chelsee. 'Not who you *want* to see. It shows you the person you *need* to see.'

'So, it's not really *all*-seeing then?'

'Look, do you want it or not?' snapped Chelsee.

'Yes! Absolutely. But how do I choose who I need to see the most?'

'You don't. The All-Seeing-I will know. Just give your heart to it.'

Alex ran his fingers over the shining metal. 'Thank you,' he said.

'Now, it's time for you to go,' Chelsee said with a brave smile.

They walked outside into the warmth of a summer morning. Chelsee grabbed her daughter and hugged her tightly.

'Goodbye, Mum,' said Lorca brightly. 'See you soon.'

Alex, Lorca and Fetlock set off, the path quickly leaving the town of Howden Leeth behind and winding among fields dotted with flowers. They walked through the morning, the sky darkening, threatening rain. Eventually, the clouds opened and they took cover under a tree and sat nibbling lunch until the rain stopped.

They were about to get up when suddenly Fetlock froze.

'Wait!' He stared out across the field in front of them. 'If I'm not mistaken, we are about to see something remarkable.'

Alex squinted. It looked like a perfectly ordinary muddy field.

Then he heard something. Slowly swelling up from the ground was music.

Lorca gasped. 'Can it be?'

A moment later, Alex saw the field come alive. Though it wasn't the field itself – it was *worms*, countless in number, wriggling out of the ground to greet the warm summer rain. More than that, they were singing – the most beautiful song Alex had ever heard in his life.

His eyes filled with tears. 'What . . . is it?' he managed to ask.

But Fetlock and Lorca were unable to speak, their own eyes brimful, so Alex simply gave himself over to the worms' song, letting it flood him with happiness and joy, his heart a cathedral of wonder, every fibre of his being aching with love. Words he didn't understand answered questions he couldn't speak, filling an emptiness he didn't even know he had. On and on the ethereal song went, until it reached a perfect crescendo and then finally died away. The choir fell silent and the worms wriggled back below the mud.

'That,' Fetlock said, 'was the Chorus of the Worms. It happens only once a year, when the conditions are just right. It's a good omen for our quest.'

For a while, they walked on in silence, feet squelching in the wet earth, each lost in their own memory of the music, but eventually they found their voices and they began chatting again. When Lorca went to scout ahead, Alex sidled up to Fetlock.

'One thing I don't understand is why Chelsee let Lorca come on this quest,' he said. 'If she's so worried about her, why didn't she just tell her she couldn't go?'

Fetlock thought for a while before he spoke.

'Because it is fated. Because Lorca is part of the story now. As are you, and as am I. And what would the world be without stories?'

Alex wasn't certain that was a proper explanation, but it would have to do. 'Thank you, Fetlock,' Alex said, reaching out towards his companion's head.

Fetlock snarled. 'Try to pat me and I'll bite your hand off!'

'I'm sorry!' Alex jumped back. 'I thought dogs liked getting patted.'

'Not this one.'

Falling back behind Fetlock, Alex thrust his hands into his pockets. His fingertips brushed metal. With everything going on, he'd forgotten about the All-Seeing-I. He pulled it out and opened it. The mirrored surface shone in the sun, then began to cloud over. It was working!

Alex's heart pounded. Who would the All-Seeing-I decide he needed to see the most? Gran? Sienna? The Father of Flies?

Slowly, the clouds parted and Alex could see . . .

Axel Stormward.

On the toilet.

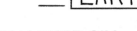

CHAPTER SIX

CONCERNING WARLOCKS AND MARRIAGE PROPOSALS

'By the gods,' Axel said, striding into the kitchen and sitting at the wobbly plastic table. 'That was the most palatial Brown Throne ever to host my heroic buttocks. Now – back to this luxurious breakfast you promised me.'

'It's Weetabix as usual,' Gran said, rolling her eyes.

Axel spooned the cereal into his mouth and grimaced. 'You call this gruel "weetenbisk"?'

'Weet-A-bix. And you have it every day. Now, look, I've got to get to work and –'

'Where I come from, this slop would not be fit to feed the goats. And if you tried, they'd tell you exactly what they thought of it.'

'What do you mean, "where I come from"? And if you don't like it, I'll get rid,' Gran said, reaching for his bowl. 'I don't have time for your play-acting.'

'No!' Axel said, pulling the bowl away. 'I need strength to complete my quest, so I must eat this mushy weetenbisk!' He grimaced as he forced down another spoonful. 'Now, get me some ale to wash the foul taste of this sludge away!'

'You what?'

'Ale, woman! Do you have any ale?'

Gran took a deep breath. 'Alex, you are only twelve years old. I'm not giving you ale. Especially not for breakfast. God, you're beginning to sound more and more like your father.'

'As I have told you many times, my name is Axel, not Alex. And twelve winters is age enough, so get me my ale, crone!'

'If you "crone" me one more time,' Gran said, raising a very straight finger millimetres from Axel's nose, 'then, role-playing or not, I'll skin you alive! You get me?'

Axel sniffed. There was something in this woman's steely voice that suggested she perhaps ought not to be crossed. Despite her only being tiny, her anger somehow made him feel smaller than her and caused his legs to weaken. Clearly, there was dark magic at work. He decided to change tack. He unleashed one of his most charming and heroic smiles.

'I get you.'

'Now wipe that stupid smirk off your face and get ready or you'll be late for school. I've got to get to work. And I can't find my bus pass,' she added, a look of concern crossing her face.

'I shall prepare with great speed,' Alex said, jumping to his feet. 'But first . . . What is this "school" of which you speak? I do not have time for distractions if I am to complete my quest.'

'What quest?' Gran replied, baffled.

Axel pulled out his tiny scroll again. 'My Impossible Quest!'

He squinted at the words on the parchment.

An evil genius bars your way,
A new war game you now must play.
Far from the sound of battle horn,
A challenge fresh, of brains not brawn
Awaits across the chequered board,
Far from the screaming goblin horde.
Two realms are crossed, two quests unfurled –
Defeat the father, save the world.

'What can it mean?' Axel eyed Gran. 'Are you an evil genius? You certainly don't *look* like one.'

'Lord, give me strength,' Gran groaned, covering her face with her hands.

Alex looked up from the All-Seeing-I with a gasp.

'Gran thinks that person is me? How does she not realize? He's . . . he's . . . an idiot.'

Lorca, who had come back from scouting ahead, peered into the All-Seeing-I.

'Ah! *That* is Axel Stormward. You do look remarkably similar. But see his muscles? His proud, heroic bearing and magnificently wavy hair? How could I have mistaken you for him?'

'Hush!' exclaimed Alex. 'I'm trying to watch!'

Axel scowled in disbelief.

'So, you say they do not teach swordsmanship, jousting or dragon riding at "school". What *do* they teach then?'

'Good question. Nothing much useful, from what I can tell,' replied Gran. 'Now get changed quick, else you'll be late.'

Axel shook his head. 'I am content with what I am wearing.'

'You're not going to school in *that*,' she said, pointing at his leather armour. 'Leaves nothing to the imagination. Where's your uniform?'

At that moment the doorbell rang.

'That'll be Sienna,' Gran said. 'And that means you're late. So, get ready or I'll flay you alive!'

'Alive?' Axel gasped.

'Come on! Shift yourself.' She opened the front door. 'Morning, lovie,' she said to Sienna, who was blowing on her hands to keep them warm.

'Y'all right?' replied Sienna, bustling in. 'Freezing out there.'

'I should warn you, Alex still isn't quite himself this –'

Sienna stood stock-still.

'I don't believe it. I convinced myself it was a dream . . . but it's not.'

'Ah, come on, Alex! Move yourself!' Gran bellowed. 'Sienna can't be standing around all day waiting for you.'

'Mrs A,' Sienna said slowly. 'This isn't –'

'Exactly!' shouted Gran. 'This isn't the time for messing about, Alex. I won't tell you again – get changed!'

'I will not wear the uniform of school!' Axel crossed his arms defiantly.

Gran turned to Sienna and sighed. 'You tell him. I've got to get to work.'

Sienna squared up to Axel. 'Your gran's right. You can't be wearing *that* for school. And what are those tiny leather circles for anyway?'

'They are my nipple protectors,' said Axel. 'And that's dragonskin, not leather.'

'Why on *earth* do you need to protect your nipples?' Sienna asked.

'A nick on the nipple from a sword edge can be exceedingly painful,' Axel replied, as if this was the most obvious answer in the world.

'Look, Mrs A,' Sienna said. 'I know this is gonna be difficult for you to believe, but this in't Alex. I mean, look at how muscly he is . . .'

'Why, thank you for noticing.' Axel flashed his biceps. 'I forge my body at the Furnace of Fortitude, honing it to be the hero the world needs.'

'I think he's been working out,' said Gran.

'Working out what?'

Gran gave a sigh. 'What *is* wrong with you? Did you bang your head, Alex?'

'What is wrong with *you*?' Axel snapped back. 'My

88

name is not *Alex*. It is *Axel*. Axel Stormward. And I am on a quest! She knows!' Axel nodded at Sienna. 'She saw me arrive. Didn't you?'

'He's right!' exclaimed Sienna. 'This isn't our Alex.'

Gran stared at Sienna. 'Don't be so bloomin' daft, love. Course it's Alex.'

'Honest, I'm not being daft. I think something really weird has happened. I think our Alex and Axel . . . they've somehow swapped.'

Gran closed her eyes and let out a long sigh.

'Sienna, you can't feed his delusions.'

'But –'

'There's no buts. No ifs. This is Alex. My grandson.' Gran flung her arms up in the air. 'Anyway, I can't be doing with this now. I can't find me glasses, I've got bills up to here, and I am *not* having him hang around the flat all day in his leather armour! So, both of you get yourselves to school. NOW!'

And with that, she stormed into the living room.

Sienna walked over to Axel, put a gentle hand on his arm and spoke gently. 'Right, your – I mean *Alex's* – gran really doesn't get it. So until we work out what's going on, you're gonna have to pretend to be Alex. So, come on. Go and get ready for school.'

Axel looked at Sienna's hand on his arm, then into her eyes, and then back at the hand. 'Wherever you go, I shall follow.'

'Okaaaaay,' Sienna said uncertainly. 'Does that include school?'

'I shall follow you to the ends of the world! Such beauty I have never beheld. Your skin, 'tis the colour of –'

'If you say chocolate or coffee, I will actually punch you.'

Axel shook his head. 'I don't know what those things are. Your words are as full of mystery as your night-dark eyes. Oh, wonderous maiden, my heart shall not rest until you are mine.'

'You *what* now?!' said Sienna, blinking in disbelief.

'What is your name, sweet lady?'

'It's Sienna, and you need to –'

'Sienna. Such a beautiful name. Like a song to my ears. Tell me, Sienna, is your hand promised to another?'

'Of course not, I'm twelve years old!'

'Well, then,' said Axel. 'It is settled. I shall marry you.'

'Oh. My. God.' Alex groaned and covered his eyes. 'No. No, no, no. I actually can't watch!'

'Well, why don't you stop then?' Lorca asked.

'Don't be ridiculous! Obviously, I'm not going to stop. I need to see what this idiot does next!'

'Marry me? You'll do no such thing!' Sienna blasted. 'Now, get yourself ready!'

Axel winced. 'You know, you have the face of an angel but the voice of a devil!'

'Ex-*cuse* me?' Sienna replied, crossing her arms.

'Your voice,' replied Axel, wincing again. 'It is harsh and guttural, unbefitting a fair maiden. But with guidance and training, you may yet learn the manner of a lady.'

'Right,' said Sienna. 'I've just about had enough of your nonsense, Axel Leather-nipples.'

'Axel *Stormward*. And they're dragonsk—'

'WHATEVER! It's nearly eight thirty. I'm going to school and *you* are coming with me. I need to keep an eye on you.'

'One moment, my princess! I shall dress forthwith in the uniform of school.'

Axel ran off, leaving Sienna in stunned silence.

A few moments later he returned in Alex's lost property uniform, which miraculously fitted him even worse than Alex.

'What hellish garb is this?' Axel said, pulling at the too-tight jumper. 'Never in my life have I worn such ugly and restrictive clothing.'

'Well, that's what you have to wear, so don't moan,' Gran said, coming out of the living room, glasses in hand. 'Oh, and Alex?'

'Yes?'

'Take the sword off.'

'But *why*?' Axel whined.

'I've told you already. You can't take a sword into school.'

Axel took off his sword, shaking his head. 'Utter madness.'

'Now get out of here and give us a minute's peace,' Gran said. 'I can't think with all this racket.'

At that moment, the doorbell rang again. In the frosted glass was the unmistakable silhouette of Irving.

Sienna flung the door open and dragged Axel out of the flat. Axel dug in his heels as he saw Irving – the small, round frame, the shock of dark hair, the black coat and tight drainpipe trousers.

'Is this warlock accompanying us on our quest?' he demanded.

'You what?' Irving said.

'Yes!' replied Sienna. 'He's coming with us.'

'Fine.' Axel glared at Irving. 'But do not try any of your dark magic on me, warlock. I am fully trained in magic repelling.'

Irving stood, mouth flapping like a beached eel. 'What's got into you, Alex?'

'Guessing you didn't check your messages last night,' Sienna said. 'So there's a *lot* I need to tell you. Something's wrong. This is not –'

'Something is indeed wrong!' interrupted Axel, looking around the street. 'Where is my horse?'

'Your *horse*?' Irving asked.

'Yes, my horse,' snapped Axel impatiently. 'My mount. My noble steed. I need a steed to carry me on my quest! I cannot simply *walk* like a common peasant. I am a *hero*.'

'W-wha–' stammered Irving.

'Hero or not,' said Sienna, 'there is no horse. We walk. Get used to it.'

'W-what's going on?' Irving asked, as they set off.

Sienna turned to Irving and placed her hand gently on his arm. 'I know this is going to be difficult to believe, but something happened last night.'

She recounted the events of the previous evening.

'So, you're saying Alex got sucked into some sort

of . . . vortex?' Irving whispered in disbelief. 'And swapped with *him*?'

Sienna nodded. 'I know how it sounds. But it's true.'

'I . . . I don't believe it. It's impossible.'

'Yes! Exactly! Impossible!' said Axel, grinning excitedly. 'An Impossible Quest.'

'Oh yeah, he keeps banging on about a quest too,' Sienna said, as they speed-walked down the high street.

'It is not just *a* quest,' said Axel. 'It is an *Impossible Quest*. And I think your friend Alex has somehow got himself mixed up in it.'

'I saw what happened to Alex,' said Sienna. 'It wasn't his fault! He just got . . . sucked in!'

'And swapped places with me,' said Axel. 'Just as I was handed my Impossible Quest.'

'I can't believe I'm saying this,' said Irving. 'But it sounds like this quest thing might be important.'

'There! You see! The warlock believes me!'

Sienna gave a huff. 'Right. Fine. We'll talk about your quest at lunch. But first you need to get through the morning without anybody thinking there is owt wrong with you.'

'There *is* nothing wrong with me!' replied Axel. 'In fact, I'm amazing!'

'You'd better be an amazing actor, cos if you keep on like this you'll probably get locked up, and then you'll never complete your quest, so you need to at least *try* and act normal.'

'What is normal?' Axel asked. 'Is the warlock normal? Are you normal?'

Sienna rolled her eyes. 'Look, just keep that flappy mouth of yours shut, yeah? Or you are going to end up in a *lot* of trouble.'

'Do not fear, my sweet Sienna. You have my word.'

Axel kept his word for less than two minutes.

'What are these noisy metal beasts?' Axel cried as they approached the school gates. 'What strange magic powers them?'

'You mean . . . cars?' Irving asked.

'Are they powered by your dark magic, warlock? Truly, I have been cast to a strange land. Great gods alive!' Axel screamed, covering his head. 'What is that huge creature in the air? Some fearsome Fire Drake?'

'It's a plane,' Sienna said. 'And he's not a warlock!'

'What is he, then? A sorcerer?'

'No! He's just a goth. His name is Irving and – oh, *please*, you have to be quiet now. Nathan Jones is coming towards us. Just try not to attract attention.'

'You wish me to blend in?'

'Yes!'

'Like the Black-Cloaked Spies of Wazzon-Free?'

'Yes! Nathan's the actual worst.'

'I shall be as silent as the Mute Monks of the Murmuring Mountains!' whispered Axel, as Nathan stepped up to them.

'Where do you geeks think you're going?' Nathan asked.

'Well, let me see,' Sienna replied. 'It's a school day, we're all dressed in school uniform and we're standing outside school ... Can you hazard a guess? Let's go, guys.' She pulled Axel by the arm.

'What is a "geek"?' Axel whispered to Sienna. 'Is it a type of hero?'

Nathan gave a braying laugh. 'No, geek. I wasn't saying you're a hero.'

'Well, I am one.'

'Come on, let's go,' urged Sienna. 'You promised . . .'

Nathan burst out laughing again. 'You? A hero? You wish.'

'I do not wish,' Axel replied. 'I *am*. Fully qualified. Grade Nine, actually.'

Nathan cracked up into a storm of laughter.

'Do you mock me?' Axel asked.

Nathan creased over, laughing even more.

'I feel he might be mocking me,' Axel said to Sienna.

'I feel you may be right,' Irving said. 'I recognize cruel taunts when I hear them.'

'Pleeeease,' pleaded Sienna. 'Let's just go.'

'Yes, I am,' said Nathan, squaring up to Axel, a full head higher than him. 'I *am* mocking you. And what are you going to do about it?'

'You are too puny to be worth my while,' Axel said. 'Does the mighty bear care about the worm?'

A tiny laugh escaped Irving, and his hand shot up to cover his mouth. Nathan glared at him.

'Sorry!' squeaked Irving.

Nathan turned his attention back to Axel. He gave him a sharp shove. 'Who are you calling a worm?'

Sienna jumped in between them. 'Leave it, Nathan. Now, come with us, *Alex*,' she shouted, pulling Axel away.

'Aww, your little girlfriend is saving you,' Nathan sneered.

'She is not my *girlfriend*,' Axel shouted back. 'We are betrothed!'

Nathan roared with laughter once again, as Irving and Sienna dragged Axel away.

'Come on,' pleaded Sienna. 'Just stop talking before you make it any worse.'

'Yeah, run away again, coward,' Nathan shouted.

Axel stopped walking. '*What* did you call me?'

'You heard. You're a coward.'

And then, before anybody could say another word, Axel Stormward strode back to Nathan, seized him by the shoulders and lifted him clear above his head.

'Put me down!' Nathan squealed, wriggling furiously.

'If you say so,' Axel roared, and threw Nathan head first into the large wheelie bin standing just inside the school gates.

Sienna's and Irving's jaws dropped.

'Now, let us go,' said Axel, clapping his palms together. 'My quest awaits.'

'You'll pay for that, Always!' Nathan shouted, as they walked into school. 'You're dead meat!'

Irving turned to Sienna.

'Now *that* was the coolest thing I have ever seen.'

'Oh my God.' Alex gave a groan, his face wracked with despair. 'I am completely dead when I get back to school. My life there is officially over. That idiot is ruining everything.'

'Do not worry,' Lorca said, putting a reassuring

hand on his shoulder. 'It does not look as if you had much of a life anyway.'

Alex turned away. Lorca had a point. As he thought of Nathan trying to climb out of the wheelie bin, covered in muck and bin juice, Alex couldn't help but feel the swell of something deep inside him. A feeling he hardly recognized.

A feeling of triumph.

In the deepest, dankest corner of the lowest cellar of the castle lay a trapdoor, illuminated by a single burning torch.

Footsteps echoed in the dark and a tall, gaunt man approached, cockroaches skittering about his feet. The light of the torch cast his waxen face with a sickly, yellow pallor.

He bent over and lifted the trapdoor. A shout rang out from the blackness below.

'Let me out of here, you fool! You don't know what you are doing!'

The man licked his bottom lip with a lizard-like darting tongue.

'I'm afraid to say, old man,' he replied. 'I know *exactly* what I am doing.'

'Please! Let me out of this infernal place!' cried the Narrator. 'The White Death is spreading, faster and faster! You must give me the book back! I must return to telling their stories!'

'You know I'm not going to do that. But we do need to talk.'

The man pulled the flickering torch from the wall, and carefully stepped down into the dark hole.

The light revealed a tiny stone cell and an old man, half-naked and chained to the wall, his hands high above his head. Across his body crawled hundreds of spiders – in his hair and over his eyes and his mouth.

'Remove your creatures,' the old man ordered.

The gaunt man gave a short laugh. 'You can't control me, Narrator. Not any more. But if it allows you to speak freely . . .'

He muttered a few words, and the spiders crawled from the old man's face and body.

'Now, set me free, Gloam.'

'Ahh, my real name,' the man said, pulling a stool from the corner of the cell. 'Few know it. But of course *you* do. Because you gave it to me, didn't you, Narrator? My name and my story. Do you remember?'

The Narrator did not reply.

'Well, allow me to remind you. Remind you of my story. Of the life *you* wrote for me. To begin with, you wrote that my mother would die giving birth to me. And that because of that, my father would always hate me. Often, he would forget to feed me, but he never forgot to beat me. That was until one spring morning, when he fell into the river, swollen with icy meltwater. I watched as he swirled through the churning foam, screaming for my help. I did not give it. He was swept away, never to be seen again. This was the story you wrote for me. I was eight years old.'

Felonius Gloam shifted on his stool. 'After that, I grew up hungry, cold and utterly alone. For ten years I had no home, but I was not the only frightened, hungry child on the streets. There were many, many more. You wrote their stories too. So much pain and misery. Why?'

'I created life!' protested the Narrator. 'There was always beauty and light.'

'Yes, and the brighter the light you made, the deeper the shadow it cast. You wrote more. When I was nineteen, I met a girl and we fell in love. She bore me a child – a son, fair and strong. Happiness, at last, or so I thought. But one starless night, she fled from me, taking my son. I tracked them down eventually, but by that time, she had poisoned my son against me. She had stolen him, and with him my last naive belief that there could be happiness in this world.

'Since that day, I have sought nothing but power. I studied dark arts, old magic. I learned to control insects, and that taught me how to control humans, who are no better than creatures that crawl in the dirt and mud. As my power increased, Narrator, you wrote another twist into my tale – a deadly disease that should have been the end of my life. Death called for me, but I would not listen. I was too full of rage, too full of anger towards the one who had written for me such a bleak, pointless life. At you, Narrator. You.

'Using the darkest spells, I forced my soul to live again. And live I did –the magic tore me from your grasp, tore my story from your Book of Lifetales. Free, I could finally tell my own tale, live my own life. And I have used it to get my revenge upon you, and this world of pain you have created. To do that, I needed your Book. Now I have it. And once you teach me how to use it, *I* will control the story of Aërth.'

'Never!' shouted the Narrator.

Gloam smiled thinly. 'Then the White Death shall spread unchecked, and all shall die. You have the power of life and death. Show me how to use the Book! Give me that power!'

'No,' replied the Narrator. 'I can only shape life, not create it. I merely tell a person's story, I do not end it.'

'Teach me how to shape life then!'

'I cannot simply teach you.' The Narrator hung his head. 'You do not understand. There are deeper powers at work.'

'No. *You* do not understand. Your time is over, old man. You created a world full of pain and cruelty. Broken bodies and broken minds. I will start this world afresh. Rid it of all the people that exist now. They are so . . . *damaged*. I shall scrub the world of illness, poverty and deviance. Humans – so defectively made. The possibility to be angels, they act like beasts: murderers and liars, grasping about in the mud for wealth with their filthy, greedy hands before they die a pointless death. No more. I will create a new world of beauty and harmony. Of perfection. It will be a heaven upon Aërth. And I shall be a far more benevolent ruler than you. All I need to create this paradise is for you to teach me how to use the Book of Lifetales.'

The Narrator shook his head. 'I will not help you.'

Gloam shrugged. 'Then I shall teach myself. It will take longer, but I have time. The White Death cannot touch me. And you can stay here and rot, knowing that all the lives that you crafted are gradually fading out of existence, one by one, like dying stars.'

Felonious Gloam stood, climbed out of the cell and whispered a word. Even before the trapdoor had closed, the spiders were crawling back over the old man's face, as he wept in the dark.

CHAPTER SEVEN

A VISIT TO THE HEADTEACHER

'Right,' said Sienna, as she hurried Axel down a crowded corridor after registration. 'First lesson is history. Irving's meeting us there.'

Axel growled in frustration. 'I need to be looking to the future, to my quest, not wasting my time studying the past!'

'I've told you, we'll talk about your quest as soon as we can. So, for now, you *need* to get your head down,' hissed Sienna. 'And keep that trap of yours shut.'

'A trap?' Axel gasped, looking around.

'Your *gob*,' Sienna clarified. 'Keep your *gob* shut.'

Axel's eyes narrowed. 'My *what*? I have no idea what a gob is, nor indeed how to shut it.'

'Yeah, that much is obvious.'

'Right,' continued Sienna, as they arrived at a classroom door. 'We're here. Now, Mr Grover's really not to be messed with, so *please* –'

'Is it a type of goblin?' asked Axel, his brow furrowing.

'You what?'

'Is a gob a type of goblin? Because I would not want to face a horde of goblins without Aëthelmrir.'

'Ethel what?'

'Aëthelmrir. My sword. My constant companion in all my heroic tasks.'

Sienna's eyes gleamed. 'Actually, your *heroic task* right now is to be as quiet as possible.'

'My heroic task is . . . to be quiet?' Axel asked suspiciously. 'That doesn't sound very brave.'

'It *is* brave! It's desperately important that you are quiet! I'm relying on you. Alex is relying on you. *Everyone* is relying on you. So do not speak unless spoken to. Can you manage that?'

Axel bowed. 'For you, sweet Sienna, I shall be as silent as a moonbeam over a sleeping forest.'

'Thank you.'

'It shall be my honoured duty!' he boomed. 'When a beautiful damsel –'

'Stop booming!'

'Why? Has the heroic task already started?'

'Yes!'

'Ah!' Axel held a finger to his lips, then gave Sienna a wink.

Sienna opened the door and walked in. Axel followed and she pointed to an empty seat next to Irving.

'Hail, warlock!' Axel boomed again. 'I hope you haven't been casting any dark spells recently.'

Irving shrank into his chair, his pale face getting a rare flash of colour.

Nathan and his gang had occupied the back row. Their leader, still grubby from his bin-dumping, glared at Axel. But Axel remembered his promise and ignored them.

'These chairs are so tiny,' he whispered to Sienna, shifting uncomfortably. 'I feel very unheroic. Can you get me a throne?'

'No!' sputtered Sienna angrily. 'You're not having a throne.'

Mr Grover, the history teacher, a man with a reputation for being as prickly as his moustache, walked in. To Sienna's great relief, Axel had the good sense to keep his gob shut. And to keep it shut until the end of the lesson. Almost.

'Now, before we go,' Mr Grover said, 'can anybody give me one of the causes of the Second World War?'

Nobody raised their hand.

'Come on. Anybody? You, boy.'

To Sienna's horror, she saw the teacher was pointing at Axel.

'Me?' Axel replied.

'Yes, you. Come on, we haven't got all day.'

'You want me to tell you the cause of the Second Great War of the World?'

'Yes!' snapped Mr Grover.

'Well, it was when the Frost Giants of the Mountains of Nephroth invaded the Golden Plains of Sharuh-Din, killing every elf that resided there.' Axel shook his head sadly.

Sienna's face dropped in horror. The rest of the class tittered nervously. Mr Grover approached Axel, moustache twitching furiously.

'Do you think that's funny?'

'No!' Axel said, outraged. 'It was very sad! Thousands of elves wiped out overnight. Senseless.'

The class burst out laughing, led by a braying Nathan. Sienna buried her head in her hands as Irving looked on in horror.

Mr Grover bent over the desk until his face was centimetres from Axel's. His voice simmered with barely restrained violence.

'Always, if you don't get out of this room and go to the headteacher's office right this second, I will not be held responsible for my actions.'

'One should always be held responsible for one's

actions,' replied Axel seriously. 'For a hero must be judged on his deeds, not his words.'

'GET OUT!' screamed Mr Grover. 'This INSTANT!'

Sienna's hand shot up. 'Sir, I'm not sure Alex is feeling too well, so maybe I should take him?'

'Whatever.' Mr Grover waved a dismissive hand. 'Just get him out of here.'

'What were you thinking?' Sienna demanded, as they trudged down the corridor towards the headteacher's office.

'He asked me!' protested Axel.

'Well, if Miss Spreckley asks you anything, don't mention Frost Giants or elves or golden plains, just tell her you've been feeling funny since breakfast. Here we are. Now you knock on the door and wait to be called.'

Axel frowned. 'Knock? Like a nervous servant? Would it not be better to just march in, to show her I am not to be trifled with?'

'That would be a really bad idea.' Sienna knocked lightly on the door.

'Come!'

'I don't know why I'm bothering saying this,' said Sienna. 'But please – remember Alex. Remember the quest. Act normal!'

'I think your idea of normal is very different to mine,' Axel muttered, then puffed his chest out. 'And now to face the danger inside!'

Before Sienna could say another word, Axel barged into the office.

Miss Spreckley, a sticklike figure with long, poker-straight hair and huge round glasses, sat behind a desk, her fingers steepled beneath her chin.

'Ha!' roared Axel. 'I was expecting a demon! I didn't realize you were just another old crone!'

'*What* did you call me?' asked Miss Spreckley dangerously.

'I called you an old crone,' said Axel slowly. 'WOULD YOU LIKE ME TO SPEAK MORE LOUDLY?'

The headteacher slowly took off her glasses and stared at Axel. 'Let me tell you what will happen if –'

Axel interrupted her with a gasp, his face suddenly enraptured. 'You are a fortune teller? How wonderous! Pray, forgive me and share your wisdom, oh ancient one! Can you help me with my quest? Allow me to read it to you . . .'

Axel pulled the little scroll out of his pocket.

'Alex, stop!' Miss Spreckley interrupted, her hand aloft. Her face softened and she spoke gently. 'Are you quite well? You are behaving rather oddly. Have you been hit on the head recently?'

'Many times!' replied Axel proudly. 'You can't go through nine levels of hero training without a few blows to the helmet.'

Miss Spreckley nodded slowly. 'Right. Well, I think I may need to talk to your grandmother about your . . . situation. Is there somebody who can help you home after school?'

'Yes! Sienna can guide me. She waits outside.'

'Excellent. Well, I suggest you head back to class for –'

'We are betrothed.'

Miss Spreckley blinked. 'Pardon?'

'Sienna and I – we are to be wed.'

'You and Sienna are *engaged*? I find that very hard to believe.'

'So does Sienna. She is a very lucky young lady.' Axel gave the headteacher one of his most charming smiles. 'Good day!'

Axel rushed out to Sienna, who was waiting in the corridor.

'OK?' she asked. 'You didn't say anything too odd?'

'No! All completely fine. She *might* have suspected there was something amiss when I mentioned our betrothal, but I think I got away with it.'

Sienna glared at Axel suspiciously. 'Hmm. Come on. Let's go. It's double maths.'

'Is double maths fun?' Axel asked hopefully.

Sienna's lips quirked into a smile.

'Definitely.'

'You lied to me,' Axel moaned to Sienna, clutching his head as he stared at the page in front of him. 'This is a torture so evil, no mortal can withstand it!'

For an hour, Axel had wrestled with the sums set by the teacher but was no closer to solving them than when he had started.

Sienna shushed him. 'Remember the quest!' she whispered. 'Soon we can start planning.'

When the bell finally went, Axel gave a groan of relief. 'Is . . . it . . . over?' he asked, his gaze hollow.

'Yes,' said Sienna. 'It's over.'

'Thank the gods! Sweet, blessed relief!'

'Until tomorrow.'

'What?!'

'Come on, let's find Irving and grab some lunch – then we can talk quests!'

'Ah!' exclaimed Axel, as they made their way into the canteen. 'Lunch! I cannot wait to see what delicious food is served here! After such gruelling work, we will certainly be rewarded with the finest delicacies in the land!'

'Riiight,' said Irving, as they collected their trays and sat down.

'What do you call this?' Axel eyed his plate warily and prodded it with his fork.

'Macaroni cheese,' Irving said.

'Does it always smell like this?'

'It does at this school,' Irving muttered.

Axel took a mouthful and grimaced. 'It tastes like sick and misery.'

Irving grinned. 'You're right there!'

'If the cooks served this in the Hallowed Halls of Heroism, they would be thrown in a dungeon.'

'Yeah, well, we don't have any dungeons round here,' replied Sienna.

'More's the pity,' said Axel. 'Now, we must discuss my quest.' He pulled the tiny scroll from his pocket.

'Wait a second,' Irving said, holding his hand up. 'Before we start – Sienna, are you sure about all this?'

'About what?'

'This . . . *swapping* thing. Alex and Axel . . . I mean, I can see that this isn't the Alex we know, but I find it hard to believe . . .'

Axel put down his fork and spoke in a lower voice.

'I understand this might be difficult for you to comprehend, warlock, but, for just one moment, dismiss from your mind all thought of what is possible and what is not. Imagine that the impossible could happen. *Has* happened.'

'OK, but do you not think Alex's gran might have noticed?'

'You know how busy she is, Irving,' replied Sienna. 'She's distracted. She's got a lot on her mind. And Alex does look like him.'

'Pah!' snorted Axel. 'A puny version of me with all the heroism drained away, and hair not nearly so magnificently wavy. Perhaps if I'd had every one of my muscles sucked out by the Screaming Leeches of the Lakes of Lurking Light we might be mistaken for each other, but –'

'Oi, that's my friend you're talking about!' snapped Irving. 'But *how*, Sienna? You love science: how does this fit into science?'

Sienna scratched her head. 'Yeah, so, I've been thinking. Alex and Axel swapping could fit into the multiverse theory. Maybe some sort of rip in the fabric of the universe allowed them to fall between worlds.'

'Oh, come on!' Irving scoffed. 'You're saying that Alex has swapped places with some sort of interdimensional cosmic twin? That doesn't make any sense.'

Sienna threw up her hands. 'Irving, *nothing* makes sense if you stop and think. *Life* doesn't make sense. You are just a meat bag sitting on a huge rock hurtling through the vastness of infinite space. A meat bag made up of a bunch of molecules and electricity that have somehow managed to collect together and realize they're alive.'

'Ha!' laughed Axel. 'She called you a meat bag. Good one!'

Irving glared at Axel and was about to answer back, but Sienna continued, 'But if they *have* swapped places because of a multiversal fluctua– because of *magic* – then they can swap back. But I think only Axel can tell us how. So – want to tell us what you know?'

'Finally! Here is my quest.'

Axel unrolled the scroll for the others to see.

An evil genius bars your way,
A new war game you now must play.
Far from the sound of battle horn,
A challenge fresh, of brains not brawn
Awaits across the chequered board,
Far from the screaming goblin horde.
Two realms are crossed, two quests unfurled –
Defeat the father, save the world.

'What does it mean?' asked Sienna. 'Evil genius? A new form of battle? And defeat which father?'

'Silence!' Axel held up a hand. 'I shall now enter my Mind Dungeon, where my mighty brain shall do battle with this infernal riddle and force it to reveal the answer.'

Axel closed his eyes and scrunched up his face.

Before Sienna or Irving could say a single word, he opened his eyes again.

'Nope. Nothing. In a surprising turn of events I don't think any of us saw coming, my mighty brain has been defeated.'

CHAPTER EIGHT

A TRAGIC AND EARLY END

'Alex,' said Fetlock. 'You need to put the All-Seeing-I away.'

'No!' protested Alex. 'Just five more minutes! Axel's trying to escape from school by climbing out of a classroom window!'

'You cannot waste your life staring at this device, Alex,' said Fetlock. 'It is said that if you use the All-Seeing-I too much you can get oval eyes.'

'My eyes are already oval!'

'Alex . . .'

'OK, in a minute. He's trying to challenge a toilet to a duel!'

'Now, Alex! We need to get going. We must focus on this world. Our first great challenge is approaching: the Silent Forest.'

'Fine,' Alex huffed, putting the All-Seeing-I in his pocket.

'Yes!' Lorca grinned. 'Let's get to the *really scary* Silent Forest then.'

'Do not speak of it so lightly,' Fetlock warned.

'Why, what's so dangerous about it?' asked Alex.

'It is . . .' said Fetlock. 'Really quiet.'

Alex shrugged. 'Doesn't sound that bad.'

'You don't understand. The Silent Forest is really, *really* quiet.'

'Sounds rather nice, actually,' Alex replied. 'I'm quite looking forward to a bit of peace and quiet.'

'Ha!' snarled Fetlock. 'Let's see how you feel when you are in the very depths of a noiseless nightmare.'

'Do not fear –' Lorca gave a confident laugh and patted the weapon at her side – 'for, with my sword, all will be well.'

'Silence is not an enemy that can be fought with a blade,' Fetlock warned. 'For the battle is inside your own mind . . .'

'An axe, then,' Lorca said. 'I shall use my heaviest axe, if my sword will not work.'

'An axe?' Fetlock's eyes widened. 'What use would an axe be against your own mind? You going to bash yourself on the head with it?'

'Yes, if that is what is needed!'

Fetlock sighed, shaking his head. 'Let us go. The Silent Forest lies one day north from here.'

'Then northwards we shall go!' announced Lorca, striding off.

'Lorca,' called Fetlock. 'You're going south.'

'I knew that – I was just testing you.'

An hour into the walk, they were deep inside a thick wood.

'Is this the Silent Forest?' whispered Alex.

'Does it sound particularly silent to you?' Fetlock cupped a paw to his floppy ear. 'Hark! Birdsong, crickets! This is just a totally normal forest. Trust me, when we reach the Silent Forest you will know.'

They walked down a mulchy track that weaved through the trees for much of the day until dusk began to settle on them like falling ash.

'We must be careful,' Fetlock whispered, his whiskers twitching. 'For dusk is the most dangerous part of the day. The in-between time, when creatures slip from one realm to another.'

'Like chickens,' Lorca said. 'And stick insects.'

'No,' replied Fetlock slowly. 'Evil creatures.'

'Chickens can be evil,' Lorca said. 'I was attacked by one once. It wouldn't stop pecking my toes.'

Fetlock put a paw to his lips. 'Hush!' he whispered, his ears flattened. 'I hear something.'

'What's going on?' Alex asked nervously.

Lorca loosened her sword in its scabbard. 'Fetlock senses danger!'

Alex's breath quickened, his heart pounding. He placed his hand on his own sword uncertainly. 'Danger? What is it?'

'You don't know what danger is?' Lorca asked, looking at Alex as if he had half a brain.

'Of course I – never mind!'

Fetlock suddenly began running in circles, sniffing the ground.

Lorca gasped. 'Fetlock has caught the scent of something. Something *evil*!'

Alex felt his legs weaken in terror.

And then he saw it – a flash of grey, running between the trees.

Fetlock bolted after it.

'What is it?' Alex squinted, heart pounding. 'Where did it go?'

'I don't know,' replied Lorca. 'Be on your guard!'

A moment later, Fetlock loped back through the trees towards them, his tail down.

'What was it?' Alex asked, terrified of the reply.

'Hobgoblin?' asked Lorca eagerly. 'Ghoul? Dire wolf?'

'Squirrel,' said Fetlock.

'A *squirrel*?' Alex rolled his eyes. 'Oh, for *goodness'* sake!'

'Do not underestimate squirrels,' Fetlock growled. 'They are creatures of pure malevolence and spite. With really tempting fuzzy tails.'

'I thought we were in mortal danger and it was just a bloomin' squirrel?!' Alex stomped off. 'This is going to be a long quest.'

That evening, the campfire crackled as night closed slowly around them. Fetlock was curled up, eyes closed. Alex sat and stared into the dark. After a moment, wisps of colour began spreading across the night sky.

'What's that?' Alex asked, squinting.

'Oh,' Lorca yawned. 'That's just the Nightlights. Happens all the time.'

Suddenly, Alex did not need to squint. The sky was awash with colour – every colour imaginable – wave upon wave, rippling through the sky. Vivid pinks to shining golds, electric blues to vibrant greens undulated across the blackness of space.

'That's incredible,' Alex murmured. He'd seen photos of the Northern Lights but this was something else.

'Yeah, you get used to it.' Lorca shrugged. 'Now, go to sleep, Soft Alex. You need your rest. And I shall take first watch.'

'Why did you call me Soft Alex?'

'Because we are on an Impossible Quest, of course.' Lorca picked up a stick and swiped it through the air. 'We should have memorable nicknames. For people will talk of our deeds forevermore, down through the never-ending generations.'

'I'm not sure I want to be known forevermore as Soft Alex.'

'Well then, perhaps Feeble-Arm Alex?' suggested Lorca. 'Because you have not been blessed with a single muscle.'

'Can we not –'

'How about Mouse-Boy Alex? For whenever danger appears, you make a squeaking noise, like a terrified –'

'No! Can we just stick to plain old Alex, please?'

'But you aren't old?' said Lorca, her face furrowed in confusion. 'You are plain, though. How about Plain Young Alex?'

Alex sighed and lay back, listening to the crackle of the logs burning.

'Tell me about where you come from,' Lorca said,

prodding the fire with her stick. The smoke curled above them, into the night.

'It's hard to describe,' said Alex. 'It's like here but also totally different and –'

'Do you have goats?'

'Yes, but they don't –'

'And do you have cows?'

'Yes, but –'

'OK, that's all I wanted to know.'

'That's *everything*?' Alex sat up, incredulously. 'You meet someone from a completely different world and all you want to know is whether we have goats and cows?'

'Yup.'

'Unbelievable.'

'You get used to it,' Fetlock muttered, eyes still closed.

Lorca sighed. 'Very well, tell me about your family.'

'Well, there's only me and Gran,' Alex replied. 'My mum died when I was only two. I'm lucky, though; I've always had this great memory for stuff, and I can remember loads about her. Her eyes, and her hair, and her voice as she sang songs to me. I never knew my dad. I only found him last year. But ... well, he doesn't want anything to do with me. He's got his own family.'

Lorca said nothing, so Alex continued. 'But me and Gran manage fine. Although she's not getting any younger and she has to work so hard. And we owe money and I'm worried that we're going to lose our flat. So, yeah, I really need to get back to her.'

'I'm sorry,' Lorca said. 'Truly. And I shall do all that I can to help you find your way back home.'

'As will I, Alex,' Fetlock added. 'As will I.'

Alex wanted to thank them both but didn't trust his voice not to crack. Instead, he lay by the dying fire, his brain awhirl, until he dropped into sleep like falling from a cliff: sharp, swift and deep.

Alex woke to the smell of something roasting.

'Good morning, Plain Young Alex,' said Lorca, handing him a plate of charred meat.

Alex's stomach was rumbling at the aroma, so he accepted the plate and started chewing. The meat was tough and kept getting stuck in his teeth.

'What ith thish?' he asked, picking a particularly stubborn piece from between his molars.

'Fetlock nearly caught another squirrel. But it got

away.' Lorca nodded at their canine companion, who was looking extremely pleased with himself. 'But then he managed to catch a rat.'

Alex spat out the food and went off behind a bush to be sick.

So it was, with an emptier belly then when he had woken, Alex set off with the others for the Silent Forest. Fetlock trotted next to Alex as he walked, head down, feeling hungry and dejected.

'Not a fan of rat, then?' Fetlock said, a glint of humour in his eye.

Alex shot him a glare. 'No, Fetlock. I'm not.'

'Me neither. It's just . . . Well, I can't catch squirrels any more.' Fetlock sighed. 'In my prime, I was the bane of squirrels, but the older I get, the faster they seem to become. I think my squirrel-catching days might be over.'

After that, Fetlock fell quiet for a while.

The weather worsened. Apart from a brief hour where spring burst forth and flowers bloomed across the path, the clouds got thicker and more ominous the further they went.

'That'll probably be the last season-changer we see.' Fetlock shivered. 'We don't tend to get them further north than the Isle of Cloudreach.'

They arrived at Cloudreach a little later, a town

built entirely on a great lake. On the outskirts, small boats were connected by gangplanks, children running helter-skelter across them. Dominating the centre of the lake, vast buildings towered above the water, interlinked walkways curling between them like arteries. Huge arched bridges crossed each other, spanning the whole of the lake, but the bridges into and out of the town had been closed.

'Everyone's panicking because of the White Death,' said one of the guards, a man with a beard the size of a fully grown badger, shaking his head sadly. 'People leaving the city. Thieves coming in to loot. All a waste of time, if you ask me. Which nobody does. Everybody's done for, anyway. I mean, look . . .'

He gave a hollow laugh and held up a trembling arm for the three to see. The Mortmark had spread all the way up it and his whole arm was pale enough to see through. 'How long do you think I have left? Ah, don't answer. Nobody knows, so I have no idea why I'm asking a mangy old dog and two children.'

They left Cloudreach behind and crossed gently rolling hills, springy with moss and dotted with purple flowers, which opened and closed as if breathing. Alex tried not to grumble too much, especially about his increasingly weary legs and hungry belly, but as the afternoon wore on the brisk wind brought a chill with it, which began to seep into Alex's bones.

'It's cold outside,' Lorca said, giving a shiver.

'Yes, we know,' Fetlock said. 'We *are* outside.'

'Exactly. That's how you know it's cold outside. When you're outside and it's cold,' Lorca said.

Fetlock stopped and stared at Lorca. 'Exactly how many times were you dropped on your head as a baby?'

The two bickered on until, underneath a darkening bruise of a sky, the scenery gradually began to change; it flattened out, grass making way for blood-red earth, a stark white path cutting through to show the way. Fetlock gave a low warning growl.

'We are approaching the Silent Forest,' he said, his ears flattened.

A short while later, a gate appeared in the distance. As they approached, Alex could see a tall figure, kohl-eyed and dressed head to toe in black feathers. He held a staff in one hand and in the other a red shield emblazoned with a white tree.

'A dire-elf!' Fetlock breathed.

'That's an *elf*?' whispered Alex.

'Yes, and the worst sort. Born of the night and, well, just really miserable creatures. And they are the biggest gossips, so tell them *nothing* of our quest.'

'I *can* hear you, you know,' shouted the dire-elf. 'We also have exceptional hearing.'

Fetlock rolled his eyes.

'Want me to take off his head?' whispered Lorca, drawing her sword.

'I'd like to see you try!' shouted the dire-elf.

'Put your sword away, Lorca,' Fetlock said. 'We shall talk with him.'

'Gah! I've had no sword action this whole quest,' Lorca said glumly, sheathing her weapon.

They walked closer to the dire-elf until he held up a hand.

'Halt!' he shouted. 'I am Rattlepike, Guardian of the Silent Forest. None shall pass through this gate, for certain death lies beyond.'

'Blast it!' said Lorca, stamping. 'A tragic and early end to our journey. Now we must head home, our heads hanging in shame.' She fell to the ground, tears streaming down her face. 'Our quest has failed!'

Fetlock looked at her, his small black eyes wide in disbelief. 'Lorca, what are you talking about? We can just walk around him.'

Lorca looked up and wiped her eyes. 'We can?'

Fetlock gestured to the gate. Sure enough, it stood alone with no fences on either side.

'Yes!'

'No!' boomed Rattlepike. 'You shall not pass, for certain death lies beyond and –'

'Yes, yes, you've said that already,' Fetlock replied. 'But there's nothing to stop us going round you, is there? Through this huge, unfenced field right here.'

To demonstrate, Fetlock stepped off the path and walked around the gate.

Rattlepike looked deflated.

'I *suppose* not . . .' he said with a sigh. 'I told them it was a mistake to fire Finble the Fencekeeper, but they didn't listen to me.'

'Well, then. We shall be on our way,' said Fetlock.

'You're still going into the Silent Forest?' asked Rattlepike, looking shocked. 'The dire warnings of certain death are usually enough to put people off.'

Lorca stood forward, puffing her chest out. 'But we are not *most people*! We are not afraid of certain death! We laugh in the face of –'

'Wellllll, hang on a minute.' Alex held up a hand. 'Let's not be too hasty here. I mean, certain death doesn't sound *great*. Maybe we could try going *around* the Silent Forest and avoid the whole "certain death" thing?'

Fetlock shook his head. 'That would add days to

our journey. Time we simply do not have. We only have eleven days left to find Felonius Gloam.'

Alex closed his eyes. 'OK. We'll go through the Silent Forest. How bad can a bunch of really quiet trees be, anyway?'

'A brave decision.' Lorca placed a hand on Alex's shoulder and gave it a friendly squeeze. 'Perhaps I have misjudged you.'

'Thank you.' Alex winced. 'Now can you let go of my shoulder? It's quite painful.'

Rattlepike eyed Alex. 'Hang on – are you not the mighty hero Axel Stormward? Did I not watch you defeat the dread Slavering Urr-Slug?'

Lorca rolled her eyes. 'No. This is not Axel. *This* is Alex.' Lorca lifted Alex's arm up. 'See! No muscles.'

Rattlepike raised his eyebrows. 'Yes. Not a single one. Oh, I nearly forgot!' Rattlepike slapped his forehead. 'Do try and avoid the dread monster that lies in the heart of the Silent Forest.'

'Pardon?' asked Alex.

'I'm such an old forget-me-knot!' said Rattlepike, slapping his forehead. 'Totally slipped my mind. There's a monster in the Silent Forest. Ophion is its name – and it is a cruel, evil beast.'

'You're the Guardian of the Silent Forest and you

forgot to warn us about the cruel, evil monster?' Alex asked.

'Easy mistake!'

'Not really.'

'What manner of beast is it?' Fetlock asked.

Rattlepike gave a shudder. 'An ancient one that has been here since before the first tree in the Silent Forest took root. It crawls and slithers and is always hungry. And it delights in providing the most agonizing of deaths.'

'Yes!' whooped Lorca. 'Time for me to do some hero-level protecting!'

Alex gave a groan of dread.

'If I face the ancient slithery monster,' Lorca continued, 'I might be allowed to skip my Dangerous Quest! Gah! I knew I should have brought my best battleaxe.'

'Come,' said Fetlock. 'Let us be on our way. The sooner we leave, the sooner we will reach the Infinite Palace.'

'You're travelling to the Infinite Palace?' Rattlepike asked.

Alex nodded. 'Yes, we must speak with the Finding Engine.'

'Well, even if you do make it through the Silent Forest – which you won't because you will die horribly – the Finding Engine won't speak to you unless you give it the word of passage!'

Alex raised his eyebrows. 'You mean a password?'

'Yes! A word of such devious complexity t'would be impossible to guess, even if you had nine lifetimes!'

'Do you know it?' asked Alex.

'I do!'

'Well, can you tell us what it is?'

Rattlepike shook his head. 'Never! Not even if you cross my palm with silver!'

Lorca unsheathed her sword and stepped forward. 'How about I cross your *neck* with silver?'

'Lorca!' Fetlock barked.

'Please.' It was Alex's turn to step forward. 'Our quest is both perilous and vital for the whole of this world. If you give us the passw– I mean, the word of passage, one day we will repay you for the favour.'

'So polite!' exclaimed Rattlepike. 'But you are going to die in the Silent Forest, so it's pointless.'

'Well, if we're going to die, then you might as well give it to us anyway,' Alex shot back.

Fetlock gave him a look which suggested he was beginning to think there was more to Alex than met the eye.

'Gah! I cannot argue with that logic,' Rattlepike

said. 'Fine – listen carefully, for only once shall I say it. The word of passage is . . . Password123.'

'*Password123*?' groaned Alex. 'I could have guessed that. Unbelievable.'

'But the word is useless anyway,' said the dire-elf. 'Because even if you do make it through the Silent Forest, which you won't, you will die crossing the Endless Chasm before you ever reach the Finding Engine.'

'It's all doom and gloom with you, isn't it?' Lorca said. 'Well, Mr Dreary-Elf, we *have* to make it across. Because we need the Finding Engine to tell us where the Father of Flies is, so we can stop the White Death.'

'I told you not to say anything about our quest!' cried Fetlock, but Rattlepike's face had crumpled.

'My brother Dismil was taken by the White Death just yesterday,' said Rattlepike sadly. 'Along with many other dire-elves.' He pulled out a small piece of parchment and handed it to Alex. 'Take this. One false step in the maze above the Endless Chasm and it will collapse, plunging you to your death. This map shows the only safe path across. Guard it with your life!'

Alex glanced briefly at the parchment – a map marked with many symbols – before Lorca snatched it from him.

'As your guardian and protector, I shall look after that.'

'Now, begone and good luck, brave travellers,' Rattlepike said. 'I hope your inevitable deaths aren't too agonizing.'

The three set off, leaving Rattlepike behind. Shortly after, the Silent Forest came into view – a row of bone-white, leafless trees, skeletal-limbed and stark against the red earth and grey sky. They approached, but stopped on the edge of the treeline.

'Are we sure about this?' Alex asked, trying to peer in.

Fetlock nodded, with little conviction.

'It will be *absolutely* fine!' Lorca drew her sword and held it above her head. 'Onwards, to certain agonizing death!' she shouted, and charged into the forest.

Fetlock shrugged, and then followed Lorca.

Alex swallowed nervously, then he too stepped forward.

CHAPTER NINE

THE SILENT FOREST

It was like putting his head under water. Everything became muffled. Alex felt a pressure on his eardrums and a light, regular thumping. He clung desperately to the sound until he realized with horror what it was – the soft, wet beating of his own heart. A few steps in, the pressure released, but only to be replaced by . . . nothing. All sound had disappeared. No chirping birdsong, no wind-rustled leaves. It was pure, dead silence.

Lorca turned to say something to Alex, but although her lips moved, no sound came out. She grasped at her throat, her eyes wide, then clutched at her ears. Alex tried to call out to her, but his own voice had vanished too. With no alternative, they walked onwards, deeper into the silence.

Sounds Alex never knew existed, like the static rush of the sun or the long, slow breath of the Earth, were gone. Only now did he understand what true silence was. It was more than the simple absence of noise; it was as if sound had never existed, as if he had lost a part of himself. He remembered the non-silence outside the forest and realized it had been music, a symphony of beautiful noise.

On they walked, further into the white trees. With each step, the dread Alex felt that he would never leave became stronger. He had lost all sense of time. How long had he been in this forest? Minutes? Hours? Days? He touched his face and found, to his surprise, that it was damp with tears. Feeling his mind slipping away, and in desperation, he turned to his companions, but Fetlock and Lorca had completely disappeared.

Panic clutched at his heart.

Alex let out a scream, utterly noiseless.

And then he saw it.

A great white tree, standing alone in a clearing, and wrapped around the bone-pale trunk, coiling itself around the branches, was a huge yellow snake, thicker than a man's leg.

Ophion.

The snake fixed Alex with a cold stare, its tongue flicking, and then, to his horror, it spoke.

Come to me.

Alex didn't *hear* the words – they were inside his mind.

Come to me.

The three words were like a fire, consuming all other thoughts. It was as if he and the snake were all that was left at the end of the world. And Alex understood: the snake was not just older than the forest, it was as old as time itself.

The forked tongue flickered again, tasting the air, and Alex felt Ophion inside his mind, tasting his thoughts.

Come to me, it repeated. *For you shall never leave this world. You shall never see home again. So, come to me. And I shall give your quest an end.*

Alex didn't want to; the words struck terror in his heart. But they were impossible to resist. The monster was right – he was never going to get home, so why not simply give up? He felt himself moving towards the snake. A few more steps and he would be within striking range, the fangs ready to puncture his skin and inject agonizing venom through his body.

Across the clearing he saw Lorca, her face blank, walking steadily towards Ophion too, her sword held loose by her side and her eyes closed. She was completely under the creature's spell, Alex realized in horror. She was walking to her death.

Without thinking, Alex charged towards Lorca. Racing across the clearing, he threw himself forward, knocking her off her feet, just as the snake struck. Its fangs snapped at the air where Lorca had just been standing.

Lorca and Alex tumbled to the ground, and this seemed to break Lorca's trance. She snatched up her sword and rolled to her feet. Alex, though, was left flat on his back. Ophion reared up, towering above him. Alex held his breath, waiting for the inevitable bite, but Lorca ran in front of the great beast and swiped at it with her sword, driving it back.

Alex sprang up and pulled Lorca away from the serpent. She had bought them some time, but he knew they had to get away, and Lorca understood too. They started running, their steps silent, their movements sluggish, as if the air was as thick as oil.

Alex could feel Ophion giving chase. Even without turning, he knew it was nearly upon him, and fear drove him to run faster than he had ever run in his life. That's why he didn't see the tree root; it took his foot and he went tumbling to the ground. He sprawled on to his back and the snake was upon him.

Ophion reared up again, and Alex felt his sword trapped beneath his body. He could see the exposed belly of the snake. All he needed to do was pull his blade out and plunge it deep, but fear had paralysed him.

Then, out of nowhere, in a flash of fur, Fetlock was on the monster's back, sinking his teeth in. Ophion snapped around, but Fetlock sprang away.

Lorca was dragging Alex to his feet, pointing frantically. They ran and ran, hand in hand, jumping over roots and ducking under branches. To their left, Fetlock ran, tearing under and jumping over branches. Finally, in front of them, Alex saw a break in the trees – the edge of the Silent Forest.

Suddenly, Ophion cut in front. But Alex dived over its back and, with his final ounce of strength, broke through the line of trees and out into the open. Looking back, he saw the great snake skulking back into the depths of the dead forest, unwilling to leave its home.

Alex fell to his knees. Under his hands, there was grass, and all around him was sound. It rushed into his ears – wind and birdsong, his own ragged breath and the sound of joyful laughter: it was Lorca, collapsed next to him.

Fetlock slumped down beside them, panting.

'I'm too old for this,' he growled.

Alex grinned and then realized he had tears streaming down his face.

'I'm sorry,' he said, choking.

Fetlock turned to him. 'What on Aërth do you have to be sorry for?'

'I would have died if you hadn't saved me.' Alex felt his cheeks burning with shame. 'I just couldn't move. Courage isn't my strong point.'

'Courage takes many different forms, Alex,' Fetlock said. 'You have been dragged from your world to an entirely new one and thrown into an Impossible Quest. I think you have faced up to that with great bravery.'

'Also,' Lorca added, 'if everybody was brave, there would be no place for heroes. So it's good that we have the not-so-brave to make us look better.'

'Thank you, Lorca. That is not helpful.' Fetlock sighed.

Alex couldn't help but grin. 'Well, one thing's for certain. I am glad to be with you two!'

'And we both are too!' Lorca grinned back.

'So,' Alex said. 'Where to now?'

Felonious Gloam turned the last page and set down the Book of Lifetales.

Finally the Narrator's scheme was clear. He had made an exchange. A boy had been taken from this world and replaced with a boy from another. One with the power to stop Gloam's own plan.

'Clever, Narrator . . .' murmured Gloam. 'But desperate.'

Gloam pondered for a moment. The boy must be found, and fast. His own spy-flies might do it, but it would be better still to use the eyes of every person on Aërth.

'Screed!' he called.

An instant later, Tarka Screed was at his side.

Gloam fixed her with his black eyes. 'I have discovered what is causing the White Death.'

'You have?' Screed exclaimed. 'What?'

'A boy has come from another world,' Gloam said. 'He brings the White Death with him and spreads it wherever he goes. Send out messengers to every town and city, and set a large reward. The boy must be found. And then we must put an end to him, one way or another.'

Screed saluted and left. Once again, Gloam opened the Book of Lifetales.

Once again, he took up his quill and scratched words on to the pristine parchment.

And, once again, the words disappeared in front of him.

With anger flashing in his eyes, he strode through the Nest to the lowest part of his lair and into the Narrator's cell.

'Your little plan to thwart me by bringing the boy from the other world,' Gloam spat. 'I'm sorry to say that will soon be over. Already my spies are hunting him. And when they find him, well . . .' He toyed with the dagger on his belt. 'I think you know what comes next in his story.'

The Narrator inhaled sharply in fear. 'But he's only a child! You cannot –'

'You were the one who brought him here, you old fool! What did you think would happen?'

'Please. Leave him be, for pity's sake.'

'It's too late for that.'

'I'll give you what you want!'

Gloam gave a hollow laugh. 'Well, then. Tell me, old man, how do I write in the Book of Lifetales?'

The Narrator gave a triumphant smile. '*You* cannot. For only one with the blood of a Narrator in their veins can harness the power of the Book.'

Gloam's reptilian gaze flicked to the Narrator's face. 'Blood, you say? Well, then I need a small gift from you.'

Gloam slid the dagger from his belt.

The Narrator tried to scream, but Gloam's hand shot to his mouth and muffled it before one left his lips.

Gloam leaned over and whispered in the Narrator's ear. 'And when I have it, I will finally be able to begin shaping reality to *my* design. I will end this ugly, broken world that you made and build a better one. All will be beauty. And all will be thankful.'

Gloam's eyes gleamed and he clamped his hand harder over the Narrator's mouth as he made the first cut.

CHAPTER TEN

THE IMPOSSIBLE QUEST

'I am Axel Stormward, flayer of evil and slayer of wolves! Now push me higher, Irving! Wheee!'

'Axel, it's time to get off the swing,' Sienna said, her arms crossed.

'Five more minutes!'

Irving pushed the swing harder, his pale face looking like nothing more than sour milk.

'No! Now!' Sienna barked. 'We need to finish talking about how to complete your quest.'

Axel jumped off the swing and landed nimbly in a crouching position, then sprang up. 'Yes! And save your weakling friend!'

'Stop calling him that,' growled Irving.

'You are angry,' Axel said, putting a hand on Irving's shoulder.

'I'm not,' said Irving, knocking the hand away.

'You are. I can tell. I'm very sensitive to emotions,' Axel said.

'You *what*?' laughed Sienna. 'Course you are!'

Axel ignored her and gave Irving a look of sympathy. 'You're a grumpy warlock today. Perhaps you did not have your weetenbisk . . .'

Irving glared at Axel. 'Do you know what I like about you?'

'What?' Axel asked.

'Absolutely nothing.'

'Are you angry because I am betrothed to Sienna? Perhaps you also love her.'

'What? *No!*' shouted Irving.

'WOULD YOU JUST DROP THE WHOLE MARRIAGE THING!?' roared Sienna.

'To settle this,' Axel said. 'We should wrestle in manly combat for Sienna's hand.'

'What? No –'

'Why not? We can strip to our undergarments here.' Axel started unbuckling his trousers.

'NOBODY IS STRIPPING TO THEIR PANTS!' shouted Sienna. 'DO YOUR TROUSERS BACK UP, FOR GOD'S SAKE! Can we just have a sensible conversation for *one single* minute?' Sienna shook her head in despair. 'Now, without threatening to strip to your pants, or going on about your wavy hair, is there anything else you can tell us about how you got here, so we can try to work out what on earth is going on?'

'Earth? Is that the name of this place? I come from Aërth,' said Axel. 'I was in the Hallowed Hall of Heroes, training for the final level of heroism – the tenth. I had just been handed my Impossible Quest and was polishing Aëthelmrir, when –'

'Polishing Ethel who?' asked Irving.

'Aëthelmrir. His magic sword,' Sienna explained flatly.

Irving raised his eyebrows. 'I can't believe I am being forced to listen to this with my own two ears.'

'Well,' continued Axel. 'I was polishing Aëthelmrir when I was plucked up from where I stood, sucked through a glowing tunnel where I crossed paths with your friend, and then ended up here. An adored hero thrown into the life of an ordinary, boring child. The shame!'

'Now, look,' Sienna said, anger flashing in her eyes. 'Alex is *not* an ordinary, boring child. And he doesn't have an ordinary, boring life.'

'Really?' Axel's face crinkled with doubt. 'Are you *sure*?'

'Yes, I'm sure,' huffed Sienna. 'He may not be a sword-swinging hero like you, fighting monsters or whatever, but he's good and kind and he has to face up to proper real-life problems, which he does without being a colossal doughnut like you, banging on all the time about being a hero. So don't come here with your arrogant nonsense about "ordinary and boring"!'

A heavy silence fell until finally Axel broke it with a quiet voice.

'What is a doughnut? Is it a word for somebody who is strong and handsome?'

'Never mind what a doughnut is,' snapped Sienna. 'Look, I'm sorry for snapping, right? It's just sometimes you properly wind me up.' Then she said in a softer voice, 'And I'm worried for Alex.'

'You should be. Aërth is a *very* dangerous place, full of deadly threats that can easily kill the weak and unwary.'

'That's not helpful!'

'But,' Axel spoke carefully. 'I'm sure your *brave* and *strong* friend will be completely fine with all the highly lethal monsters.'

'He will be,' said Irving, uncertainly. 'Definitely,' he added, even more uncertainly.

'Anyway,' huffed Sienna. 'Do you want to know what I'm thinking about this quest or what?'

'Pah!' scoffed Axel. 'Thinking is for those who are feeble of arm. Thinking is for weaklings such as book readers and guardians of libraries. I need *action*!'

'Well, I've been thinking about what was written on

your scroll and I reckon it's all to do with Mr Abiss, Alex's dad.'

Irving's face clouded in confusion. 'Alex's dad?'

'Yeah, so Alex's dad is not a nice guy,' Sienna continued in a low voice. 'Not at all.'

'I know the feeling,' muttered Axel.

'Why? Is your dad –'

'I do not wish to speak of him,' Axel interrupted, his face suddenly dark. Sienna chose not to press further and carried on.

'So, Mr Abiss abandoned Alex and his mum when Alex was just a baby. Didn't want owt to do with them. So after his mum died, Alex was brought up by his gran. She's been a mum and a dad to him, really. And while they haven't got two pennies to rub together, his dad's living in this big, fancy house on the other side of town. Now, before he got . . . swapped, Alex told us his gran owes money. Like, a lot. They have to find twenty grand in less than two weeks, or they're going to lose their home.'

Axel gasped. 'Truly?'

Sienna nodded. 'And, meanwhile, his dad is sitting there with pots and pots of money, not giving them nothing.'

'Not even one pot of money?' asked Axel, outraged.

'Err, nope . . . Not even one. Well, Alex's gran is too proud to beg for help. And I don't blame her neither. She'd rather try and make it on her own. But Mr Abiss could help them in a second, if he wanted. He won't, though, cos he's *evil*. And that's where it gets interesting. Irving, tell Axel how he made all his money.'

'He's a brilliant chess player who invented some groundbreaking new computer stuff, like this big AI thing,' Irving explained. 'Did all the coding himself. When it comes to computers, he's a bit of a . . . *genius*! An evil genius!' Irving clapped. 'Sienna, *you're* the genius!'

Axel gasped. 'Of course! Sienna, I am here to *defeat* you, not to marry you!'

Irving and Sienna looked at each other in disbelief.

'You're *so* close, Axel,' Sienna said. 'But no. *Mr Abiss* is the evil genius. He's been evil to Alex his whole life, is a genius, and getting money from him is totally impossible!'

Axel put his hands on his hips and stared into the distance mysteriously.

'Impossible, you say . . .?'

'What you doing?' Sienna asked.

'I'm staring into the distance mysteriously,' replied Axel.

'Well, why you doing that?'

'Because, sweet Sienna, you are right – this *is* my quest! My *Impossible* Quest. I shall save Alex's home by defeating his evil genius father! Just like it says: *Defeat the father, save the world!* We must find this evil genius. And when we do, I'm going to take his money. Every last pot of it. And if he resists, I will show him exactly how much of a doughnut I really am!'

'Oh, Axel!' Sienna laughed, but then the smile fell from her face, fast as a guillotine. 'You really reckon Alex might be in danger then, wherever he is?'

Axel nodded. 'If he has taken my place in Aërth, as I have taken his here, then, yes, he will be in grave danger.'

'Then we'd better get on with your quest and get you two to swap back as quickly as possible.'

'Yes!' shouted Axel.

The school bell began to shrill.

'But first,' Sienna said, 'we have to finish lessons.'

'Noooo!'

'Maths ... science ... geography ... These tortures are almost beyond endurance,' Axel said glumly, as they walked home after school. 'I do not think I am cut out for your world. I wish to return to my own as quickly as possible.'

'Believe me,' Irving said. 'That is *exactly* what we want too.'

'You have a kind heart, Warlock Irving,' Axel said, clasping Irving's cheeks in his hands. 'I feel you and I are going to be the very best of friends.'

'Well, I'm not so sure –'

And then, much to Irving's dismay, Axel pulled him into a hug.

'You're squeezing me,' wheezed Irving.

'Yes. It feels good, does it not?'

'It's a bit . . . tight.'

Axel ignored Irving and kept hugging him, with his eyes closed and a beatific smile.

'When . . . will it . . . finish?' Irving asked.

'Any minute . . .' Axel said, still squeezing. 'Now!' And he let Irving go.

Irving snatched in a breath, said a quick goodbye and scuttled off as they reached Alex's flat. Sienna knocked on the door.

Gran opened it, her hair tousled.

'Oh, hi lovie,' she said to Axel and gave him a kiss. 'Hi, Sienna. Come on in, chuck. Want a brew? I've just made a pot.'

Sienna nodded, and Gran disappeared into the kitchen.

"Ere y'are,' she said, planting two mugs on the rickety coffee table in front of the sofa.

'Thanks a mill.'

'How you doing?' Gran asked Axel. 'Feeling any better?'

'I have had a day of torments no person should suffer, thank you for asking,' Axel replied.

'Rough day at school?'

'Double maths is a horror that not even the Torturer Chief of the Ravaging Throngs of Ulun-K'man would dream of inflicting.'

Gran gave a long, tired sigh. 'You still not back to yourself, are you?'

'I am completely normal,' Axel said, and gave a wink to Sienna.

'I know things are difficult right now, love.' Gran gave Axel a smile, but tears glistened in her eyes. 'Reckon you just don't want to face up to reality, so you're disappearing into a bit of fantasy. You want to escape. And I don't blame you one little bit; sometimes I want to escape too. Well, you stay there in your fantasy land for a while, if you like. I'll be right here for you, waiting.' A single tear finally spilled and she wiped it quickly with the back of her hand. 'Now, come here and give us a hug!'

Gran buried her face in Axel's hair, as she pulled him close. Axel hugged her back, trying to hide his face too, but not before Sienna saw tears falling down his own cheeks.

Finally, Gran pulled back from the hug, slapped her thighs and stood up.

'Now, we can't sit here scriking all day. Sienna, you're welcome to stay for dinner, if you like?'

'Oh yeah, cheers.' Sienna smiled. Then she added uncertainly, 'I can give you some money, if you like.'

'Don't be daft. If I can't afford to give you a bit of scran, then God help me!'

'OK,' Sienna said, smiling again. 'I'll text my mum and tell her.'

'Fish fingers and chips all right?'

Sienna gave a thumbs-up. 'Great.'

'By the gods!' Axel looked horrified. 'What sort of monstrous creatures inhabit your seas? Fish with *fingers*? Can it be?'

Gran rolled her eyes and headed for the kitchen. The moment she had gone, Axel leaned towards Sienna.

'Sienna, you must *never* tell anybody what you have seen here today,' he whispered urgently.

'What you talking about?' Sienna asked.

'Just now, I was . . . overcome with emotion,' Axel said, his face full of shame. 'I do not know what is wrong with me. Perhaps I am tired.'

'Give over! There's nothing wrong with expressing your feelings.'

'Do you really think so?' Axel stifled a sob. 'Oh gods, I'm starting again! Look at me! A Grade Nine Hero, crying like a babe!'

Sienna rolled her eyes again. 'Oh, Axel, you big numpty. What we going to do with you? Now let's go and have some dinner, yeah?'

Axel nodded, but his heart ached with a sadness he could not explain.

Walking through a dense canopy of trees, Alex stopped sharply, tears suddenly flowing down his cheeks.

'Is something the matter?' Lorca asked, gently. 'I mean, apart from being torn from your family and friends and thrust into a totally new world full of danger and a high risk of death?'

Fetlock rolled his eyes. 'Lorca!'

'I don't know,' said Alex. 'I just suddenly feel really sad. I think I miss my gran.'

He quickly wiped his eyes and they continued walking, but for some reason thoughts of his father sprang to Alex's mind, as unbidden as the tears. 'Lorca, can I ask you a question?' he asked, finally.

'Of course. You may ask me anything. As long as it's not where I went to the toilet earlier. I shall take that secret with me to the grave.'

'No! I didn't – Anyway, I was just wondering . . . I didn't see a dad where you lived.'

'That is correct. He was not in the hovel.'

'Ah,' said Alex. 'So we're the same then. No dad living with us.'

'Ha ha! No!' Lorca laughed. 'My father doesn't live in our hovel because he's dead.'

'Oh.'

'Yes, he got eaten alive by rabbits.'

'*What?*'

'Yes. The Man-Eating Rabbits of Mellowmere Meadows.'

'I'm so sorry,' said Alex. 'That's awful.'

'It was,' agreed Lorca, matter-of-factly. 'To die on a lowly Really Dangerous Quest was particularly tragic. But I'm sorry about your terrible father leaving you,' she added gently.

'Thanks,' said Alex, swallowing the ache in his

throat. 'So am I. What about you, Fetlock? Do you still have your parents?'

'No.' Fetlock shook his furry head. 'My mother died when I was just a pup. My father, though, lived a long and eventful life. Died at the ripe old age of thirteen.'

'Thirteen?' Alex gasped. 'That's not very old.'

'It is for a dog.'

'Yes, I suppose so.' Alex thought for a moment. 'How old are you, Fetlock?'

'Twelve.'

'Ah,' said Alex awkwardly.

Fetlock grinned. 'Don't worry, Alex. I know I have little time left. When the Orb foretold that some of us might fall during this quest, I thought that I would not be too sad if it were me.'

'Don't say that!' He struggled to find stronger words of comfort for Fetlock, as anxiety squeezed his chest.

He did not have to struggle for long, though, as they broke through the cover of the trees and Fetlock pointed a paw at a ridge in the far distance. 'Behold – the Cliffs of Tanishmoor. Home of the Infinite Palace . . . and the Finding Engine.'

CHAPTER ELEVEN

THE WORST POSSIBLE DEFEAT IN BATTLE

'I have a *what*?' asked Axel.

He had woken feeling gloomy, and his new friends' arrival to take him to school had not lifted his spirits.

'A test,' replied Irving.

'What sort of test? A test of bravery? Strength? Honour?'

'No. Maths.'

Axel's heart sank. 'Ah.'

At that point, Mr Sunshine jumped on the sofa, hissed at Axel and swiped at him with a claw.

'I have faced many a malevolent creature, but that *thing* –' Axel pointed at Mr Sunshine, nursing a new scratch on his arm – 'is made of purest evil.'

Gran bustled in. 'I'm late for me shift! See you later, Alex, love.'

'Wait!' Sienna shouted after her. 'You're still wearing your slippers!'

Gran stopped and looked down at her feet, an expression of surprise on her face. 'Lordy, that's a senior moment. I don't know what's got into me these days. I haven't got time to think!'

She kicked off her slippers, squeezed into her shoes and was out of the door a second later.

'And *I* haven't got time for maths tests when I am on a quest to defeat an evil genius,' growled Axel.

'Yes, but defeating Mr Abiss and saving Alex's home won't be much good if you ruin the rest of his life,' said Irving. 'You have to keep pretending to be him, and that means school and tests and all that stuff.'

'You know, you are a funny-looking little warlock, Irving, but you can be very wise,' Axel said.

Irving rolled his eyes. 'Lord spare me.'

Axel's brow furrowed. 'I am beginning to think that Alex and I are connected in some way. What each of us does affects the other. I feel what he feels.'

'Is that possible?' Irving asked Sienna.

Sienna shrugged. 'Anything's possible, I guess. But if that's true, it makes it all the more important you stay positive. Now, come on!'

As they approached school, Axel saw Nathan and his gang glancing their way and whispering to each other.

'I can see them plotting,' he said to Sienna. 'I can see you plotting!' he shouted at the gang, and then back to

Sienna he said, 'Should I taunt them? I have been preparing some *brutal* taunts.'

'No! Come on,' said Sienna. 'Save it.'

'Yes, I must get on with the quest!' Axel punched his palm.

'Yeah, I know, but first we've got to go to history.'

'No,' cried Axel. 'Not history! That Mr Grover . . . I have faced many a malevolent creature, but that *teacher* . . .' He seethed. 'That teacher is made of purest evil.'

'Forget about him,' Sienna replied. 'It's the maths test you need to worry about.'

Axel put his hands on his hips and laughed loudly. 'Ha! A maths test will be no match for my heroic brain!'

Irving gave a hollow chuckle. 'We'll see about that . . .'

At the end of the maths lesson, Axel bounded up to Sienna and Irving, clutching his test and grinning from ear to ear.

'The teacher was *astonished*,' he declared gleefully. 'She said she had never seen answers like mine.'

'So, you did well?' Sienna asked, trying to disguise her disbelief.

'Yes! I got –' Axel checked his test – 'four per cents! Is that good? It sounds good.'

Sienna gave him a sympathetic smile. 'It's ... It could be worse, Axel.'

Axel pumped his fist. 'Yes! I am mastering school after all!'

'Well, that's good,' said Irving. 'Because this was only the practice for the big end-of-term test next week.'

'I have to do this again?' Axel gasped.

Irving nodded. 'This school focuses far too much on maths for my liking. Where are the nineteenth-century poetry lessons? We haven't studied Poe once. And I am still furious they rejected my request to do extra-curricular taxidermy.'

Axel ignored Irving. 'You're saying I have to do the test *again*?'

'I'm afraid so. And this time you'll have to do better.'

'*How much* better?' Axel asked slowly, fear creeping into his eyes.

Irving looked at Sienna. 'Do you want to tell him?'

Sienna gave Axel another sympathetic smile. 'Quite a bit better.'

'Like, ten per cents?'

'No ... more like fifty.'

'FIFTY PER CENTS?!' Axel shouted, causing students to turn and stare. 'Have you lost your mind? That's not possible. I only got four today! And fifty per cents is . . . is . . .' Axel's faced creased in concentration as he tried to calculate the difference. 'Well, it's a *lot* more.'

'Yeah. And the thing is, if you do badly, you – *Alex* – could be dropped down a set. So you can't let that happen. For Alex's sake. Just think of it as another bit of your Impossible Quest,' Sienna suggested.

Axel's brow furrowed again. 'You are right. I must do well for Alex. But how on Aërth can I meet this new challenge?'

'You're just going to have to sit down and learn.'

Axel narrowed his eyes. 'Sit down and learn? That sounds like the most difficult quest I have ever faced.'

'Well,' said Sienna, 'you can't use your fists to solve every problem.'

'And they do say the pen is mightier than the sword,' Irving added.

Axel roared with laughter.

'A pen being mightier than a sword! That is a very funny joke! Imagine – going to battle against a ravaging horde of night-orcs with only a pen! Irving, you are too funny!' Axel slapped Irving on the back, wiping tears of laughter from his eyes. 'But enough of this ribaldry! We must turn our minds to the *actual* Impossible Quest: how to defeat Alex's evil genius father and take his pots of money!'

'I told you before.' Sienna sighed, as they walked out of the classroom. 'He doesn't *actually* keep his money in pots.'

'Well, where does he keep it then?'

'In the bank,' Irving said.

'Well then, we shall go to this "bank" and take his treasure from there.'

'You can't!'

'Why can't I?'

'Because they have guards.'

'Then I shall take Aëthelmrir,' Axel said slowly, as if he was talking to a rather obtuse child. 'And cut off their heads!'

'I don't think that would end well,' said Sienna, squeezing her way down the crowded corridor. 'Look, you're supposed to be doing an Impossible Quest, right? Well, it can't be impossible if you can just use a sword on everything and everyone. You need to use that ... *unique* brain of yours. You need to think of another way to defeat Alex's dad.'

'By the gods on high, you might be right ...'

But before they could discuss that any further, Miss Spreckley appeared. 'Ah, I've been looking for you, Always.'

'Always?' replied Axel, looking confused. 'We only met yesterday.'

The headteacher shook her head. 'I need to speak to you.'

'Why? You have an evil foe to vanquish?' Axel asked, hopefully. 'Mayhap a dragon to slay?'

'Not quite,' replied Miss Spreckley. 'I'd like you to see the school counsellor. He has an appointment free right now. Off you go.'

As Miss Spreckley walked away, Sienna grabbed Axel and whispered to him urgently.

'Please, Axel, don't say anything about the quest to the school counsellor. Act normal. Remember – nobody can suspect you aren't Alex. So, don't say *anything* weird.'

'Do not worry,' Axel said, with a wink. 'My lips are sealed.'

'And so that's how I defeated the Goblin Prince of the Darklands and recovered the Gauntlets of Ogre Power and the Tiara of Endless Misery,' Axel said proudly, sitting up on the sofa. 'What are you scribbling on your pad, mind-doctor?'

Mr Manischewitz, the school counsellor, didn't speak but just kept writing furiously. Then he stopped, lay back in his chair, stared at the mouse-nibbled ceiling tiles and chewed his pen for a long time.

'Riiiiiight,' he said finally. 'This might be a *little* beyond my pay grade.'

'Agreed. A puny old man such as yourself would be no match for a Goblin Prince.'

'I didn't mean fighting a Goblin Prince! And I'm only forty-five,' Mr Manischewitz protested.

'Come, come, that's nearly dead,' said Axel dismissively. 'In my world we would leave you atop a mountain for the buzzards to clean your bones.'

'That's it! I give up!' Mr Manischewitz threw up his arms in despair.

'You yield?' said Axel. 'Very well. I bid you good day!' And he marched out of the office.

The bell had rung for the end of break, and the corridor was once again packed with children. After looking both ways, Axel realized he didn't know where to go.

He stepped up to a tall Year 11 boy. 'Pray tell, do you know where the fair maiden Sienna is?'

'Shut up, you massive weirdo,' he sneered and walked off.

Well and truly lost, Axel was wandering the corridors when a foot caught his from behind and he suddenly found himself flying face first to the floor.

Before he had a chance to get up, he was pinned to the ground. It was Nathan Jones and his gang, all of them. Two were sitting on his legs while the others held his arms down.

'Where do you think you're going, Always?' sneered Nathan.

'Get off me!' strained Axel. He used every ounce of his strength, but there were just too many of them.

'Not so tough now, are you?' Nathan hissed.

'Let me up and I'll show you how tough I am!'

'We'll let you up. Once I've taught you a lesson for messing with me!' Nathan laughed, squatting above Axel's head.

'Oh gods, no!' cried Axel, as he realized what was about to happen. 'No, no, noooo!'

Some time later, Sienna finally found Axel sitting in the corner of the playground, his head in his hands.

'Y'all right?'

Axel said nothing.

'The counsellor meeting went fine, yeah?' asked Sienna, sitting down next to him.

'Yes,' came the muffled reply.

'You didn't say anything weird or owt like that?'

'No.'

'It's just there's a rumour going round that Mr Manischewitz handed in his notice.'

Axel finally lifted his head. 'Well, it's nothing to do with me!' he snapped.

'All right. What's got you so grumpy?'

'Nothing,' Axel answered, grumpily.

'Come on, what's up?'

Axel closed his eyes, his face creased in pain.

'Something ... something happened to me,' Axel replied.

'What?'

'I ... cannot say.'

'You can tell me anything,' Sienna said. 'Don't worry.'

'I ... I have been defeated. In battle. In the worst possible way.'

'What happened?' demanded Sienna. 'What battle?'

'I can hardly speak the words. The shame!'

'Go on.'

'It was that villainous Nathan Jones and his followers. They tackled me from behind. Held me down. And then ...' Axel closed his eyes. 'And then Nathan Jones crouched above my face and expelled a wind of such power and pungency upon it that it left me senseless! Oh, the shame!'

Sienna knew better than to laugh, but it took her a moment to compose herself before she could reply.

'Axel, getting face-blasted – that's not your fault!'

'But what sort of hero am I, that can be so easily defeated?' Axel wailed.

'You know,' replied Sienna. 'There's actually loads of different types of heroes. And not all rely on their muscles all the time. A hero isn't somebody who never gets defeated, Axel. A hero is somebody who gets back up after he's been defeated and fights on. Even after a face-blasting.'

Despite his misery, Axel felt a bubble of hope rising in his chest. 'You think so?'

'Are you a hero or not?'

'I'm a hero,' said Axel, in a tiny voice.

'Well, then. Now's the time to prove what you're made of.'

'Yes!' shouted Axel, pumping his fists.

'You ready to show 'em who's boss?'

'Yes! Yes! I am! Now kiss me, Sienna,' Axel cried, puckering his lips.

'Don't push your luck!' Sienna pointed a threatening finger at Axel.

Axel grinned back and then, his smile fading, he stared into the distance.

'You like staring into the distance, don't you?' Sienna said.

'I do. It allows my brain to work. And I have been doing some thinking of my own, although I shall not make a habit of it. It is now clear that Nathan Jones is evil.'

'Yeah, but trust me, he's no genius, if that's what you are thinking.'

'Perhaps, but we can't take that risk. I think I should kill Nathan Jones.'

'Woah, steady on! Dial it back a notch, yeah?'

Axel didn't appear to be listening. 'And dismember all his followers. Just to be on the safe side.'

'Look, nobody is dismembering anybody, all right?' squawked Sienna. 'Or you'll land up in jail, and then where will you be with your Impossible Quest?'

'You are no fun, Sienna.'

'Dismembering is not fun, Axel.'

'As my future wife, you are going to have to learn that dismembering *can* be fun. Under the right circumstances.'

'Well, not here,' snapped Sienna. 'End of!'

'Nobody?' Axel gasped. 'Ever?'

'Nobody. Ever.'

Axel looked utterly crestfallen.

'Now, are you ready to go back to the quest? Every minute we waste is another minute closer to Alex losing his home!'

Axel nodded firmly. 'I am ready.'

'Great, well, after school me and Irving are coming round yours, and we're going to figure out what to do about Mr Abiss. And it's not going to involve swords.'

'And not a moment too soon,' Axel said, when Sienna and Irving knocked for him after dinner. 'You have saved me from a truly terrible fate.'

'I only suggested you have a bath,' Gran shouted from the kitchen. 'Or a shower.'

'And, as I told you, the rain is my shower and the lakes are my bath!'

'There's not a bloomin' lake for miles,' Gran snapped, appearing behind Axel. 'And I'm not having you standing outside in your underpants with a loofah the next time there's a bit of drizzle! What'll the neighbours think?'

'I'll have a word with him.' Sienna grinned. 'All right if we go out?'

'Please. Take that boy away before I throttle him. It'll buy me a minute's peace before I have to get to the jewellers,' Gran added, her eyes watering.

Sienna's face creased in concern for a moment, before she grabbed Axel, dragging him outside before the threatened throttling occurred.

'Where are we going?' asked Axel.

'To find Alex's dad,' replied Sienna.

The sky was as grey as the buildings around them as they walked – hands in pockets, shoulders hunched against the cold – until they reached a bus stop.

'Look at us,' said Axel. 'Three friends on a quest. The brave adventurer from a far-off land, the beautiful maiden and the . . . the . . . miserable warlock?'

Irving rolled his eyes. 'I am *not* a miserable warlock!'

'Well, what can you be, then? A miserable peasant? The brave adventurer, the beautiful maiden and the miserable peasant? I mean, it's not traditionally what's in the legends, but it might work . . .'

Before Irving could reply, the bus arrived.

'You want me to mount this mechanical monstrosity?' Axel asked nervously.

'Come on, *brave adventurer*! Do you want to meet the evil genius or what?' Irving laughed. Axel gave him a glare in reply.

'You'll be fine.' Sienna gave him an encouraging smile. 'Go on.'

A few moments later, Axel was sitting in the front seat of the top deck, nose pressed against the window, doing considerably better than fine.

'Wheeeee! By the gods, this is the way to travel,' he said, beaming.

Irving shook his head. 'He's like a Labrador puppy.'

'What are we going to do when we get to Mr Abiss's lair?' Axel asked, bouncing up and down.

'Just scope it out, I reckon,' replied Sienna. 'Hopefully get some ideas.'

Axel shook his head. 'I think I should just go the traditional route and challenge him to a good, old-fashioned duel to the death.'

'How many times have I told you, Axel?' Sienna said slowly, stressing every word. 'You – aren't – allowed – to – kill – people – here.'

'Not even a little bit?'

'Not even a little bit!'

'I hate this place.'

'So you are going to need to defeat him using your brain,' said Sienna.

'Gah! My heroic brain keeps forgetting that detail. Gods, who lives *there*?!' Axel was pointing at a large block of flats. 'A king, perhaps?'

'No. Lots of people,' Irving said.

'How many?

Irving shrugged. 'Like, maybe a thousand?'

'A thousand people? Living in one building?' Axel looked aghast. 'They must have tiny homes. Like mice.'

'That's where *I* live,' said Sienna coldly. 'Do I look like a mouse to you?'

Axel looked at Sienna. 'No, but you must be very poor.'

'You know what,' replied Sienna, staring at Axel. 'You're right. We don't have much. Nor does Alex. Or Irving. So, yeah, I come from nothing but I'm going to make something out of myself. That's *my* quest. And it's a lot harder than fighting goblins and trolls or whatever. So you'd best wipe that pitying look off your face before I *knock* it off.'

They sat in silence for several minutes, the streets gradually becoming wider and the houses older and grander.

Eventually, the bus pulled up at a stop and the three got off. They walked down an avenue of even fancier houses until they reached the end. The house that stood there was the hugest Axel had seen.

'Now a king could live *here*.'

'Well, a king doesn't,' Sienna said. 'But Alex's dad does.'

'Mr Abiss lives here?' Axel gawped. 'And yet Alex and his grandmother have no money? How is that fair?'

'It's not,' replied Sienna. 'That's the point.'

Axel walked up to the great black gates, topped with brutal-looking spikes, and pressed his face through.

'And he got all this from . . . chess?'

Irving nodded.

'What *is* chess?'

'It's a game.'

Axel frowned. 'And in this world you can make money from a game? It must involve great danger.'

'Not really. It's just –'

'So, how do I gain entry to this palace?'

'You can't,' Sienna said. 'Last time Alex came here, his dad slammed the door in his face. And remember – he's going to think you're him.'

Axel shook his head. 'Let's see how impossible this quest really is.'

And before Sienna or Irving could stop him, he began to clamber over the gate.

'Wait!' Sienna cried.

'No! The time for waiting is over!' Axel roared.

'But –'

Before Sienna could finish her sentence, Axel had clawed his way to the top of the gate, gashing his arm on one of the spikes, and hurled himself over on to the other side.

'Made it!' He gasped with exhaustion, holding his hand up weakly.

'But ... it isn't locked,' Sienna finished, and she opened the gate and walked in.

Axel groaned and dusted himself down. 'What sort of evil genius doesn't lock his portcullis?'

He stormed to the front door and banged on it with his fist.

'Open up, evil genius! Let me into your palace!'

Silence.

'Try the bell,' whispered Sienna.

'Where's the bell?' asked Axel.

Irving rolled his eyes and pressed the small button next to the door. A tiny tinkle came from within.

Silence again.

'I think I prefer thumping,' Axel said, banging the

door with his fists again. 'It's a bit more dramatic, don't you think? Certainly more heroic.'

The door suddenly swung open.

'WHO THE HELL IS BANGING ON MY DOOR?!'

The three were confronted with a bristling beetroot of a man, red of face, bald of head, with an angry moustache topping a petulant, thin-lipped mouth.

'Oh. It's you again.' The man gave Axel a withering look. 'I told you before. I don't want to see you.'

'Hello, father!' Axel grinned. 'I think we need a little chat.'

CHAPTER TWELVE

THE
INFINITE PALACE

For the rest of the day, Alex, Lorca and Fetlock walked towards the Cliffs of Tanishmoor, wading through a series of babbling brooks, their feet tickled by silver fish that glinted in the sunlight like promises.

Slowly, Alex felt his earlier sadness disappear, replaced by something akin to happiness. Danger felt far away. But then a cloud passed over the sun and the temperature dropped abruptly, and his mood changed again.

What am I doing? Alex thought. Deep down, he knew they were walking to their doom. What use were his new friends going to be? A girl who couldn't defeat a bucket and an arthritic dog, against the all-powerful Father of Flies?

The cliffs loomed ever larger, stretching to the horizon. As they approached, Alex could see that carved into their face was a pair of great towers – two soaring sentinels, vast grey slabs of impossible height – and, between them, a door of a size Alex's brain could not quite grasp. Fifty Alexes could have stood on each other's shoulders and still have walked through it.

'The Infinite Palace,' Fetlock whispered, his voice laced with reverence.

All three fell into silence, intimidated by the sheer scale of what lay ahead. Guarding the door, and dwarfed by it, were a pair of soldiers. Both were standing straight as a pencil, smartly uniformed and holding pikes.

'Our luck is in! There are only two of them,' whispered Lorca. 'Finally, some sword action. I shall run them both through before they know it!' She quickly drew her blade.

'What are you doing?' growled Fetlock, grabbing her backpack in his teeth before she could break into a run.

'I'm going to kill the guards! With my sword,' she added unnecessarily, pointing to the weapon.

'You're not going to kill anybody,' said Fetlock. 'Put your sword away.'

'But how will we get in, if we don't kill the guards?' said Lorca, her face dancing between confusion and disappointment.

'How about we try just *talking* to them before we run them through with our swords?' suggested Fetlock.

'Yes, please.' Alex nodded his head vigorously. 'No killing anybody unnecessarily. Definitely just talking.'

Lorca sighed and sheathed her sword. 'That sounds like a terrible plan. I *hate* just talking,' she said, crestfallen. 'I'm telling you now, you'll regret it.'

'Look,' said Fetlock. 'How about this for a compromise: if they don't let us in, then maybe – *maybe* – we'll let you kill them?'

Lorca broke into a wide smile. 'Aww, brilliant! Thank you, Fetlock. You're the best!'

'Right,' said Fetlock. 'Come on, then.'

Alex began praying – really hard – that the guards would let them in.

'Good day,' said Fetlock to the guards. 'We seek entrance to the Infinite Palace.'

The guards were very similar-looking. Both had dark hair, both had blue eyes. One had a moustache, though, as thick as winter bear fur, and one didn't.

'On what business?' said the moustache-less guard.

'We wish to consult the Finding Engine.'

'Absolutely not!'

'Yesssssss!' said Lorca, pumping her fist. 'Stabby time!'

'Wait,' growled Fetlock at Lorca.

'Please,' said Alex desperately. 'We are on a very important quest. And it really would be best for every*body* if you let us in.'

'Don't care. I don't like the look of you and you're not coming in,' the moustache-less guard snapped.

Just as Alex feared the worst, and Lorca was reaching for her sword, the moustachioed guard jumped in.

'Please excuse my friend,' he said, glaring at the other guard. 'He lacks manners. Among many other things. Allow me to introduce myself – I am Captain Couth. And this fellow next to me is Captain Kempt. We are the Doorkeepers of the Infinite Palace. Now, you say you wish to enter . . .'

Alex nodded.

'Well, then. One chance we shall give you, and one chance alone,' Captain Couth said. 'You must solve our riddle.'

'Oh, here we go,' said Captain Kempt, rolling his eyes. 'This *again*.'

'Yes, this again!' Captain Couth shot a glare at Captain Kempt and then continued. 'Answer this riddle, traveller. One of us can only tell the truth. The other only lies. You –'

'It was *one* lie!' Captain Kempt shouted, hands on

hips. 'And you bring it up EVERY SINGLE TIME! I have apologized AGAIN and AGAIN!'

'Tell these nice people what you did, then,' said Captain Couth, motioning to Alex, Lorca and Fetlock with his pike.

'No, I won't,' said Captain Kempt, folding his arms and looking away.

'Well, *I* will then. He told me that my pet cloud-hamster died peacefully in his sleep. Turns out, though, that *he* –' Captain Couth jabbed an accusing finger at Captain Kempt – 'accidentally trod on him. Squashed him completely. I only discovered the truth because I found some of Sergeant Fluffy's fur on the sole of his boot.'

Captain Couth bit his fist, trying to stifle tears.

'I said you'd regret not letting me kill them,' whispered Lorca.

Fetlock stepped forward and put a paw on Captain Couth's leg. 'Sir, I'm sorry for your loss. Sergeant Fluffy must have been a fine cloud-hamster.'

'The best,' sniffled Captain Couth. 'Such a cute little face!'

'I'm sure. But we are in a most dreadful hurry. We are trying to find the answer –'

'Pah!' Captain Kempt laughed. 'Everyone seeking

answers comes here. What makes you think you are worthy to consult the Finding Engine?'

'Because,' replied Alex, 'it's really important. We —'

'Everyone thinks the answers they seek are important, but they are usually asking the wrong questions,' Captain Kempt said.

'Please,' Alex pleaded. 'We're trying to find out how to stop the White Death.'

A silence fell.

Captain Kempt was about to speak, but Captain Couth shook his head slowly and pulled up his sleeve — the White Death had spread all the way up his arm, and the whole limb was nearly invisible.

Captain Kempt's eyes filled with tears. 'It's got worse?'

Captain Couth nodded.

'Since when?'

'Just last night.'

'So fast,' Captain Kempt whispered.

Captain Couth nodded again. 'I'm sorry.'

'You have nothing to be sorry for,' Captain Kempt said. And then, without taking his eyes off his partner for a moment, he continued, 'Go. Enter the Palace. May the gods speed your quest.'

Alex's eyes pricked with tears. There was so much

anguish in this world. All caused by Felonious Gloam. They had to stop him and the accursed White Death he had unleashed. He glanced over at Fetlock and Lorca with a look of grim determination. They nodded back, words unnecessary between them.

Leaving the two captains in silence, Kempt still cradling Couth's disappearing arm, they walked up to the colossal doorway. Lorca gave the doors a mighty push, they creaked open and the three stepped inside the Infinite Palace.

The inside of the palace was so cavernous it almost defied description. Every way Alex turned, he stared into an inky darkness, as if he was looking into a bottom-less ocean. Hanging above their heads was an enormous wind chime: a thousand metal tubes fashioned into the shape of a teardrop. An unseen breeze stirred it, and it rang – no, *pulsed* slowly, again and again – with a sonorous, throbbing chime which vibrated inside Alex's chest. He felt ant-like, and when he spoke it was in a reverential whisper.

'Who built this place?'

'Nobody knows,' said Fetlock. 'It is said that –'

'It was gnomes,' Lorca interrupted, matter-of-factly.

'You think gnomes built . . . all this?' Fetlock replied.

'Yup.'

'You think gnomes – tiny creatures who spend most of their days fishing – built the largest building on Aërth, of unfathomable size and wonder, housing the Endless Chasm and the Finding Engine?'

'Yup. Gnomes. Definitely.'

Fetlock shook his head. 'I sometimes wonder what goes on in that head of yours.'

Though the palace was silent apart from the throb of the wind chime, they were far from alone; tall, hooded figures slid silently past them, heads down.

'The Keepers of the Infinite Palace,' Fetlock murmured.

Lorca shook her head. 'Gnomes.'

'Gnomes? They are two metres tall!' spluttered Fetlock.

'Giant gnomes!' Lorca gasped. 'Can it be?'

'No, it can't be.'

'Fetlock,' whispered Alex. 'What's the Endless Chasm?'

'*That* –' Fetlock pointed to a huge, perfectly circular hole in the floor, the size of a small lake, with a spiral staircase climbing above it – 'that is the Endless Chasm.'

They edged nearer, and the closer Alex got, the more his head began to swim. He crept up to the lip of the chasm and looked down into an abyss.

'I can't see the bottom,' Alex whispered. He felt dizzy – almost as if he was upside down, staring into space.

'That's because there isn't one,' Fetlock replied. 'It goes on forever. Endless, you see.'

Lorca stared into the abyss, wide-eyed. 'I feel like it's staring back at me.'

'No bottom? That's impossible!' exclaimed Alex.

'Well, let's not try to find out, eh? Now – shall we go to the Finding Engine?'

There was only one direction to go and that was up – up the spiral staircase which encircled the Endless Chasm. As Alex took the first step, though, he realized something startling – it appeared to be floating, suspended in mid-air. There was also no rail or bannister to hold on to. A few steps later, Alex made the mistake of looking down. The Endless Chasm yawned beneath him, and his knees began to tremble. Onwards they climbed, though, round and around the never-ending hole.

After a while, Fetlock stopped and sat down. 'Blasted knees,' he grumbled. 'Not what they used to be. Give me a moment.'

'Course,' said Alex. 'Take your time.'

A short while later, Fetlock dragged himself to his feet and they continued climbing. From the bottom of every step hung a bulb to light the way and Fetlock's brow crumpled in suspicion.

'What strange magic creates these lights?' he murmured.

'If I'm not mistaken, it's electricity,' said Alex.

Fetlock gasped. 'The power of lightning? I hear it kills with a touch . . .'

'Only if it touches you while you're touching the ground,' Alex replied. 'We learned about it in science.'

'What beings could control such power?' mused Fetlock.

'Gnomes,' Lorca said. 'My dad told me.'

'Enough about gnomes, Lorca,' Fetlock snapped. 'Hold your tongue!'

Fetlock's black nose twitched, and he started sniffing the air.

'Isth ith another thquirrel?' Lorca whispered, and Alex turned to see her holding the tip of her tongue.

Fetlock then sniffed harder. 'The air smells different up here. I think we have nearly reached the top. Onwards!'

'Can I leth go of my tongue firstht?'

'Yes!' Fetlock snapped.

The three climbed on, higher and higher, until they arrived at the top, all jelly-legged and panting.

A vast platform stretched out in front of them, covered in a mosaic of squares. Each square had a symbol on it. Below the platform, unseen, was the Endless Chasm.

'This is the maze which Rattlepike told us about!' Fetlock said.

'Do we really have to cross it?' Alex gulped.

Suddenly, from behind them came a soft click, and the steps they had just ascended slid silently into an unseen wall, leaving no way back down.

'Well, I guess that answers *that* question,' Alex said.

'Remember,' Fetlock said. 'Rattlepike said it's vital we follow the path on the map. We must cross using the squares with the correct symbols or else we shall plummet to our deaths. Hand us the map, Lorca.'

'The what?' Lorca asked.

'The map. The map Rattlepike gave us.'

'Ah, that. There's a small chance I *might* have burned it. A large chance, in fact.'

'You did *what*?' growled Fetlock.

'Last night when I was lighting the fire, I was looking for kindling and I found some scrumpled paper in my pocket and ... Well, you can finish the story yourselves, really.'

'UNBELIEVABLE!' shouted Fetlock. 'How are

we going to get across now without PLUNGING TO CERTAIN DEATH?'

'I think I can do it,' Alex said in a small voice. 'I can remember the way.'

'How?' Fetlock asked.

'I looked at the map for a second when Rattlepike gave it to me. And I'm . . . Well, I've always been able to remember things really well.' Alex closed his eyes. 'I can see the symbols in order: bird, flame, flame, sword, flower, axe, flower, weird monster-looking thing, bird, flame, axe, weird monster thing.'

'You remember all that from just one glance?' Fetlock asked. 'You're amazing, Alex Always.'

'Let's see if my memory is as good as I hope it is.'

Alex grimaced and hopped on to the square showing an image of a bird. He held his breath, bracing himself for the ground to crumble beneath him, but it stayed steady.

Ahead was a diamond symbol, a shield and a flame. Alex stepped on to the flame and gave Fetlock and Lorca the thumbs-up. Slowly, symbol by symbol, Alex hopped across, closely followed by the other two, until they reached the far side.

The three whooped in relief.

'Well done, Alex, I knew we wouldn't need that map,' Lorca said. 'Clever forward-thinking by me.'

Suddenly, a light flickered on, revealing something extraordinary and unexpected.

'It's a computer!' Alex laughed.

Indeed, sitting on a desk was a computer, glowing in the dim light, and next to it a printer.

'A what?' asked Fetlock.

'The Finding Engine is a computer. We have these in my world. I know how to use it.'

Fetlock raised an arched eyebrow. 'There is more to you than meets the eye.' He motioned Alex to the computer. 'Well, go ahead then.'

Alex gave a grin and approached the desk. It was a computer, though unlike any he had used before. The screen was black and there was a flashing green cursor. It looked incredibly old-fashioned.

'I think it just wants me to say something.' Alex shrugged and typed `Hello`.

A moment later, the response appeared in green on the screen.

`greetings. please enter the password.`

Alex remembered the password that Rattlepike had given them and typed it in.

`Password123`

The Finding Engine whirred for a tense moment until the response appeared.

password correct. what is your question?

Alex thought, and decided the simplest question would be the best.

How do I defeat the Father of Flies?

Another moment later, a response appeared again.

please wait. searching infinite worlds and infinite answers for best possible solution.

The computer hummed.

'What do we do now?' Fetlock asked.

'I guess we just wait.' Alex shrugged his shoulders.

'Excellent!' said Lorca.

'What's excellent about waiting?'

'It's one of my top three skills,' replied Lorca. 'Along with punching and fighting.'

'I think punching and fighting might count as one. But how is *waiting* a skill?'

'I can sit and completely empty my mind of all thoughts,' said Lorca, tapping the side of her head. 'Not a single thought.'

'Somehow I'm not surprised you don't find that difficult,' said Fetlock.

But before Lorca's waiting skills could be put to the test, a new message appeared.

your answer is ready. would you like to print? y/n.

Heart-pounding, Alex hit the Y key. Immediately, the printer started whirring and clacking, startling both Lorca and Fetlock, who jumped back in surprise. A moment later, the printer stopped.

please take your answer. exit down the stairs, which have now been restored.

Alex snatched up the paper and read it aloud. 'It says, "Of all possible paths, the only possible solution is this: to defeat the Father of Flies you must journey to the Far North, where the winter nights last forever, and cross Emocean, the great Sea of Feelings. On its farthest shore, clinging to the Black Cliffs, you will find an ancient castle called the Nest. There, before all stories end, you must recover the Book of Lifetales and rewrite the story of Aërth."'

'That seems pretty simple,' Lorca replied. 'I guess it really is up to you to save the world then, Alex. And I shall be right at your side.'

'Yeah, but it doesn't say how I'm supposed to get the Book off Gloam, though, does it?' Alex sighed. 'Could have been a bit more helpful on that front. Oh, hang on, there's more on the other side ... "Your quest complete, the Book can send you home. But know this: if you write in the Book of Lifetales, your own story will be forever entwined with this world, and you will never be able to leave. And always remember – a memory given is a memory taken."'

Alex's blood ran cold.

So, I have a choice, he thought miserably. *Save Aërth and never see my own home, or go back to Earth and let this world and everybody in it die ... How can I possibly decide?*

Retracing their path through the maze, Alex, Lorca and Fetlock finally stepped out of the gloom of the Infinite Palace, blinking in the bright sunshine, to be greeted by the sound of crying.

It was coming from Captain Kempt. He was kneeling on the ground, above the pale body of Captain Couth.

'It's the White Death,' Captain Kempt said, tears streaming down his face. 'It's spread so fast ... Do you know how to help him?'

Alex could only shake his head, his mind empty.

Kempt's face was stricken with misery. He shook Couth, choking back the tears. 'Wake up! I ... I cannot bear to live without you.'

Captain Kempt fell forward, sobbing into the chest of Captain Couth.

'Come,' whispered Fetlock, placing his paw on Alex. 'The best thing we can do for them is head as swiftly as we can for the Sea of Feelings and then onwards to the Father of Flies.'

Alex knew Fetlock was right. Completing their quest was the best way to help Couth – and all those like him – before they disappeared forever.

'Their only hope rests on our shoulders and our foolhardy but very heroic quest,' Lorca said.

No, Alex thought, full of despair. *Not our shoulders.* **My** *shoulders . . .*

CHAPTER THIRTEEN

A BATTLE OF WITS

As he looked into the furious eyes of Mr Abiss, a sudden and unexpected shiver of despair rippled through Axel.

'I've nothing to chat to you about,' Mr Abiss growled. 'And I believe I asked you not to bother me again. Now get off my property.'

'He only wants to talk to you,' Sienna said.

'I'm sorry, who are *you*?'

'That is Sienna,' shouted Axel. 'And she is my wife!'

'WHAT?' Mr Abiss's face turned from red to purple.

'Well, *wife-to-be*,' corrected Axel.

'I think not!' Sienna said, crossing her arms.

'What are you blethering on about? You're just a child! Why are you here?'

'I am here,' Axel said, flicking his hair. 'On a quest.'

'A *quest*?' Mr Abiss said, eyes narrowed.

'Yes. So I suggest you let me into your palace before I bring a world of trouble down upon your shiny head.'

Mr Abiss glared at him. 'You can have five minutes. But you two,' he said, pointing at Irving and Sienna, 'stay outside.'

A moment later, Axel was padding through the house behind Alex's father, into a vast, soulless room, all white walls, white sofas and white carpets, with a polar-bear-skin rug in front of a fire.

'This is quite the palace you live in, evil genius – I mean, *father*. Did you slay that bear yourself? That must have been quite the battle.'

'What do you *want*?' Mr Abiss sighed.

'I have come here to take your treasure.'

'Pardon?' Alex's father blinked.

'And I am not going to use a sword,' Axel said proudly.

'What sword? Have you lost your mind?'

'No, but you are about to lose your pots of money.'

'Ah, I knew it!' Mr Abiss exclaimed triumphantly. 'I knew the first time you came to see me that money was what you're after. Well, you're not getting another penny from me. Nobody ever gave me handouts of cash when I was your age. I had to work for it. And so should you.'

'I *shall* work for it! Not with my muscles, which is a great shame, because they are plentiful, but with my heroic brain.'

Alex's father buried his face in his hands. 'Leave now.'

'Hear me out,' replied Axel. 'For I come to offer you a bargain. Face me in a battle of wits. If I win, you shall give me enough treasure to buy Alex's – sorry, *my* – grandmother's flat.'

'And if you lose?'

'Then I give you my word, you will never see me again.'

Mr Abiss peeked out from behind his hands.

'What type of battle of wits?'

'You may choose.'

'Well, then. I choose chess.'

'Ah, chess!' exclaimed Axel. 'The game of great danger!'

Mr Abiss ignored him. 'The National Chess Tournament is being held in town next week. It has a first prize of fifty thousand pounds. Beat me, and I'll double it, then you'll have *earned* the money fair and square. Lose, and you never bother me ever again. Deal?'

Mr Abiss held his hand out.

Axel shook it vigorously. 'Deal.'

Mr Abiss let out a sharp laugh. 'You do realize I am the favourite to win? I'll be glad to have you out of my life for good. You are no child of mine, Alex.'

At those words, Axel staggered back as if he had been punched.

'I see nothing of myself in you,' continued Alex's father. 'I can hardly believe you are mine. And now you think you can beat me at chess? Impossible.'

At the sound of that final word, Axel gave a wide grin.

'We shall see . . .'

'You agreed *what*?!!' Irving said.

They were walking back to the bus stop and Axel had just reported with no small delight his conversation with Mr Abiss. 'You want to beat Alex's dad at chess?! It's not impossible like defeating some great, ugly monster in hand-to-hand combat. It's properly impossible!'

'Anything can be done if you just *believe* . . .' Axel said.

Irving scoffed. 'That's just something they say to children. Do you even know how to play chess?'

'No, but you can teach me.' Axel beamed.

Irving groaned again.

'But Alex's dad is a *Grandmaster*.'

'Then *I* shall become a Grander Master!'

'In EIGHT DAYS?' Irving said, eyes wide in exasperation. 'It literally cannot be done. That's like rolling a dice and getting seven. Or flapping your hands really fast and flying. It's . . . it's *impossible*.'

'Precisely,' said Axel, waggling his eyebrows up and down. 'An Impossible Quest.'

'You have *no* idea what the word "impossible" actually means, do you?' Irving said.

'Nobody ever said an Impossible Quest was going to be easy,' replied Axel, putting his arm around Irving.

'Argh! You're infuriating!' Irving snapped, shrugging off the arm.

'Don't forget,' Sienna added gently. 'You've got the maths test to prepare for, too.'

'An evil genius father to defeat! Chess to learn! Infernal mathematical puzzles! And bullies to destroy! All without using so much as a dagger.' Axel grinned. 'Truly the stuff of heroes.'

Irving looked at Sienna and shook his head in despair. Sienna gave a warm laugh in reply.

An hour later, they were back at Alex's flat, and Irving was teaching Axel the rules of chess.

It was not going well.

'So, this horse thing –'

'It's called a knight,' Irving replied.

'You knight your horses?' Axel roared with laughter. 'Come along, Sir Horsey! Let us take his pawn –'

'You can't do that,' Irving groaned. 'That's not the way knights move.'

'Well, then, I shall . . . move my queen here.'

'You'll lose it if you do.'

'Well, it's not as if I am losing my king!' laughed Axel.

'The queen is the most powerful piece on the board.'

'Ha ha!' boomed Axel. 'The queen the most powerful! This is your wonderful sense of humour again, is it not, Irving?'

By the end of the evening, Axel had finally learned the rules, but was still by some way the worst player Irving had ever seen.

'He's finished. Done for!' Irving sighed. 'He's never going to complete this Impossible Quest. And that means we are going to be stuck with the great, lumbering idiot forever.'

'Which great lumbering idiot?' asked Axel.

'You!'

'That's not very nice,' Axel said. 'You're a very angry warlock today.'

Irving flung his hands in the air. 'I just want my friend back!'

'And the longer you're stuck here, the longer Alex is stuck in Aërth. In danger,' Sienna said, chewing a knuckle. 'So if this really *is* the way to complete your quest, Axel, then you need to concentrate.'

'Do not fear, concentration is my strongest weapon and I shall – oh, look! A pigeon on the windowsill with unfortunate feet! Look! He is staring at me with his beady eye –'

'AXEL! CONCENTRATE!'

Axel jumped and immediately turned his attention back to the board in front of him.

Despite considerable practice, Axel's skills did not improve. Irving kept beating him, game after game.

'I am beginning to think I may have been a little rash with this bet,' said Axel glumly.

'You don't say,' Irving shot back.

'Never mind.' Sienna gave Axel an encouraging smile. 'It's late now. We can pick it up tomorrow. It's Saturday, so we can work at it all day. Sleep on it and I'm sure you'll wake up a different player.'

That night, Axel dreamed of a vast chequered field.

Stood next to him on one side was Sienna, wearing a crown, and on the other was Irving, riding a horse. Beyond Sienna, he could see a boy, head turned so Axel could not see his face. Next to the boy, a girl and a dog stood.

Axel tried to talk, but before he could open his mouth he felt breath on his neck. There was someone behind him, but he was so terrified he couldn't move. And then he looked down and saw, as he knew he would, insects, thousands of them, crawling up his body to his face, his mouth . . .

Axel woke, sweating, a scream caught in his throat, to the sound of Irving and Sienna talking to Gran.

'Right, I'm late for me shift. Alex isn't up yet, so you go and give him a kick.'

That woman, Axel thought, *works far too hard for a crone.*

But before he could think any more about it, Sienna and Irving were in his room, the chessboard was back out and he was losing to Irving again.

And again and again and again.

Eventually, Axel jumped up in frustration.

'Argh! I mean, who cares for this stupid, stupid

game? Moving these stupid little pieces around this stupid board? It is a game for people with weak, spindly arms and no courage whatsoever!'

He glared pointedly at Irving.

'Don't be such a sore loser,' Irving said.

Axel tipped the board over, shouting, 'I am *not* a sore loser! I just *hate* losing!'

A gloomy silence fell upon the room, only to be broken by the shrill ring of the doorbell, followed by a hard banging on the door.

'Somebody is keen to enter,' Axel said. 'Let us see who has such desperate need.'

He got up, quickly followed by the other two, and opened the door to find two men outside. Both were a head taller than him, both in black leather jackets, and both with faces like they had just had their pints spilled at pub-closing time.

The slightly larger of the two spoke first.

'Your mum or dad in?'

'My mother is far away from here,' Axel replied. 'I miss her greatly. She is the Sorcerer-Queen of Aërth. I do not speak of my father. Ever.'

'Yeah . . .' the man replied, uncertainly. 'Well, we are licensed to enter this address to take possession of property for unpaid debt owed by a Mrs Always.'

'Oh no!' said Sienna. 'They're bailiffs. They're here to take Alex's gran's stuff!'

'They are thieves?' Axel gasped.

'Sort of,' Sienna said.

Axel drew himself up to his full height, put his hands on his hips and eyed the two men.

'If you wish to take the crone's meagre belongings, you shall have to cross me. I would not try that if I were you.'

'Why not?' the shorter one laughed.

'I am a fully trained Grade Nine Hero,' Axel replied, prodding the man in his barrel chest. 'With an advanced diploma in henchman-dispatching.'

The man gave a more nervous laugh this time. 'You what?'

'You should also know I have single-handedly defeated a horde of rampaging Mud Trolls and bested a slippery Steam Giant in just my undergarments.' This was met with confused murmurs from the bailiffs. 'And I swatted thirteen Rainbow Fairies in less than a minute. That's a record for my village. Admittedly they aren't *that* dangerous, but they can give an itchy bite.'

The other bailiff held up his hands, a smirk on his face. 'Look, I can see you aren't someone to be messed with.'

'You are an excellent judge of character,' Axel said.

'Hang on a minute, you aren't even allowed in here anyway, are you?' Sienna pointed a finger at the two men. 'We're children and there's no adult here.'

The smirk fell from the bailiff's face. He looked like he wanted to tear Sienna into two.

'You're correct, Little Miss Clever Clogs. We aren't allowed to enter this property without an adult present, so why don't you just tell Mrs Always that she has eight days to pay the debt she owes – twenty thousand pounds – or we will return and evict her and whoever else lives here.'

'Ha!' crowed Axel triumphantly. 'Scuttle away, cowards! And do not darken my domain again!'

He slammed the door.

'That was a lesson in the art of fighting without fighting,' Axel said. 'With some foes, you can see the fear in their eyes, so it's easier to win a battle in the mind. It doesn't mess your hair up that way.'

'Come on,' Irving said, smiling. 'Let's go back to chess.'

'Gah, that cursed game!' Axel snapped. 'I thought it was supposed to be deadly dangerous, not deathly boring!'

Sienna snapped her fingers.

'Ah, but it *is*, Axel! Danger runs through the heart of this game.'

'What do you mean?' Axel asked, looking deeply sceptical.

'It's like you said,' continued Sienna. 'You're fighting with your mind. You have to think of a game of chess like a miniature war!'

'Now, war I *do* know!' exclaimed Axel. 'I had to learn all about it!'

'I thought you didn't go to school?'

'Well, no, I didn't go to *school*. But I had many years of hero training at AAGH.'

'Aagh?'

'Yes – the Academy for Aspiring Great Heroes. Where every hero must study the Three Chief Pillars of Heroism: swordplay, warfare and haircare. I mastered all three almost by the time I could walk. In fact, I could fully shampoo and condition before I could crawl.'

'OK, good,' said Sienna. 'Well, you need many of the same skills used in warfare when playing chess. You need to plan ahead. Work out what your enemy is going to do. Find their weaknesses.'

Axel's eyes lit up. 'I got a B+ in finding my enemy's weaknesses.'

'There you go! Sometimes you need to dominate by attacking. At other times, if your enemy is cunning, you will need to defend until the moment is right to strike.'

'I see, I see! Let us play!'

And then something remarkable happened; within a few shocking minutes, Axel beat Irving at chess.

Irving sat motionless, his jaw wide open in shock.

'I don't believe it. He beat me. He actually beat me. If the Chess Club hears about this, I'm finished.' Irving gave his head a little shake. 'You were lucky. Play me again.'

Twenty-four moves later, Axel had defeated Irving again.

'Argh!' shouted Irving. 'Stupid game!' He jumped up and stormed out of the room.

Axel gave a grin to Sienna. 'I think Irving might be a sore loser as well.'

Irving stormed back in.

'Again!'

They played twenty-seven more games that day. The score was twenty-eight wins to Axel and one draw. As each game finished, Irving became increasingly pale.

At the end of the last, he stood up and stared mournfully out the window, muttering, 'I don't believe it. I just don't believe it.'

'You see,' said Axel, slapping him on the back. 'Anything *can* be done if you just believe.'

'I'm glad to hear you say that,' said Sienna, grinning. 'Because now it's time for some maths revision.'

'Noooooooo!'

Felonius Gloam put down the goblet and wiped his mouth.

He was close to mastering the Book now. He could feel the power coursing and curdling through his body. The Narrator's final gift – his blood.

That was the end of it. The last drop.

Before him cowered a man. The wretch's name was Finbar Rake and he lived up to his name, being almost entirely skin and bone.

'Please, master,' Rake begged. 'Have mercy!'

'This is not a world for mercy, Rake,' returned Gloam coldly. 'But the world I shall create will be. And your sacrifice may make it possible.'

He turned to the Book of Lifetales. Dipping a quill in an inkpot, he wrote:

Finbar Rake: heart explodes and dies.

Nothing happened.

Gloam cursed. What was he doing wrong? Could it be that the Narrator had told the truth? '"I merely tell a person's story,"' Gloam murmured. '"I do not end it."'

Well, no matter. The White Death was taking care of *that* problem. Without their stories being told, the population of Aërth was dying, and dying fast. Soon, all would be gone, save Gloam himself, who had long since freed himself of the Book's power and the child the Narrator had brought to challenge him.

Gloam pursed his lips thoughtfully.

But if he could not cause death, perhaps he could at least cause suffering? At his feet, Rake whimpered, as if reading his thoughts. Gloam picked up his quill again and began to write.

Finbar Rake: suffers a most terrible case of scarlet wolfpox.

Rake screamed. Instantly, tell-tale red welts had begun to appear on his body. Soon the agonizing shivers would begin. And then the last symptom, the most terrifying – the long, mournful howling of the wolfpox sufferer – would be heard echoing through the Nest.

Whether the man would die might not be within his power, mused Gloam, but perhaps that didn't matter.

He may not be able to take lives, but he could now control them.

And the next to feel his power would be the boy who was sent to defy him. His human agents had returned no word of the mystery boy, but Gloam had other spies at his disposal. He began whispering, and raised his arms aloft, his eyes pure white.

His words were soon answered. Flies, countless numbers of them, buzzed around him until it was impossible to see him within the frenzied black cloud. Gloam stepped forward, the cloud of flies moving with him. And then, slowly, his feet left the ground.

CHAPTER FOURTEEN

MOONLINGS, RATS, BADGERS AND FLIES

Thick roiling clouds, heavy with rain, had mushroomed across the sky, so Alex, Lorca and Fetlock had taken cover in a dilapidated barn on the edge of a deep-green field which disappeared down a sloping valley to a watery horizon.

Alex stared into the distance as the first heavy drops began to fall. He had taken to staring into the distance more and more often. It allowed him to think more clearly, and, he thought, it gave him something of an air of mystery. Lorca was busy cooking dinner; she had caught *something* (Alex did not dare ask what), skinned it and built a fire. Fetlock was sat next to Alex, and together they watched the rain slowly get heavier, the smell of cooking meat wafting through the air. Finally, Lorca gave both of them a bowl of steaming food and they ate in silence, gazing into the early evening rain.

'Sort of rain that soaks you, this,' Lorca said after a while.

Fetlock rolled his eyes. 'What sort of rain *doesn't* soak you?'

Alex grinned as the two continued to bicker.

After dinner, Lorca gave Alex his nightly sword training. He thought he was getting a little better. The weapon felt lighter in his hand and he was able to swing it with more force. He lay back afterwards, panting, and stretched. He felt rejuvenated after the food and exercise. Stronger too. All this walking was clearly having an effect.

'We should rest here for the night,' said Fetlock. 'While we have cover.'

Nobody argued.

Lorca had found a pile of old sacks at the back of the barn and spent the rest of the evening putting stuff into one.

'What are you collecting?' Fetlock asked, trying to look.

Lorca snatched the sack away. 'Erm . . . Nothing. Just some . . . useful stuff. Necessities. For the journey.'

'Well, they better be useful,' Fetlock said. 'We need to travel light.'

'They are. *So* useful.'

Fetlock sniffed. 'What's that smell? Is it coming from the sack?'

'No!' Lorca said. 'I think there might be some . . . cow dung nearby.'

Fetlock hmmed, curled into a ball with a creak of old bones and almost immediately started snoring.

After a while, the rain cleared, so Lorca and Alex took two of the sacks outside and lay down under a depthless black sky pricked by a million glittering, icy stars. *It's strange*, Alex thought. *Back home, I'd memorized every constellation in the sky; yet here, I don't recognize a single one.* They climbed into their sacks like makeshift sleeping bags and Lorca wriggled over, worm-like, until she was right next to Alex.

'Do you ever wonder what they are?' she whispered.

'The stars?'

'Yeah. My mum says they are lamps lit every night by Sky Giants.'

Alex smiled. 'They aren't. They're actually all suns and planets.'

'Millions of suns and planets like ours?'

Alex nodded. 'The ones that twinkle are suns and the ones that don't are planets.'

Lorca stared at him for a moment, then burst into hooting laughter. 'You're a funny one, Alex Always, and no mistake.' Lorca let out a short sigh. '*I* think they are holes to heaven. I think when my father died, his soul went up into the sky and into the next world through one of those holes. And I'll follow him when it's my time.'

Alex smiled to himself. 'That,' he said, 'sounds like as good a theory as any.'

As they watched, a brighter light appeared in the sky, flitting high above their heads: a bird, starling-like, but glowing brightly with a warm, yellowy light.

'Oh!' Lorca gasped. 'A moonling!'

More and more moonlings began to flock above them, countless numbers, dazzling against the black, darting and weaving, until they were a vast, phosphorescent murmuration, a shimmering cloud, swooping and diving and dancing as one, painting mercurial smoke-shapes across the sky.

Eventually, the cloud swept off into the night and the spectacular show was over, leaving Alex and Lorca in the dark, with just a silent heart-memory, a held-breath shared secret locked tight inside them. They smiled at each other and rolled over, each lost in their own thoughts.

And as Alex drifted towards sleep, quicksilver blooms of light fireworked behind his closed eyelids.

He woke as the first fingers of dawn choked the last breath of night from the indigo-streaked sky that stretched above the barn. He shivered against the cold, which had crept up from the ground and settled deep into his bones. A single bird called in the distance, a solitary, mournful song.

Alex shivered again and shifted closer to Fetlock, who was now snoring happily next to him. The old dog must have come out to join them during the night. Alex reached out and stroked Fetlock's long, brown ears. Fetlock stopped snoring and gave a gentle sigh, his black nose twitching.

Suddenly, his eyes sprang open.

Alex sprang back, holding his hands up. 'I wasn't stroking you!'

But Fetlock didn't seem to care. He jumped to his feet, sniffing the air frantically, then bolted behind the barn.

Alex crawled over and gave Lorca a sharp shake.

'Wake up!' he whispered, but Lorca just groaned.

'Come on!' Alex shook her again. 'Something's wrong.'

'Whassamatter?' Lorca rubbed her eyes.

'Fetlock smelled something.'

'It'll be last night's dinner. Roast Mountain Rat always gives me terrible wind.'

'No, it's not that. It looked serious.'

Lorca sprang out of her sack.

'Well,' she said, stifling a yawn. 'Whatever the danger, I'm ready with my sword!'

'That's not your sword. That's a broom handle.'

Lorca looked at her hand and jumped in surprise. 'Fair point.'

A few seconds later she had replaced the broom with her sword, just as Fetlock rushed back, panic in his eyes.

'We have to go!'

'What? Why?' Alex asked. 'What's going on?'

'No time to explain.'

The three ran into the barn and grabbed their gear.

'Quickly!' Fetlock urged. 'This way. And whatever you do, don't look back.'

As anybody who has ever been told not to do something knows, this was the worst possible advice.

'What *is* that?' Alex asked, squinting back.

It was a distant cloud, ink-black and threatening, and Alex knew immediately there was something horribly wrong with it. It wasn't just that it was moving unnaturally fast, or that it was moving towards them against the wind. It was that, even though logic was screaming that it couldn't be so, Alex couldn't deny what his ears were telling him: there was a ferocious buzzing coming from the cloud.

The buzzing grew into a roaring hum and Alex realized in horror what was flying in their direction. It was a cloud of insects: a Stygian shadow of flies arrowing towards them. The buzzing had now turned into a roaring hum. And then, inside the cloud, Alex saw something he would never ever forget as long as he lived. Inside the mass of insects, the flies had coagulated, forming themselves into a shape – with arms out-stretched, the figure of a man.

'It's Gloam!' screamed Fetlock. 'Run!'

'No!' shouted Lorca, holding her sword aloft. 'I shall fight them!'

'Don't be ridiculous!' Fetlock yelled, over the ferocious sound of the flies. 'You can't fight them! You will die.'

'Ah! But what a glorious death!'

'Not really. It would just be stupid. Now, hurry!'

'Do you know what?' said Lorca in a wounded tone. 'I don't think you trust me very much.'

Fetlock growled. 'Now is really *not* the time for this! Run!'

Lorca rounded on Fetlock indignantly. 'You don't think I can defeat them, do you? But that's why I was fated for this quest by the Orb of Exposition – to fight!'

'I absolutely *do* trust you,' said Fetlock. 'But this isn't a couple of underfed Pygmy Goblins, this is magic powered by Gloam himself. A whole battalion of heroes couldn't stop them.'

'Well, then I shall die protecting Alex!'

'I don't want you to die protecting me, I would much prefer you to live,' Alex screamed over the noise of the flies. In the depths of the cloud, the shape of Gloam seemed to raise a hand to point at him. 'Now can we *please* run?!'

'Fine!' harrumphed Lorca. 'But when the songs are written of our great quest, let it be known Lorca Stonearm was *not* happy about running away.'

'You don't have to be happy about it,' shouted Fetlock. 'Let's just go!'

And all three started running.

The cloud was gaining on them, though, at terrifying speed.

'Come on!' shouted Fetlock, who was by far the fastest. Alex was almost as quick, but Lorca was much slower than both, struggling under the weight of the sack of supplies she had thrown over her shoulder along with her backpack.

'Drop the sack!' shouted Fetlock.

'I can't! It's the essentials for the journey.'

'Like what?'

'Some rocks, a small set of ceremonial drums and a dead badger.'

Fetlock looked like he wanted to tear Lorca's throat

out. 'WHAT?! WHY? Actually, forget it – just dump the sack!'

'Dump it?! The badger hasn't even started to smell yet. Well, not much.'

'Lorca, a Felonious Gloam made of flies is nearly upon us! Dump the sack!'

'Gah! They're such lovely looking rocks!'

'DUMP IT!'

'Ugh, *fine*.'

But before Lorca could do so, the flies were upon them.

It was as if the world was suddenly screaming. All Alex could do was keep running, his legs thundering on the ground, eyes and mouth closed.

Then he slipped and fell, sprawling forward, and suddenly every centimetre of his body was crawling with glistening flies, flowing over him like seething black oil. Although all Alex wanted to do was scream, he did not dare open his mouth. But that didn't stop the flies from crawling into his ears and up his nose. And deeper still, inside his mind.

'I know you,' he heard the flies buzzing. 'I know where you are – and where you are going . . .'

A hand pulled him up. Lorca dragged him to his feet as she swung her sword around her head.

'Die, tiny beasties!' she yelled, then coughed as she swallowed a mouthful of flies. Alex staggered and then they were off again, running desperately.

'I am coming for you, Alex Always!' Gloam hissed. 'You have travelled to this world only to find your death!'

Ahead of them, Fetlock scrambled to a halt. They had come to the edge of a ridge, with a steep ravine below. They were trapped.

And then an idea hit Alex.

'Give me the sack,' he yelled to Lorca.

She threw it at him and Alex thrust his hand inside, into soggy, damp fur. He pulled the dead badger from the sack, the smell assaulting him. Immediately, the flies around him thickened, drawn irresistibly to the foul stench. Alex stepped back to the very brink of the ravine.

'No!' he heard Gloam hiss, as he realized Alex's plan.

With one almighty heave, Alex flung the badger off the edge.

The flies shot after it, unable to resist the sweet smell of rotting meat, diving down to the stream far below and out of sight. Alex collapsed to the ground, panting. Fetlock slumped beside him.

'No!' cried Lorca, aghast. 'That was our dinner! Why did you chuck it away?'

Fetlock stared at Lorca. 'Because it got rid of the flies!'

Lorca seemed about to protest, but then her eyes widened.

'Oh yes! I mean, *of course*. That's why I brought it. Just in case we needed to distract a cloud of flies in the shape of Felonius Gloam. That was exactly my plan all along.'

'Those flies did something to me,' Alex announced, distraught. 'They got in my brain. Gloam knows where we are now. And where we are going.'

Fetlock gave a low growl. 'Well, then, we must move. We should put as much distance as we can between us and the flies. And we are still a day's travel from the shore of Emocean.'

Alex nodded and pulled himself to his feet. He didn't need to be reminded that the clock was ticking; the warning from the Orb of Exposition was still sharp in his memory.

Only eight days to go until the end of the world.

CHAPTER FIFTEEN

ESCAPE TO EMOCEAN

They walked in leaden silence, Alex shuddering and itching at the memory of the flies crawling inside him. They trudged through field and village and crossed river and valley, and with each step the temperature seemed to drop. The green hills turned grey, thick clouds hanging low above them, obscuring their peaks. The fields hardened under their feet, full of brittle ridges of earth and sharp rocks.

'Our destination is the other side of those hills.' Fetlock pointed at a range that was looming ever larger. 'Beyond lies the Sea of Feelings.'

'You *absolutely* sure about crossing Emocean?' Lorca asked, uncharacteristic nervousness adding a quaver to her voice.

'We have no choice,' replied Fetlock. 'It's the quickest way to Gloam.'

'First the Silent Forest, now the Sea of Feelings,' Lorca said. 'This is *quite* the journey.'

'And it is far from over.'

Fetlock kept pushing the two humans harder, not allowing any rest stops in case the flies had followed them. Eventually, just as Alex's legs were about to give out, they arrived at the foot of the hills.

Much to Alex's dismay, they were considerably higher than they had looked from far away. In fact, their jagged peaks looked more like mountains.

'We will rest a moment to get our strength back, then we climb,' Fetlock said. 'What do we have to eat, Lorca?'

'Nothing, because *somebody* threw the badger I was saving for dinner over the edge of a cliff.'

'It was rotting!' protested Alex.

'No matter.' Fetlock held a paw up. 'We shall have to go without.'

After a mercilessly short sit-down, they were up and climbing. On and on they trudged, step by weary step, as the daylight slowly slipped away. The shale became loose underfoot, sending them slipping back one step for every two they took. Eventually, they reached a thick bank of damp cloud that reduced visibility to an arm's length.

On they plodded, the freezing fog soaking them, deadening the sound of their feet on the crunching rocks, until Fetlock finally announced they had reached the top and should rest until morning.

Alex fell to the ground, his legs jelly. He didn't think he could ever move again. He closed his eyes and, before he knew it, there was the sound of a crackling fire, and something roasting on a spike.

'What meat –'

'Best not ask,' Fetlock interrupted.

Alex nodded. It looked suspiciously like rat. Again. His rumbling stomach overrode every other concern, though, and a few minutes later he was chewing happily on more gristly meat of unknown origin.

Night came gently, the surrounding fog slowly darkening until all was black. Sleep escaped Alex, though, so he peered through the night, ears pricked for any sign of the Father of Flies, accompanied by the sounds of snuffling and snoring from Fetlock and Lorca. Once he was sure they were asleep, he pulled out the answer that the Finding Engine had given him and squinted in the dying firelight to reread the final paragraph.

```
your quest complete, the book can
send you home. but know this: if you
write in the book of lifetales, your
own story will be forever entwined
with this world, and you will never
```

```
be able to leave. and always remember —
a memory given is a memory taken.
```

That last sentence still had him baffled, but the rest did not. The impossible choice he faced was perfectly clear – save this world or go home and leave it to its fate.

Alex crumpled the paper back into his pocket, sick at heart. Never had he felt so alone, so far from his friends and his gran. He stared into the thick fog, tears running down his face. He tried to stifle the sound of his sniffling, but he could see Fetlock's eyes open, glinting in the dark. He padded over and curled up next to Alex. They lay in silence, both watching the fire.

'This morning,' Fetlock whispered, 'you stroked my ears.'

'Yes, I'm sorry, but –'

'It was nice. You can do it again.'

Alex wiped his eyes with the back of his hand and began to stroke the soft fur. Fetlock gave a low sigh.

'Fetlock, remember what the Orb foretold? That some of us might die on this quest. Is that definitely going to happen?'

Fetlock gave another sigh, but this time it was one of aching sadness.

'I fear so. But if we succeed in stopping this cruel plague destroying our world, it will be a sacrifice well made.'

'I really don't want anyone to die,' Alex said, miserably.

'Nor me, Alex Always. Nor me.'

A moment later, Lorca crawled over to them, shuffling close until they were all cuddled closely together in a ball.

The three fell asleep, just like that, in a warm huddle: a girl, a boy and a dog in front of a fading fire.

When Alex woke, each muscle in his body seemed to ache. He could still feel every rock he had slept on. They set off on their descent, hungry, exhausted and not a little grumpy.

They lumbered through the damp morning cloud, Alex's and Lorca's wet clothes clinging to their shivering bodies, Fetlock's fur sodden and stringy. The cold was becoming sharper, biting at their faces and hands. Finally, to their great relief, they broke through the base of the clouds and could see into the distance once again.

And there, twinkling on the horizon, was Emocean. The Sea of Feelings.

The way to the Nest, where Felonius Gloam lay.

It was if the mountains themselves crashed into the sea. A great rainbow arced across the water. And huddled on the shore, glinting in the morning sun, lay a town, its harbour filled with ships. The town itself was all curves – there was not a single sharp edge to be seen – and each building was painted the brightest white, tumbling down to the shore like the rolling crest of a breaking wave.

The sight gave Alex a swell of hope in his heart, and by the look on Fetlock's and Lorca's faces, and the extra burst of speed in their legs, they felt the same. A few hours later they had reached the outskirts.

'You two see if you can get fresh supplies,' said Fetlock. 'I will find us a ship. Meet me by the harbour in an hour.'

'Come on,' said Lorca. 'The market is this way.'

'How do you know?' asked Alex. 'Have you been here before?'

'Nope, but I can smell the fish . . .'

Lorca's nose led them through a warren of streets to a small square where, to Alex's surprise, life seemed to be going on as normal despite the Mortmarks clearly visible on people's hands. A noisy crowd of market traders were selling seafood, the likes of which Alex had never seen: fish of every size, colour and type imaginable, seahorses the size of dogs, crabs glistening metallic gold in the cold sunshine.

In fact, the fish were much more colourful than the people, who were dressed completely in white, including white masks which covered their mouths. It gave them a sinister air. While Lorca haggled for some supplies, Alex felt a curious feeling that he was being watched, catching one of the fishmongers staring at him for just a moment too long.

'Let's go and find Fetlock,' he said, as Lorca handed over a few coins and pocketed a pungent package of dried fish.

They were setting off down a small ginnel, following their noses towards the harbour, when two men suddenly jumped out in front of them.

'Hello, strangers!' sneered one, two eyes peeping out above his mask.

'What do you want?' Alex asked, trying to hide the tremor in his voice.

'We've been told to look out for three travellers,' rasped the other man, stepping closer. 'A boy, a girl and a dog. And here you two are. There's a reward for your capture, you see.' Here, Alex and Lorca looked at each other in horror. 'The Father of Flies is most interested in meeting you.'

Alex stepped backwards, reaching for his sword, his hand shaking.

'Now, now, none of that,' said the first man. 'I see from your trembling arm, you are no fighter. Come quiet and we won't have to hurt you.'

'*You* won't have to hurt *us*?' Lorca drew her blade. 'I'll have you know I'm a famous hero. Now you two best scamper along before I run you through!'

The two men looked at each other, then at the fierce girl in front of them with the steady arm and the look of steel in her eyes, and chose to run.

Lorca was about to give chase, but Alex grabbed her arm.

'No, Lorca.'

'But they are so . . . killable!'

'Leave them,' said Alex. 'We need to find Fetlock and leave this place. We are being hunted now.'

'Gah! Fine!'

To Alex's relief, he could see the crashing sea at the end of another narrow alleyway and they hurried along it, an icy wind whipping at their hair. But as he reached the beach, Alex saw something which sent a fresh shiver down his spine.

Bodies, row upon row, lay stretched out on the shingle, staring sightlessly into the sky. Each was in the latter stages of fading; the nearest to Alex was so pale he could see straight through the body to the pebbles underneath. The rising tide was already lapping at the bodies nearest the water.

So this was how victims of the White Death were treated here. Left out for the sea to carry them away into its depths. Alex shuddered. Even Lorca seemed lost for words. They turned and hurried towards the harbour, not looking back.

There was no sign of Fetlock yet, so they sat next to each other on a small pier, swinging their legs, staring at the waves below them, churning with frozen daggers of ice.

'What's so bad about this sea then?' Alex asked.

Lorca gave a small shrug. 'I've heard stories, that's all. About how it messes with your head, makes you feel things. Apparently it's not too bad near the shore, where they do the fishing and stuff, but further out it's supposed to be worse.'

Alex could believe it. Even here he could sense the sea somehow pulling at him, as if he was at the top of a roller-coaster, about to plummet. He stared down at the roiling ice and foaming black water and could almost feel invisible arms drawing him in . . .

Lorca grabbed his arm.

'Come on, maybe let's not sit here,' she said. 'Look, there's Fetlock.'

The grizzled old dog was walking along the harbour with a grizzled old man. They hurried over to join him.

'Ah good, you're here,' Fetlock said. 'The captain has agreed to give us passage across Emocean aboard the good ship *Siren Song*.'

Alex noticed that the captain was not, in fact, a grizzled old man but a grizzled old lady with a full beard, and when she spoke it was in a voice like rough waves on pebbles.

'My friends call me Alas McClann. But you can call me Captain, because no friend would take another over the Sea of Feelings unless in the *direst* need.'

'This is the direst need,' Fetlock replied.

'So I hear,' McClann said. 'Word is, three travellers matching your description are being looked for, eh? And that there's a boy among them that's the cause of the White Death.'

'That's not true!' Alex gasped, then spoke more quietly. 'Felonius Gloam is the cause and we are on a quest to stop him.'

McClann gave a low harrumph.

'Well, an enemy of Gloam is a friend of mine. I will take you.' McClann squinted into the distance behind them. 'I suggest we move quickly, though, eh? I think you might have been found.'

Alex turned. Striding along the beach towards them was a group of soldiers, clad in chainmail armour.

Alex let out a groan of fear.

'Let's go,' growled McClann.

They didn't need to be told twice. McClann ran to a small schooner bearing the name *Siren Song*. All three followed her and jumped aboard.

'Come on! Hurry!' urged Lorca, as the soldiers got closer.

'I'm going as fast as I can!' snapped McClann, furiously pulling at ropes and unfurling sails.

Alex and Lorca pulled out their swords, Alex's heart pounding with fear.

McClann cast off the last of the ropes. *Siren Song* started edging away from the harbour, but the soldiers were so close now that Alex could see their faces. With horror, he realized they were entirely skinless, all sinew and stretched muscle, twisted in anger.

They charged into the sea, arms stretching out for the ship as it crept away from the shore. Lorca swiped her sword at them, keeping them back, but Alex clambered to the prow, desperate to get away from their clutches. Then McClann pulled at a rope and another sail unfurled. It caught the stiff breeze, billowing in the wind, and *Siren Song* suddenly surged forward, leaving the soldiers thrashing in its wake.

Lorca gave a whoop of triumph, and Alex cheered and high-fived her.

McClann glared at them. 'Calm yourselves, you fools! Have you forgotten where you are, eh? You are sailing on Emocean. It pays to keep your feelings in check. Now all of you, sit.'

They obeyed meekly. McClann disappeared below deck, a moment later reappearing with a long rope.

'What's that for?' Alex asked.

'To tie you all down,' McClann answered gruffly.

'Is that really necessary?' Fetlock demanded.

'It is.'

'Why?' Alex asked.

Alas McClann stared at Alex, her eyes colder than the black sea below them, and said words which sent a shiver of fear down Alex's spine. 'To make sure you don't kill me. Or each other.'

CHAPTER SIXTEEN

THE SEA OF FEELINGS

Siren Song pushed out into the Sea of Feelings, nudged by gentle waves. Captain McClann had finished tying the rope around Alex, Lorca and Fetlock, and was now chained to the ship's great wheel.

Aside from the lapping waves against the hull, there was silence – not even the cry of a seagull. On they sailed, the land behind them shrinking until it was a faint line on the horizon. And then it was gone.

'Who *were* those soldiers?' Alex asked.

'The Sons of Perdition,' Fetlock said. 'Gloam's most trusted followers. They are driven not by money or blood-lust, but purely by loyalty to him. And to show that loyalty, they carve off their own skin, piece by piece. You see, belief is the most dangerous weapon there is.'

Alex couldn't help but shudder, but the next moment a wave of shame washed over him as he remembered how he had fled to the front of the ship, leaving Lorca and Fetlock to fight. He tried to put on a braver face.

'Well, we got away from them, anyhow. And soon we'll have stopped Gloam too.'

Fetlock gave a non-committal growl. Lorca stayed silent. She had grown pale.

'Are you OK?' Alex asked.

'I might not be *that* used to travelling on boats.'

'Oh.'

'In fact, this might be my first time.'

'Well, it's not so –'

'And I might be feeling a bit queasy.'

'But the sea is so calm!'

'Doesn't matter.' Lorca's face had gone from pale to a shade of yellowy-green. 'I definitely feel quite sick. Really sick, if I'm honest.'

It was the worst moment for the wind to suddenly pick up, each gust sharpening the edge of the bitter cold. Icy rain started sleeting down as the waves became choppier, and the ship began to dip and rise in the water.

'I am definitely going to be sick,' gulped Lorca.

Alex let out a short laugh. He felt bad for Lorca, but the look on her face *was* quite funny.

Lorca retched, but nothing but a groan left her mouth.

Fetlock eyed her warily. 'Captain! Captain McClann! We have a problem here!'

'Deal with it yourselves!' McClann shouted, without looking round. 'There's a storm coming in fast!'

Lorca burped, her skin going from yellowy-green to full-green.

'I'm going to –' She retched again.

Fetlock starting tugging at the rope, trying to get further away from Lorca. The waves became steeper, *Siren Song* swooping and rising in the water. Captain McClann was wrestling with the wheel, struggling to keep it straight.

'Don't you dare be sick on me!' Fetlock snarled at Lorca, rain flattening the fur on his usually kindly face into an angry mask. Alex let out a giggle, and his hand shot up and covered his mouth in shock.

'Lorca!' he shouted, giving her a huge grin. 'Turn around so you aren't sick in the boat!'

This was not good advice, though, for just as Lorca swung around to face the sea, the vomit exploded out of her. It sprayed from Lorca's mouth in a huge curving arc, showering Fetlock full in the face.

Fetlock froze in horror, sick dripping off him.

'My . . . fur!'

'I'm sorry!' wailed Lorca. 'Please don't be angry with me!'

'My fur! It's *covered*!' Fetlock snarled, his teeth showing.

Alex let out another giggle. Fetlock rounded on him.

'Oh, you think this is funny, do you?'

'No!' sniggered Alex. 'Not at all!'

'You *do*!' growled Fetlock. 'I should kill you for that!'

'Steady on!' Alex said. 'I was only –'

Fetlock pulled at the thick rope around him. 'I'll tear your throat out for laughing at me!'

Alex's whole body flooded with joy at the sight of Fetlock growling and snapping away.

'Oh gods!' screamed Lorca. 'Somebody save us from the wild dog! He'll kill us!'

Alex watched as Lorca started crying, and the sight of his friend sobbing was completely hilarious.

'Please!' gibbered Lorca. 'Let me go!'

'Not before I get you first!' snapped Fetlock, at which Alex roared with laughter.

It was then that Alex realized what the problem was. And he thought it was the funniest thing ever.

'It's the Sea of Feelings!' he whooped, joyfulness bubbling through him. 'It's Emocean making us feel like this!'

'I don't care what it is!' snarled Fetlock. 'You're laughing at me, and I'm going to bite your head off.'

'I can't help it!' hooted Alex. 'The sea is making me happy!'

'Let me out of these ropes!' wailed Lorca, her face stricken with panic. 'I must get off this boat!'

'Don't worry, I'll put you out of your misery!' snapped Fetlock, gnawing at the rope with his sharp front teeth.

'No!' moaned Lorca, shivering and cringing.

Alex found the whole scene the funniest thing he had ever seen. Life was so absurd that laughter was the only answer. Deep down there was a part of him that knew this wasn't in the least bit amusing, that they were all in great danger, but he didn't seem to be able to do anything about it. He was laughing too much, the tears of joy streaming down his face mixing with the lashing rain.

The ship was rolling now in great waves, up and down, and Captain McClann was cowering next to the ship's wheel, head in her hands.

'What's the point, anyway?' she wailed. 'We're all doomed!'

But doom didn't seem that bad to Alex. Nothing seemed that bad any more.

On and on they ploughed, the wind whipping at the sails, driving them through the waves. Alex had no idea how long they had been on this ship. He just knew that it was the happiest time of his life and he never wanted it to end. Sheet lightning strobed around them, freeze-framing emotions on their faces – fury, terror, ecstasy and despair. Deafening thunder rolled, a calamitous clashing that shook the sky.

Ignoring the storm, Fetlock was tearing furiously at the rope, shredding the binding down to its last threads.

'One more minute and my teeth will be at your throats!' he snarled.

'He's going to escape!' cried Lorca, shaking in terror.

Alex laughed wildly once again, lifting his head up to the rain as Fetlock gave one more mighty pull at the rope, and it snapped.

Fetlock was free.

'At last!' he growled through bared teeth.

But it wasn't just Fetlock who was free; all three were bound by the same rope, and it fell to the deck for all of them.

Lorca jumped to her feet. 'Get me away from that dog!'

Everything seemed to happen very quickly then.

Lorca, arms aloft, made a running jump for the sea, but Fetlock took a flying leap and intercepted her. They tumbled to the deck in a heap.

'You're not going to cheat me out of the chance of killing you!' Fetlock snapped at Lorca.

Alex started pulling the rope off his own wrists. Although he was filled with joy at the thought of Fetlock killing Lorca, if she died it would be one less person to laugh at. He had to stop them.

Fetlock sprang to his feet and stood over Lorca.

'Prepare to die!' He howled and pounced.

Just at that moment, a huge wave hit *Siren Song*, sending all three sprawling. The ship nearly rolled over, but righted itself, scattering them all across the deck. Alex clung on to some rigging, desperately trying to stop himself from falling into the sea. All he could hear above the sound of thunder and rain and the crashing waves was Captain McClann sobbing and his own terrible laughter.

Alex, soaked to the skin, dragged himself to his feet. Lorca was crawling towards the rail and Fetlock was edging towards her. Before Alex could reach them, Fetlock jumped on to Lorca's back and plunged his teeth into her shoulder. Lorca howled in pain, then staggered forward, crashing into the rail and over it, into the freezing, churning sea, Fetlock still on her back.

As suddenly as it had come, the wind vanished.

'The tide has changed!' Captain McLann cried, shaking her head and grabbing the wheel.

In a flash, as the joy in his heart was replaced by absolute fear, Alex realized two things. First, Emocean's new tide had given him back his real emotions, and, second, his friends were about to die.

'No!' he screamed and ran to the ship's rail.

Below him, he could see Fetlock, paddling frantically, and Lorca, arms flailing.

'Help!' she screamed. 'I can't swim!'

Alex froze in terror at the sight of the churning waves below him, an icy certain death in which unknown creatures would rise up from the depths and tear at his flesh. But the terror of losing his friends was far greater. Without thinking, Alex grabbed the rope and dived into the sea.

The cold hit him like a dagger to the heart. He gasped, struggling to catch his breath, the freezing water burning every centimetre of his skin. He started swimming towards Fetlock, who was nearest, but the dog called out, 'Save Lorca first!' All the hatred and anger was gone from his eyes, replaced with anguish.

Alex swam over to Lorca, tied the rope around her struggling body and pulled her back to *Siren Song*. She clambered weakly past him and up the side of the ship to safety. Alex swung round, scanning the water for Fetlock.

Who had disappeared.

Alex swam to and fro, panic and cold clutching at him. And then, out of the corner of his eye, he caught a flash of white fur in the water. Alex thrashed towards it, heart pounding.

The fur was Fetlock, floating face down.

Alex didn't allow himself to think, in case the terror stopped him from moving. He tied the rope around Fetlock and swam for dear life back towards *Siren Song*, towing the body behind him. From up on deck, Captain McClann and Lorca pulled Fetlock aboard, as Alex climbed the ship's side.

He collapsed on deck, next to Fetlock's sodden, furry body. It was motionless.

'No!' Alex wailed. 'Wake up, Fetlock!'

He started pumping the dog's hairy chest, again and again, Lorca watching on in horror. Until suddenly, Fetlock started coughing and spluttering up water, drawing in huge gasps of breath.

Alex slumped to the deck, staring into the

sky, almost too tired to breathe, until he heard a sudden cry.

'Land ho!' cried Captain McClann.

Lorca crept over to them and laid a hand on Fetlock's paw. 'I'm so sorry I nearly got you drowned.'

Fetlock, bedraggled, his fur clinging to his small frame, dragged himself over to Lorca. 'Please,' he wheezed and gave an exhausted cough. 'I *bit* you. I am the one who should be sorry.'

Fetlock hung his head in shame, his ears flattened low.

'Nobody needs to be sorry,' Alex said. 'It was Emocean. She made us feel it all.'

And with a soft bump, Captain McClann brought *Siren Song* up to a rickety wooden jetty.

They had reached the other side.

CHAPTER SEVENTEEN

INFERNAL PUZZLES

'What have you done with her?!' Axel demanded furiously.

He pulled the mattress off his bed and hurled it across the room.

'What have I done with who?' Gran asked, her face a picture of bafflement.

Axel dropped to the floor and peered under the wardrobe. 'Where is she?'

'Where's *who*?'

'Aëthelmrir!'

'Ethel Maria? Who's she?'

'Aëthelmrir! My sword, crone! Where have you put her?'

'Firstly, call me crone one more time and you'll regret the day you were born. Secondly, I have confiscated your sword.'

'You have *what*?'

Gran folded her arms. 'I've confiscated your sword. It's dangerous.'

'Of course it's dangerous, you fusty old harridan, it's a *sword*!' Axel threw up his hands in despair. 'It's *meant* to be dangerous! Now give it back. I need it – it is my maths test today!'

'And why do you need a sword for your maths test?'

'BECAUSE IF I DO NOT PASS I WILL HAVE TO CHALLENGE MY TEACHER TO A DUEL TO THE DEATH TO PROTECT MY DIGNITY!'

'You're going to challenge Mr Chicken to a duel to the death to protect your dignity?' Gran asked, narrowing her eyes.

'If necessary.'

'Mr Chicken is sixty-seven years old, Alex.'

'Yes, but –'

'And he was so scared when a pigeon got in the classroom that he started crying.'

'Yes, but –'

'And last year he put his back out picking up a punnet of strawberries.'

'Yes, but I CANNOT FAIL THE TEST! EVERY-ONE WILL LAUGH AT ME!' Axel roared. And then, in a small voice, he added, 'And I need to pass it for Alex. I feel, deep down, he needs me to pass.'

Gran gave Axel a soft smile. 'Come here,' she said, sitting down on the mattress, which had come to rest against Alex's desk. 'Sit next to your old gran a minute.'

Axel did as he was told.

'Now, listen here, chuck,' she said gently. 'You've worked your socks off for this test.'

'I do not wear socks,' replied Axel. 'I prefer to allow my feet to breathe in a pair of heroic sandals.'

Gran ignored him. 'So you just do your best. You don't need a sword. You just need to switch that clever brain of yours on and you'll be fine!'

Axel stared at his feet.

'It is Alex's brain that is clever, not mine.'

Gran gently tapped Axel's forehead. 'Alex's brain is in here.' Her face softened. 'I don't know what's going on with you, love. Maybe it's my fault? I'm hardly ever here. I'm sorry, Alex, I really am. I'll try to make more time.'

Axel tried to reply but found he couldn't get the words out.

'But I'm proud of you and I love you very much, whatever happens in the test.'

'Thank you,' Axel squeaked.

'Are you digging your fingernails into your palms?' Gran asked.

'Yes.' Axel nodded. 'I have found that it stops me from crying. Although it's not working very well today.' He choked.

'Alex! You can't keep all those emotions trapped inside.'

'I do have a painful lump in my throat,' Axel admitted in a wobbly voice.

'Ah, love. You need to let those feelings out.'

'I don't!' protested Axel, and then gave a huge sob. He quickly covered his mouth with his hand. 'A hero should always keep his emotions to himself!'

'Don't be daft! You can be as emotional as you like and you'd still be my hero. It's a confusing time for you. You're just on an emotional journey,' Gran said. She closed her eyes and the briefest look of pain shadowed her face. 'We all are.'

Axel lifted his head and gave her a brave smile.

'I'd feel a lot better on my emotional journey with Aëthelmrir by my side.'

'No.'

'Blast your eyes, crone!'

'I am feeling a strange sensation,' Axel said, standing with Sienna and Irving outside the classroom as they waited for the test to begin. 'As if I have ... flying creatures in my stomach.'

'Butterflies?' Sienna suggested.

'No, far bigger and more terrifying than butterflies. I feel like I have ... sabre-toothed Poison Eagles in my stomach.' Axel narrowed his eyes. 'Perhaps a curse has been placed on me. An ill curse of dreadful unease cast by the darkest of dark warlocks.'

'Or maybe you're just nervous,' said Irving, rolling his eyes.

Sienna put a gentle hand on his arm. 'You'll be fine, Axel. Relax. We've done so much revision. And you only need fifty per cent.'

'I shall try,' said Axel, putting on his bravest smile. 'There. I am relaxed.'

'Good luck, loser,' sneered Nathan Jones, barging past and knocking Axel's bag off his shoulder. 'You'll need it after last time!'

Nathan stopped and turned round. 'Now I think about it, it's strange that you failed that test. Not like you. In fact, you've been acting pretty weird the last few days.' He stared closely at Axel and then shook his head. 'Well, weirder than normal, and that's saying something.' He gave a sharp laugh and walked into the classroom, followed by his gang, all hooting gleefully.

'Ugh,' said Sienna. 'Trust Nathan Jones to start suspecting you. You have to be better at acting normal.'

'Oh gods! He's right, though,' wailed Axel. 'I only got four per cents last time. How am I supposed to relax? My brain is awhirl with numbers! All this maths is making me lose my mind!'

'Calm down, Axel! You're panicking,' Sienna said.

'How dare you! Heroes don't panic!' replied Axel, panicking.

'Course they do. They just learn how to calm themselves.'

'All right, perhaps I *am* heroically panicking. What do I do? WHAT DO I DO?!'

'Just breathe, Axel,' Sienna said.

'I *am* breathing!'

'Breathe slowly!'

'I am!'

'No, you're literally panting. Breathe in through your nose. Out through your mouth.'

Axel breathed in through his nose. And out through his mouth.

'And again,' Sienna said.

Axel closed his eyes and breathed slowly again.

'Now think happy thoughts,' Sienna said gently.

'Like what?'

'Well, whatever makes you most content in life.'

'Like . . . slicing the head off a rampaging orc-chief?' Axel asked, opening one eye.

'I mean, OK, if that makes you happy, Axel . . .'

'It does. I'm relaxed.' Axel sighed sleepily, his eye closed again.

At that moment, the bell went.

'Oh gods, oh gods, oh gods!' Axel wailed. 'I'm panicking again!'

Sienna grabbed him and looked him in the eyes. 'Axel, you'll be fine. I believe in you. Now believe in yourself. For Alex's sake.'

Axel gave Sienna a nod and walked slowly into the classroom and up to his desk. The test paper lay in front of him. The numbers swam before his eyes. He closed his eyes, breathed slowly, opened them again and the numbers were still. He could read them. He could do this!

Something hit Axel lightly on his shoulder. He turned around just in time to see Nathan Jones pull back his ruler and ping something towards him. It hit him on the forehead and stuck there: chewing gum. Axel peeled it off. Nathan fired off another and it landed straight on the top of his head.

'Not my gorgeous hair!' Axel gasped, trying to pull the gum out.

'Quiet please, Always!' Mr Chicken said.

Nathan Jones gave another sneering laugh.

Relax, mouthed Sienna at Axel.

But my hair! mouthed Axel back, pointing.

Concentrate!

Axel nodded gravely and started the test. Ten minutes later, he heard a whispering from behind him.

'Psst! Alex! You're such a weirdo.'

It was Nathan, of course.

Axel gripped his pencil tighter, his face thunderous.

'And your girlfriend Sienna is an even bigger one.'

Axel snapped his pencil in fury.

Calm down! Sienna mouthed at him.

'And your hair is stupid!'

That was it.

That was all Axel could take.

With a roar, he sprang to his feet, knocking his chair backwards. Before anybody could stop him, he jumped on Nathan, sending them both flying.

Mr Chicken bolted over and pulled Axel back.

'What is the meaning of this?'

Axel, red in the face and panting in rage, pointed at Nathan. 'He . . . he said I had stupid hair!'

'That is no reason to attack somebody, Always.'

'He's lost it, sir,' Nathan said, picking himself up and clutching his arm. 'He needs a doctor looking at him. And he should be excluded!'

'Right, Always,' Mr Chicken said, hands on hips. 'Go to the Isolation Room. Immediately.'

'But, sir, the test!' Sienna blurted out, her face stricken.

'He should have thought of that before he attacked another pupil. Now out!' Mr Chicken pointed to the door.

The class fell utterly silent and all eyes fixed on Axel.

'But ... but ... my hair,' Axel said in a tiny voice.

'OUT!' screamed Mr Chicken.

Axel walked out, his face burning.

He sat in the quiet of the Isolation Room, dwelling on what had just happened. He had failed. He had failed Sienna and he had failed Alex. Never in his life had he felt so small.

Finally, the bell went for lunch. Axel was about to leave when the door opened. Mr Chicken bustled in and slapped Axel's test paper on the table in front of him. 'You have thirty-five minutes.'

Axel looked at the teacher blankly.

'Take that gormless look off your face,' Mr Chicken snapped, and then his face softened. 'You've never been a troublemaker before, Alex, so I think you deserve a second chance.'

'Oh sweet, blessed purveyor of mathematical education!' exclaimed Axel. 'Ancient, gormful, white-haired wizard of numbers! The gods on high will smile upon your bloodline for a hundred and one summers for this kindness! The name of Chicken shall be sung throughout the halls of Aërth for generations innumerable!'

Mr Chicken rolled his eyes. 'Just get on with it.'

Without another word, Axel turned back to his paper.

In what seemed like the blink of an eye, Mr Chicken said quietly, 'Pen down now.'

Axel handed his test paper over – it was a mess of scribbles and crossings-out.

He placed a firm hand on Mr Chicken's shoulder.

'My fate lies now in the hands of others. I can only hope *those* gods are as kind as you. Who knows when their verdict shall be passed.'

'If you are asking when you'll be getting the results,' Mr Chicken said. 'It'll be tomorrow.'

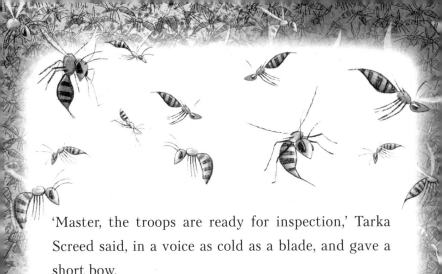

'Master, the troops are ready for inspection,' Tarka Screed said, in a voice as cold as a blade, and gave a short bow.

Felonious Gloam sighed. A pointless exercise. With the Book at his disposal, he now had a more powerful tool than any army.

He stepped out on to the balcony and looked without enthusiasm at the ragtag band of mercenaries, Furies, Weremares, bloodthirsty Nightpires with teeth sharp as needle-points, poisonous Shadow Snakes and the usual collection of Fire Dwarves and Cave Elves. But the largest group were the most deadly – the Sons of Perdition. At the front they stood, the place reserved for the most fervent believers, skinless and eyes wild with fanatical love, and Gloam felt nothing but disdain for them.

He gave one wave, to which a thunderous cheer came in response, and slipped back into his room.

'Master,' Screed said, a rare quiver in her voice. 'As

you can see, much of the army has been taken by the White Death. Fear is spreading through the ranks. Are you any closer to finding the boy?'

'My flies found him and his companions, but they escaped. The Sons of Perdition nearly had them on the shore of the Sea of Feelings, but they slipped through their grasp.'

'How?'

'Do not worry yourself, Screed. It shall all be at an end soon.' A smile crossed Gloam's face, but did not trouble his eyes.

'I am much relieved to hear it. Where are they now?'

'They have crossed Emocean. They approach Sullenbane.'

Screed inhaled sharply. 'Then we must send out more soldiers. Intercept them there.'

Gloam waved a dismissive hand. 'By all means. But now I control the Book, I think I shall also show those three the power I have in my grasp.'

'You can control the Book?' Screed gasped.

'Drinking the Narrator's blood has allowed me to gain enough control over it to change lives, but not to destroy. And, remember – the boy himself is beyond the Book's power.'

Screed gave a slow grin. 'Well, a dose of the wolfpox for his friends, then?'

The tiniest furrow disturbed Gloam's brow.

'Sadly not. To affect them directly, I need their full names to write in the Book, and that information has not been revealed to me. But no matter. I have other ways to bring death to them. It is time to wake the winged one from her slumber.'

CHAPTER EIGHTEEN

THE STORM-DRAGON

Before time began and the stars winked into existence, ancient creatures roamed the silent, frozen universe. Vast, long-forgotten beings, cold and unfeeling, that cared nothing for life or death, for their eyes saw no difference.

As the stars cooled and the planets were birthed, one such creature fell into slumber as the planet Aërth took form around it. Mountains and canyons flowered above as the creature slept. Oceans grew and vanished and grew again. Life flourished, civilizations were born and died, each nothing more than a heartbeat to the creature below. On it slept.

Until now.

It had been woken. It had been called.

Deep, deep underground, something stirred.

'Something is stirring!' Lorca gasped, sitting up beside the crackling fire.

'What is it?' Alex asked, his nerves fraying.

'Something . . . foul . . .' Lorca said, eyes wide.

'What is it?' Fetlock repeated, fur bristling.

Lorca let out a huge burp.

'I think it's the stew.' She grimaced, rubbing her stomach. 'There's only so much rat I can eat before it starts giving me a funny tummy.'

Alex threw a pebble at Lorca. 'What is *wrong* with you? You had me worried for a moment!'

The trio had left Captain McClann and the *Siren Song* and moved inland. Nearer and nearer they were getting to Gloam. Nearer and nearer to the impossible choice facing Alex – to save this world and never see his friends and family again, or to abandon Aërth to the ravages of the White Death.

To make matters worse, the temperature had plummeted even further. Whorls of snow had flurried around them as they trudged across the windswept Plains of Sullenbane, where all they had seen were rocks, slate skies and an endless, unforgiving horizon. The Plains were devoid of life, and by the time they had reached the far side, their food supply had once again dwindled to nothing and their water was down to the last dribble.

Finally, Lorca called a halt.

'We can go no further,' she said. 'So we must make a

bold choice. We should draw lots to see which of us is to be sacrificed for the other two to eat.'

'What?' Alex gasped. 'We can't –'

'The Orb said not all of us would survive. It's fated, so we might as well just get on with eating Fet– I mean, eating whoever it is we decide.'

'You were about to say my name, weren't you?' Fetlock said, eyes narrowed.

'Just a slip of the tongue,' Lorca protested. 'I'm not saying we should eat you. But now you mention it, I have heard dogs are rather delicious . . .'

Fetlock gave Lorca a warning growl.

'We are not eating Fetlock, Lorca,' Alex said.

'Well, we can't eat *you*. It's your quest!' Lorca exclaimed. 'And you can't eat me –'

'Why not?' Fetlock interrupted. 'Plenty of meat on you.'

'Because I am sworn to protect Alex. And *he* has to save Aërth. So that only leaves you.'

Alex held his hands up. 'Look, nobody is eating anybody! We keep walking until we find food.'

'Fine!' Lorca rolled her eyes. As they fell back to walking in silence, she kept sending darting glances at Fetlock while licking her lips, which Fetlock returned with snapping barks. On they trudged.

As they travelled, they saw far more fading bodies than healthy ones.

The whole world, Alex realized with horror, was dying.

They had marched as far as they could until finally, exhausted, they made camp for the night. A fire was built and a rat – welcome now – caught and roasted. After dinner, Lorca once again took Alex through his sword practice.

But although he was feeling more at one with the weapon now, Alex couldn't face telling the others that, deep down, he knew he wouldn't ever have the courage to *use* it: to slice into someone's neck or plunge it into their stomach? He just couldn't. He knew the fear would defeat him, just as it had done with the Sons of Perdition. So, he just went along with Lorca's training, ducking and swiping, jabbing and sidestepping, until he was finally knocked to the ground, Lorca above him, her sword to his throat.

'I have a gift for you.' Lorca grinned, pulling the sword away, her eyes glinting in the firelight. She pulled Alex to his feet, then pulled a sack from her backpack.

'Where did you get another sack from? How many sacks have you got?' Alex asked. 'You're like my gran when we went on holiday to Wales.'

Rummaging inside, Lorca brought out what looked like some sort of armour and held it out to Alex.

'Why haven't you given that to me before?' he asked. 'It might have been useful.'

'Ah.' Lorca held up a finger. 'Because it is the armour of a true warrior! Only to be worn by those who have proven their worth through great and terrible danger. Or who are very weak and need a bit of a confidence boost.'

'And which am I?' Alex demanded.

Lorca blinked a few times, then clapped her hands. 'Anyway!' she said, thrusting the armour at Alex. 'Put it on.'

'Now?'

Lorca nodded vigorously.

'It seems a bit . . . skimpy. And what are *these* bits for?' He held up two small circles of armour.

'Those are nipple protectors.'

'I'm sorry – *what?*'

'Nipple protectors.' Lorca snatched them from Alex's hands and held them up. 'See how they twinkle majestically in the firelight!'

'Yes, I can see that. But why do my nipples need special protectors?'

Lorca laughed. 'So speaks a man who has never faced a snapping horde of Nihilese Nipple-Nibblers.'

'Right, and nor do I intend to!'

But Alex could see a look of hurt growing on Lorca's face. 'Thank you, Lorca, for this kind gift. It's splendid.'

Lorca gave a grin in reply. The snow had started up again, wind whipping it into spiralling eddies.

'You're not going to try it on?'

'What? Now?'

Lorca nodded. 'To make sure it fits.'

Alex sighed and a few moments later was shivering in his new armour, which barely covered half his body. He lay down and pulled a blanket over himself. 'At least my nipples are warm,' he muttered.

Fetlock padded over to Alex.

'I think your new armour suits you marvellously,' he said.

Alex couldn't see Fetlock's face, but he knew the dog's eyes would be glittering with mischief.

'Very funny.'

'You practised well with the sword,' Fetlock said. 'You have a talent for it.'

Alex swallowed. 'I can't use it, though. The sword. On somebody, I mean. I don't have what it takes. I'm not brave like Lorca or fierce like you. I wouldn't have even made it through the Silent Forest if it hadn't been for you two. I'm always scared. I'm a coward. I'm weak.'

Fetlock sat down next to him.

'Alex, there is more than one type of bravery. You have been plucked from your own life and thrown into this world of untold dangers. And yet so often I see you smiling. *That* is true bravery. Perhaps you are somebody who fights with his brain rather than his arms. But know this, Alex Always – you are a fierce warrior.'

Alex nodded and, when he trusted his voice, he said simply, 'Thank you, Fetlock.'

In reply, Fetlock curled up next to Alex, nestling into his chest. Lorca joined them and, finally, with the fire spitting and crackling, the three snuggled together again for warmth, snow softly settling around them, and sleep took them one by one.

From the moment Alex woke, in the grey light of dawn, he knew something was wrong. An uneasy feeling lay on his heart. He couldn't put his finger on *what*, but he could feel something was amiss.

His stomach churning, he brushed off the snow that lay on their blankets as Lorca packed their meagre belongings. They started walking, but all day, no matter which direction they took, it felt as if they were heading towards doom. Or, more precisely, that doom was heading towards them.

A few raindrops were the first sign of what was to come. Then a vast cloud, towering on the horizon, grey as mourning, roiled and rolled closer. A thunderous rumble shook the sky and Alex clapped his hands over his ears, ducking by instinct.

And then, with horror, Alex realized that the cloud was not a cloud at all but something else.

Something huge.

Axel felt his stomach churn in a most unpleasant way. He had barely slept the night before and had woken with a strange feeling of impending doom. The school day had seemed to take forever, until now the moment had arrived, the last lesson – maths.

Mr Chicken walked into the room and all chatter stopped instantly. He solemnly circled the students, handing back the marked test papers. Sienna got hers. So did Irving. Even Nathan Jones. Finally, Mr Chicken reached Axel, slipping the test paper on to his desk, face down.

Axel swallowed, not daring to turn it over.

This was it.

This was it.

Never had Alex felt fear like that which clutched at his body in that moment.

Lorca drew her sword. Fetlock was on his haunches, teeth bared, his fur on end. Alex pulled his own sword out and held it wobbling in front of him, his arms and legs trembling.

The shape that was not a cloud gradually came into focus: a vast winged beast, silhouetted black against the grey.

Then it burst out of the cloud, and Alex let out a whimper of terror.

It swooped towards them just as a shaft of sunlight broke through the clouds, illuminating silver scales that gleamed in the golden light.

'Gods!' Fetlock yelped. 'It's a storm-dragon!'

Alex didn't even hear the first half of the name. He only heard *dragon*.

And then the dragon roared and the roar was thunder, so cacophonous it drowned all thought from Alex's brain. Once again, fear flooded his body, freezing him stock still. He simply stared, unable to move, unable to process that in front of him was an *actual* dragon, silver wings unfurled, arrowing straight for them.

And then he heard Fetlock scream. 'Run! Run, blast it!'

That broke the trance. Alex ran, just as the dragon opened its mouth. Out of its roaring jaws came not fire but lightning, a searing bolt of arcing electricity. Alex dived to the left and the bolt smashed into the ground just a few metres from him. He jumped up, began running and dived again, as the dragon sent another crackling bolt of lightning at him. This one hit a tree, which instantly exploded, sending blackened bark flying everywhere. The tree had been utterly obliterated.

Alex stood again, but the dragon soared down and landed with a ground-shaking thump that nearly knocked him back off his feet. With a war cry, Lorca charged straight towards the creature, sword aloft.

'Die, infernal beast!' she screamed.

The dragon blasted a bolt of lightning at Lorca. She ducked beyond the electricity's dreadful reach and it left behind a pile of smouldering earth where she had stood. Lorca gave a roar of triumph, but then tripped on a stone and tumbled to the ground. In two strides, the dragon was over her, Lorca lying prone, pointing her sword upward, needle-like, in the face of the monster above her.

With a howl, Fetlock made a flying leap, soaring

through the air, and managed to clamp his jaws on the dragon's tail. The dragon reared up on its hind legs, smoke curling out of its mouth, and then crashed to the ground. Despite his ferocious grip, Fetlock was thrown through the air, rolling to a stop in a dusty heap. After a heart-stopping few seconds, Fetlock picked himself up and shook himself, then suddenly stopped and stared at his right forepaw, as if there was something wrong with it.

'Fetlock! Move!'

Alex's words woke Fetlock, and he bolted straight through the dragon's legs and out behind. The dragon's flank was exposed and Lorca ran towards it, swinging her sword with all her might.

It was useless. The blade bounced off the scales like a stick against a mountain.

The dragon roared, a deafening, triumphant thunderclap that echoed across the sky, and turned to face the three friends. Eyes of death, lava-red with coal-black slits, examined them with dispassion.

And, at that moment, Alex knew all hope was lost. They could never defeat the storm-dragon. All courage was gone. Fear had defeated him.

Axel stared at the paper before him. Never had he felt fear like that which clutched at his body in that moment. The terror was greater than he could possibly have imagined.

All the faces in the class had turned to look at him.

'I shall not be defeated by fear this day!' Axel shouted.

And he turned the paper over.

There, at the top of the page, ringed in red, was his mark: fifty-one per cent.

He had passed.

He had done it! Axel closed his eyes, letting joy flow through his body.

Courage suddenly flowed through Alex's body. Courage and happiness. In his heart, he knew it was somehow linked to Axel, and as he remembered Axel, he remembered home. He remembered one of his last school lessons before coming to this world – about electricity and conductivity. He had been half-asleep, not concentrating, but still he remembered what the teacher had said, and an idea came to him. A wild idea. An impossible hope, but hope nonetheless.

'Lorca, listen to me!' he shouted. 'We have to use our swords to reflect the lightning!'

'What?' Lorca shouted.

'We'll never defeat the dragon with our weapons. We need to use its *own* weapon against it! But remember what I said in the Infinite Palace – whatever you do, don't touch the ground when you reflect the lightning!'

Lorca looked at Alex as if he had lost his mind. Then she shrugged.

'If this doesn't qualify me for my Ludicrously Dangerous Quest badge, I don't know what will.' She pointed her sword at the dragon. 'Now – have at you!'

The dragon leaned back on its haunches, gave another deafening roar, then spat a crackling arc of lightning. It forked in two, one branch towards Lorca and one towards Alex. Both sprang sideways at the same moment, angling their swords so the lightning hit the metal blades.

The bolt ricocheted perfectly off Alex's sword as he hung in mid-air, and reflected back at the dragon, straight into its wide-open maw, hurling it back, until it landed with a shuddering crash. The beast was not dead, but it was clearly hurt. It snarled weakly as it lay panting on the ground.

Alex held his sword up as a warning. 'Try it again,' he screamed. 'And this is what you get!'

But the dragon seemed to recognize it had been defeated. It flapped its wings limply and then launched into the air, flying off into the distance, giving a final plaintive cry.

Alex let out a whoop of triumph. His plan had worked! He had saved the day! He turned to his friends, only to find Fetlock kneeling by the prone body of Lorca.

'Alex!' Fetlock shouted, his voice cracking with distress. 'Come quickly!'

Alex ran over, his heart thudding. Lorca's face was blackened, her hair standing on end. Her eyebrows were singed, and her armour was charred and smouldering.

'She must have still been touching the ground when the lightning hit,' Alex moaned. He fell to his knees and looked at Fetlock, distraught. 'The Orb warned me that some of us would die, but I didn't listen. It's all my fault. My stupid plan. I've killed her!'

And then Lorca gasped and opened her eyes.

'Who've you killed? What happened? Did I have a bucket stuck on my head?'

'Oh, Lorca!' Alex dived forward and tumble-hugged her.

The friends decided to rest where they were to give Lorca a chance to get over her brush with electricity. She fell asleep almost immediately and was soon contentedly snoring.

As Alex was drifting towards sleep himself, though, he spotted Fetlock examining his paw again.

'Are you OK?' Alex asked, sitting up. 'Is it hurt?'

'It's nothing,' Fetlock said gruffly.

'Come here, let me see.'

Fetlock didn't move, so Alex went over to him. He looked down and then he understood.

Fetlock's paw – and his whole leg – was pale. Fading.

The White Death had begun to spread.

'How long?'

Fetlock sighed. 'I noticed it first during the battle with the dragon. It had covered the whole of my paw then. But it has spread already. It moves fast.'

His heart aching, Alex found he didn't have any words of comfort, for his friend or himself. Eventually, it was Fetlock who broke the silence.

'So, it looks like we will have to move faster if we are to save me. Faster than squirrels even!'

Alex tried to give an encouraging laugh at Fetlock's joke, but it rang false, and both knew it.

'Sleep now, Alex. Things will look better in the morning.'

But they didn't.

Alex woke in the first weak light of dawn. He immediately turned to Fetlock and his heart plummeted to see the dog was as pale as the watery morning light.

Fetlock sighed. 'Not good, right?'

Alex shook his head, the words once again stuck in his throat.

Lorca woke, yawned and stretched, then gave a cry of distress as she saw Fetlock and rushed over to hug him.

'Come on, enough fuss!' Fetlock said, batting her away. 'We just have to cross the Moors of Mourn and then we will reach the Black Cliffs. A day, perhaps.'

But they all knew that with the speed the White Death was taking over Fetlock, they would not make it in time. With every step he took, he seemed to fade further.

They reached the moors by midday: a plain of boggy land that stretched as far as the eye could see. The icy ground sucked at their feet as they walked, turning each step into a battle. For hours they silently trudged, each lost in their own thoughts, until snow began to fall around them, soft, wet flakes that nestled on their heads and shoulders and began to carpet the world in white.

'I . . . need to rest,' Fetlock said suddenly, and then he fell to the ground. He was as pale as the snow Alex could see falling through his body.

'No,' Alex protested, trying to pull Fetlock up. 'We need to keep moving!'

Fetlock gave a soft sigh. 'I can't.'

'You can't just give up, Fetlock!' Alex cried. Lorca stood behind him, wiping tears from her filthy face.

Fetlock gave a gentle laugh. 'It's my time, Alex. It's my time. But will you both do me a favour before I go?'

Both Lorca and Alex nodded, tears streaming down their faces. 'Anything,' choked Alex.

'Will you . . . stroke my ears?'

Without a word, Alex and Lorca knelt down next to the fast-fading body of Fetlock and started stroking his soft, floppy ears.

Fetlock gave a contented sigh. 'It doesn't hurt, you know? It feels rather like I'm drifting away on a boat on a still ocean.'

Alex sniffed. 'I'm so sorry, Fetlock.'

'You've nothing to be sorry for. I have had a good life and a full one.' Fetlock paused for a moment, watching the snow fall around him, and sadness clouded his eyes. 'I would have liked to have had pups, though. Alas, not to be. Funny – you two are as close to pups as I have had. Although ... I would prefer you to have more fur.'

Alex and Lorca both laughed through their tears. Alex leaned forward and buried his damp face in Fetlock's fading fur, smelling his scent for the last time.

Hours passed, just the two friends watching the slowing rise and fall of Fetlock's chest, and the soft snow falling around them.

Fetlock suddenly spoke with the faintest voice, his nose twitching.

'I ... see a squirrel.'

Alex choked down a sob. 'Go chase that squirrel, Fetlock.'

Fetlock's legs jerked for a moment, as if he was running in his dreams. Finally, he spoke again in the same faint voice.

'Caught it ...'

And so Lorca and Alex lay weeping, as their friend Fetlock slowly faded away until there was nothing left but snow and memories.

CHAPTER NINETEEN

A SONG OF HOPE

Axel strode out of the class, beaming triumphantly, with Sienna and Irving by his side.

'Fifty-one per cents! I defeated the test. Can you believe it?'

'Well, now you mention it,' Irving said. 'No, I can't.'

Sienna gave him a dig in the chest with her elbow. 'Actually, we *can*, Axel. We always believed in you.'

'Did we?' Irving replied. 'Because only this morning you said he had zero chance of –'

'Zero chance of failing,' Sienna interrupted, glaring at Irving.

'It turns out, *Irving*,' said Axel, giving Irving a pointed look. 'You don't *always* need a deadly weapon to pass a heroic challenge.'

'Why are you looking at me?' protested Irving. 'I never said you did!'

Axel narrowed his eyes in suspicion. 'I suppose you cast some sort of spell to make sure you did well?'

Irving huffed. 'We've been through this. I'm not a warlock. I don't have magical powers.'

'Hmm,' said Axel, eyes narrowed even further. 'Well, *I* believe you need just one thing to succeed. A brilliant mind such as mine.'

Sienna rolled her eyes.

'A brilliant mind,' repeated Axel, '*and* fabulous hair. So, you need two things, actually. And I shall now use my mighty brain to defeat Alex's evil genius father in the deadly game of chess! And possibly use my hair too.'

'You *what*?'

It was Nathan, sneering as ever, closely followed by Willard, Sniper and Simone.

Axel flinched. 'You stay back, Jones! Keep your blasted bottom away from my face!'

'Just tell us what you said and I'll leave you alone,' Nathan said, holding his hands in the air.

'I said I'm going to use my mighty brain in the chess tournament –'

'Axel, shh!' Sienna shushed. 'Don't be telling them nowt.'

'But he has said he will leave us alone if we tell him,' said Axel. 'Anyway, the tournament is on Friday evening, and it is my Impossible Quest to defeat Alex's – I mean *my* – evil genius father. I need to win the prize money so we can pay off Alex's – sorry, *my* – grandmother's debts and stop them – I mean *us* – from being evicted!'

Nathan shook his head. 'Why are you acting *so* weird?'

'I'm not! This is exactly how Alex acts normally. Sorry, how *I* act normally!'

'Hmm.' Nathan pursed his lips. 'Right. So, anyway, it's important you get to this chess thing?'

'Very, very important,' Axel replied, solemnly.

Nathan nodded and wandered off, followed by his gang.

'See?' Axel prodded Sienna. 'He left. My mighty brain is now thinking that perhaps Nathan Jones is a man of his word after all.'

Sienna gave a suspicious hmm. 'I think your mighty brain may be a bit off there. Perhaps your hair is interfering with your neural pathways. Anyway – we need to get back to yours. You seriously need to practise your chess if you've any hope for Friday!'

'UNBELIEVABLE!' said Irving, tipping the board over in fury yet again.

'UNBELIEVABLE!' he ranted. 'EIGHT YEARS I'VE BEEN PLAYING THIS BLASTED GAME!'

'Anger and violence will solve nothing,' Axel said. 'Try using your brain more. And perhaps your hair. I'm not sure your brain will ever be as mighty as mine, but with a little care and attention your hair could be not quite so . . . unheroic.'

'I'm going!' Irving pulled his scarf on.

'Come on, stay. Don't be so mardy,' Sienna said.

'Honestly, there's nothing more I can teach him about chess. He hammers me every time.' Irving buttoned up his coat. 'I've got to get to my dad's anyway. I'm staying at his tonight.'

At the word 'dad', Axel gave an almost imperceptible wince. But Sienna noticed it and later, sitting in front of the TV after they'd scoffed plates of bangers and mash, she found her moment to bring it up.

'By the gods,' exclaimed Axel, pointing at the television. 'Britain does indeed have much fine talent. Look at that dog dance! Where I come from, dogs merely talk. 'Tis a wonderous thing to see a dog dancing . . .'

Sienna took a breath and switched the TV off.

'Turn the box of illusions back on,' objected Axel. 'I must learn whether the dancing dog succeeds in his quest to reach the final!'

'Axel, I saw your reaction earlier,' Sienna said,

ignoring his demand. 'Tell me about your dad. You never talk about him.'

'And nor shall I. I do not want to even *think* of him.'

'But talking can help,' Sienna said softly.

'Oh, sweet Sienna, you do say the funniest things.' Axel smiled. But then his face shadowed over. 'My father was – *is*,' he corrected himself, 'a very bad man. He was mercilessly cruel to my mother and me. My earliest memory – I can have only been two or three winters old – was trying to comfort her. I remember trying to wipe her tears away, but I couldn't get her to stop crying, no matter what I did. In fact, I don't recall seeing her ever really smile.'

'Oh, Axel. You poor thing.' Sienna sighed.

'For whenever she did smile,' Axel continued, 'it would send my father into a rage. He would shout, "*How can you sit there grinning like a village idiot when there is so much misery in the world?*"'

'He sounds a real charmer,' Sienna said.

'Eventually, my mother could not take any more. We fled in the middle of the night, under the cover of a fierce storm. By daylight, we were miles away from my father's clutches. Free.'

Axel stopped and simply stared at the floor.

'And then what happened?' Sienna asked, gently.

'As my father's power grew, he searched and searched for us, until one day he finally found me. He demanded I come with him, said that hiding behind my mother's skirts was making me a weakling and that to become a real man I had to leave her.'

'What? That's a load of rubbish.'

'Obviously, I refused. And when he realized I was not going to change my mind he said – well, the words never left me: "You are no child of mine, Axel," he said. I never saw him again. And that was the last day I shed a tear. Until I came here, that is.'

'Oh, love!'

Axel and Sienna both jumped. Neither had noticed that Gran was standing in the doorway, listening. She walked over to Axel and pulled him into a hug.

'Alex, I know your father isn't what he should be. But me and you – we're all the family we need. You hear me?'

'I hear you,' Axel said, his voice thick with emotion. 'Thank you.'

'Good.' Gran pulled back and gave him a smile. 'Now, Sienna, love, go make us a brew and we'll watch some more telly, yeah?' She turned the television back on and pointed at the screen. 'Look, the dancing doggie made it to the final!'

But at the sight of the dog, Axel was filled with an overwhelming sadness and feeling of loss he could not explain.

It took a long time for Alex's and Lorca's tears to stop flowing for Fetlock. Although they knew they had to continue their journey, it wasn't until late in the day that they found the strength to pick themselves up and walk. They were filthy; only the tracks left by their tears showed clean.

They trudged through the endless mud of the moors in mournful silence, the only sound the lonely cawing of crows. Alex watched as one bird wheeled above their heads before plummeting out of the sky. It landed with a soft thud not far away. It was practically translucent, consumed by the White Death.

As evening fell, Lorca pulled the last of their firewood from her pack and, before their legs gave way from exhaustion, they made camp for the night next to a river running brown with mud. Lorca fell asleep quickly, but Alex was not so fortunate. Wave after wave of sadness hit him, until he felt his heart might break. For several days, he had resisted using the All-Seeing-I, but now he felt he needed the comfort of home. Pulling out the metal device, he wiped a little mud off with his sleeve, gave it a quick polish and then opened it.

'Here y'are,' said Sienna, setting the tea tray down on the coffee table.

'Who . . .?' Gran looked up at Sienna, her face clouding with momentary confusion. But then the cloud passed as quickly as it had come, replaced with a smile.

Sienna fiddled with the hem of her top. 'You feeling OK, Mrs A?' she asked.

'Yeah, I'm OK, love,' Gran replied in a way that made Sienna feel that she really wasn't OK at all. 'Money worries, you know? But then, who doesn't have them nowadays, right? And I'm just so bloomin' busy all the time. I must look exhausted!'

'You don't,' said Sienna. 'You look great.'

'She does *not*!' Axel declared.

'Axel! What is *wrong* with you?'

'The Ninth Pillar of Heroism is truthfulness.' Axel gave a tiny bow of the head. 'So, I always tell the truth, no matter how unpalatable it may be.'

'There you go!' Gran laughed. 'No arguing with *that*.'

A cup of tea and half a pack of custard creams later, Sienna had gone home and Axel was sitting with Gran in the living room. The electric fire was glowing and the TV was muted.

'So, what've you got this old thing out for?' asked Gran, nodding towards the chessboard.

'I have a wager with . . . my father. If I defeat him in the chess tournament, he will help us with the money you need.'

Gran's eyes widened in shock.

'You mean to tell me you made a bet with your dad that you could beat him at chess? Oh Alex, you daft lummox, you *know* how good he is! Blimmin' eck. He's *impossible* to beat.'

Axel looked slightly crestfallen. 'That's the whole point. It's supposed to be an Impossible Quest.'

Gran sat back, then after a moment's thought sat forward again. 'Well, maybe not absolutely impossible. I can show you a few tricks, if you like.'

Axel looked at her in surprise. 'Feeble old women play chess, too?'

'Yes, they bloomin' well do!' Gran snapped. 'I told you before where your mum met your dad, didn't I? At a chess tournament I was playing in. You've got chess in your *blood*, love, from both sides. It's probably where you get that memory of yours from.'

'Well, perhaps not, because –'

'Anyway,' continued Gran. 'I matched up against your dad enough times to learn how he plays the game. And his *weaknesses*. He might be near-enough unbeatable but . . . but . . .' She held up a finger. 'I *might* be able to teach you enough to rattle him. Reckon my brain's still fit for that.'

'Thank you,' exclaimed Axel. 'Yes, please!'

Axel speedily set the pieces up and moved first. Twenty minutes later, they were deep into a tactical battle.

'You're good,' murmured Gran. 'And who knows, one day you'll be able to take on your dad.'

'And that one day shall be very soon,' Axel said proudly.

'You certainly have the same streak of arrogance he does,' Gran said, moving her queen. 'Checkmate.'

Axel gasped, but, before he could say anything, Gran continued, 'And that's his weak spot. Using his overconfidence against him is your only chance.'

Axel raised his eyebrows.

'Tell me more . . .'

Alex snapped shut the All-Seeing-I. Although it made him happy to see Gran teaching chess to Axel, his heart broke a little to see her looking so worn out.

Misery, it seemed, crossed universes.

Alex didn't get a wink of sleep that night. Next morning, Lorca rubbed her grimy face with the palms of her hands and packed the camp away without a word.

Eventually she spoke. 'We aren't far now. A day or so, I reckon, to the Nest.'

Alex gave a sullen nod.

'One more day until the end of our journey. One more day until we defeat Gloam and save the world!'

'That simple, right?' Alex gave a hollow laugh.

'Yes! Don't worry. We'll figure out the exact details when we get there.'

Alex was glad Lorca was so confident, as he still didn't have any idea how to defeat Gloam, and now they didn't even have Fetlock's help. The only thing he knew was that, even if they did succeed, success only led to two different routes to despair – save Aërth and never go home, or go back to Earth and leave this world to die.

'I'm sorry, Lorca.' Alex sighed. 'I just feel like I can't go on. I'm too tired. Too hungry. I'm not the hero you need. I'm a nobody. I can't defeat Gloam.'

Lorca put a hand on his shoulder.

'Listen.'

'To what?'

She cupped her ear. 'There's a song on the breeze.'

'Is there? I can't hear any–'

'It's not an *actual* song,' snapped Lorca. 'It's a metaphor.'

'Oh!'

'So, listen. There's a song on the breeze, Alex. It's a song of courage. A song of hope.' She offered Alex a hand. He grabbed it and allowed himself to be pulled to his feet.

'Many a great story has been etched in the Book of Lifetales,' Lorca continued. 'Many a hero has had their tale told. Now, perhaps, it is time for one last tale to be passed down through countless winters? For now, it's our moment to write our names into the pages of history. Are you ready to write a tale of such valour that it echoes through time? For now is our time to become heroes, our time to say "*This* is who I am!" All it takes is one step. One small step towards our destiny! One step closer to doom or victory, it matters not which. Because each path leads to the same place: glory. All it takes is one step. One step to death, one step to glory! Dare you take that step with me? Dare you take that step?'

Do I dare? Alex wondered. His quest was impossible. It always had been. But there was something in Lorca's voice that had woken a feeling deep inside him. Was it hope, or perhaps courage? Was it the feeling that comes from having someone believe in you so completely they are willing to risk their life for you? Maybe it was all those things. And Alex knew his answer.

'Yes, I dare!' Alex whooped, throwing his arms in the air. 'I dare!'

'Then let us go. And face our fate together.'

They jumped and clasped in a great hug. Then Lorca stepped back.

'So, how did I do?'

'With what?'

'My Inspirational Speech.'

'You mean that was –'

'That was a Grade Seven Inspirational Speech. I wasn't sure I could pull it off; I'm normally only a Grade Five. But I thought the moment called for a bit more, so . . .'

'You did great, Lorca. You did great.'

Lorca pumped her fist. 'Yes! Grade Eight here I come!'

They started walking, following a sludgy trickle of river that gurgled next to them, and soon a smell of salt tickled Alex's nose, followed by the sight of sea in the distance, rolling grey peaks capped with white foam.

'You see.' Lorca grinned. 'Easy.'

They quickly reached the deserted coast, undisturbed by another living soul. There were signs it should have been inhabited – small, empty villages and the occasional cottage – but it was evening before they saw somebody. And, luckily, Alex and Lorca saw them before they were seen.

'More Sons of Perdition,' whispered Lorca, as they ducked down at the crest of a small cliff. Below them walked a small group of soldiers whose skinless appearance made Alex shudder. 'We must be getting close to the Nest.'

The soldiers were all clearly suffering from advanced cases of the White Death, but something drove them forward.

'What do you think they're doing?'

'Looking for us, of course.' Lorca gave a short laugh. 'Although they aren't doing a very good job of it!'

'Don't be so sure,' spoke a voice, cold as the blade that pricked the back of Alex's neck. 'My master would like a word with you . . .'

'I have an ill feeling,' Axel announced. 'As if the world itself has suddenly become horribly unbalanced.' He reached for his collar. 'I can hardly breathe . . .'

Sienna rolled her eyes. 'It's just nerves! It's natural. Just finish your flapjack and let's get to the tournament.'

Before and after school for the last few days, Axel had played chess with Gran. She'd taught him every trick she had, every technique, every move – and told him everything she knew about Alex's dad.

Finally, the day of the tournament had arrived. Axel, Irving and Sienna had agreed to go together straight from school. But the hours had stretched endlessly and, by the time the last bell rang, Axel's nerves were stretched to breaking point.

'I cannot manage my jack of flaps! My stomach is awhirl. Something is horribly amiss. It is as if a storm is raging in its depths, building and rising up through me.'

'You trying to say you're going to be sick?' Sienna asked.

'No!'

'It's just you are looking pretty –'

'Thank you, Sienna,' Axel said weakly. 'My hair *is* extra magnificent today.'

'Let me finish. I was *about* to say "pretty pale".'

'I . . . I think my connection with Alex is getting stronger,' Axel said, his face creased with worry. 'I feel he is in great danger. The day I must complete my Impossible Quest has come, and I know in my heart that Alex needs me to succeed or something terrible will happen to him. But how can I possibly succeed? I am not ready. I will fail and Alex will . . .'

The sentence hung in the air like black smoke.

Sienna gave him a smile. 'You know, I also feel things. And I feel that if anyone can do this, Axel, it's *you*. I believe in you. God knows why, but I *do*. So best start believing in yourself, yeah? Now, come on. Alex's dad won't know what hit him. Let's get Irving, then catch the bus into town.'

But Irving wasn't where they had agreed to meet. Instead, standing by the water fountain, was Nathan's friend, Simone.

'Looking for Irving?'

'Yeah,' replied Sienna. 'Where is he?'

'Follow me.' Simone walked off, without even looking back.

She led them through emptying corridors to the school basement.

'What you doing? We aren't allowed!'

'Irving's in there talking to Nathan.' Simone nodded at the basement door.

'You want us to go down *there*?'

'Do what you like. I couldn't care less.' Simone walked off, nose in the air.

Sienna looked at Axel nervously and said, 'Yeah, I'm not sure we should . . .'

But Axel had already pushed the door open. He peered down into the darkness.

Suddenly he felt a shove in his back, heard Sienna scream and he fell, arms wheeling uselessly, head first down the stairs. His head hit the bottom stair with an empty thud and all went utterly black.

'Wakey, wakey, sleepyhead!'

Axel opened his eyes, his head throbbing. In front of him, standing underneath a bare light bulb, was Nathan Jones, with the usual smirk on his face. Behind him, his gang leered from the shadows.

Axel tried to jump up but found he was unable to move. He was tied to a rickety chair. He looked around and saw that Irving and Sienna were in the same predicament, both tied to chairs, with all three chairs bound together. Irving also had a scarf in his mouth.

'Let me go!' shouted Axel.

'Let *us* go, you mean!' Sienna shouted, glaring at Axel.

'Yes! Let us go,' shouted Axel. 'But if you have to keep one of us, it should be Irving.'

'Mmmm mmphmmm mm mph!' Irving muffle-shouted.

'Cast a spell, Irving!' Axel demanded. 'Use your magic!'

'Mm mmph mm mmmmph!' Irving muffle-shouted even louder, his eyes flashing in fury.

'We won't be letting anybody go. And this should stop you shouting for help.' Nathan sneered, gagging Axel and Sienna with two more scarfs. 'Oh dear, oh dear!' he added, shaking his head. 'Guess you won't be making it to your precious chess tournament after all.'

Axel's eyes bulged, but he couldn't move.

'Pathetic,' Nathan sneered again. 'Not so strong now, are you, Always? Come on,' he said to his gang, and they filed out of the basement, barking with laughter. 'Bye, losers,' Nathan shouted from the top of the stairs. 'If you're lucky, I *might* let somebody know you're here tomorrow.'

He flicked the light off and bolted the door shut, leaving Axel, Sienna and Irving trapped in the dark, the only sound their panicked, muffled breaths.

CHAPTER TWENTY

TWO
LOSSES

The only sounds in Alex's ears were his own panicked, muffled breaths. Taking a moment to compose himself, he tried to calm them and assess the situation.

He was tied up inside a sack, trundling along in some sort of rattling cart, into which he and Lorca had been thrown, after being captured by the woman the soldiers called Tarka Screed.

'Lorca, you OK?' Alex whispered.

There was no reply. Alex felt his gut churn in fear.

'Psst! Lorca, are you OK?'

Nothing.

And then came the unmistakable sound of snoring.

'Are you asleep?!' Alex spluttered. 'Unbelievable!'

The cart abruptly stopped.

'That's it, I'm no' pullin' this thing another shrew-length!' said a high-pitched, whining voice.

'It's that blasted horse's fault, getting the White Death,' replied a second, deeper voice.

'Well, I've got it too and nobody's pulling no cart for me. I've had enough, Ned. It's too heavy.'

'Well . . . we could make it lighter,' said Ned.

'How?'

'Well, Screed only said to bring the *boy* to the Nest, didn't she, Perse? Nobody said nothing about no *girl*. So . . . what's stopping us from, you know, just doing the girl in and dumping her in the sea?'

Alex let out a gasp. He had to do something.

'Lorca!' he hissed. 'Wake up!'

Lorca snored on.

'T'would make the cart twice as light. Or half as light, is it?' Perse said. 'Go on, then. Do her in.'

Alex gave a groan. He had to get out of the sack – and fast.

It was Sienna who managed, with much tugging of teeth and twisting of the head, to get her gag off first. She gasped at the fresh air.

'I've got me mouth free!'

Irving was next.

'Axel, try and get your gag out,' Sienna urged.

'Are you sure?' whispered Irving. 'It might be easier for us to think if it stays in. Just for a while.'

'MMMMPPH-MMM PHHHMMM!' Axel mumbled, furiously.

'Fine! Pull with your teeth,' Irving said. 'Then twist your neck.'

'Oh, woe!' wailed Axel. 'Woe upon woe! What did I do to anger the gods?'

'It's not your fault,' Sienna said. 'It's Nathan and his lot.'

'I have failed. FAILED! I have been bested again. I am a weak and pathetic excuse for a hero!'

'Hey, don't be so hard on yourself,' Sienna said, twisting her head to face Axel. Their eyes were getting accustomed to the dark and they could see each other faintly now. 'And anyway, whinging in't getting us out of here. We need a plan. So let's put our thinking caps on.'

'If we all wriggle together, it might loosen the knots,' suggested Irving.

They all started moving, but after a moment Axel exclaimed, 'Pah! This is taking too long.' He stamped his feet in fury and then gasped. 'Wait! I have an idea.'

'Oh, great,' Irving groaned.

'Do not despair, my warlock friend. If I just use my . . . legs . . . like two mighty tree trunks . . .'

Axel started straining, and before they could stop him he had managed to push himself to his feet, carrying

Irving and Sienna, still strapped to their chairs, on his back. 'And if I can ... just ... get ... over ... here ...' Axel staggered across the basement like a dying beetle.

'No,' shouted Sienna. 'Put us down!'

'I just ... have to ...' Axel lumbered backwards and crashed straight into a wall – or, rather, crashed *Irving* straight into a wall.

'Stop it,' shouted Irving. 'That hurt!'

'No ...' wheezed Axel, staggering to his feet again. 'Never ... give in ... If I can ... just carry you up ... the stairs ...'

'No!' Sienna and Irving both shouted at the same time. 'Do NOT try climbing the stairs!'

'Yes ... I can ... do it!' Axel cried. 'Nothing ... can ... stop me!'

He made it up four stairs before the combined weight of Sienna and Irving was just too great. They all tumbled backwards and crashed in a heap, with Irving at the bottom of the pile and Axel on top, his arms and legs waving like an upturned tortoise.

'Except gravity.' Sienna groaned.

'STOP TRYING TO CARRY US!' Irving roared. 'I think you've cracked one of my ribs.'

'Hang on, my chair is breaking,' Sienna shouted. 'Do it again!'

'Don't do it again!' Irving yelled.

'One . . . more . . . time . . .' Axel gasped.

With all his strength, he righted himself and, with his very last ounce of energy, ran backwards, Irving-first, smashing into the wall with an almighty crack.

'My chair is broken!' Sienna yelled triumphantly.

'So is my back.' Irving moaned.

Sienna jumped up and pulled the ropes off Axel and Irving.

'We . . . are . . . free!' Axel was panting. 'My . . . plan . . . worked perfectly!'

'That was your plan?' moaned Irving. 'To half-kill me?'

'We have escaped, have we not?'

'No – if you hadn't noticed, we are still stuck in a basement.'

'Then I shall use my mighty brain again to get us out.'

'Well, I guess that means we are going to die down here then.'

'How dare you?' exclaimed Axel. 'I ought to smash your puny . . . Wait! My mighty brain has come up with an idea.'

'Wait!' Alex shouted from inside his sack.

'Wait?' Perse replied. 'Wha' for?'

'Did you say you've got the White Death?'

'Maybe a touch. But it could just be a cold.'

'I dunno about tha',' replied Ned. 'Ya look quite fadey to me.'

'If you let me out,' said Alex. 'I can stop it.'

'We ain't fallin' for that,' said Perse. 'Everyone knows you started this blasted plague!'

'That's a lie,' Alex protested. 'Let me out and I'll explain.'

'Well, we've been told that we've got to bring you to Gloam cos Gloam says you're the reason everybody's dying.'

'It's not true!' Alex shouted. '*He's* the one who has caused it. Please, you have to believe me. I'm the one trying to *stop* it.'

Alex heard the two voices muttering to each other.

'He's just a kid. What harm can he do?'

'Kill us?'

'We're dying anyway, Ned.'

There was a moment's silence, then Alex felt hands untying the sack and light flooded in.

'In just one moment,' Axel cried, his heart full of hope. 'We shall be free!'

And before the others could stop him, Axel ran up the stairs and, with one mighty butt, smashed into the door with his forehead, splintering it in two.

Axel turned to the others and gave a weak smile.

'I . . . did it.'

And then he fell backwards down the stairs, unconscious.

Alex blinked in the daylight, his head suddenly throbbing.

'Now, you keep your distance. You've got two minutes to tell us the cure or the girl gets it.'

Standing next to the cart were two young men – boys, really, not much older than Alex. They wore oversized uniforms, and both clearly had the White Death. In fact, Alex wasn't sure how they were still standing. He could practically see straight through them.

Alex quickly explained exactly why the White Death was happening, how Felonious Gloam had stolen the Book of Lifetales from the Narrator and how that meant everybody's stories had stopped being told.

'The only hope of ending this is if you let me and my friend go. We're going to get the Book back. And when we do, we can stop the White Death.'

There was a long pause.

'Do you believe him?' asked the taller guard, nodding at Alex.

'I seen him, Perse, in the Nest. The Narrator, they called him. Locked up in a cell he was. All skin and bones. So, yeah. I believe him.'

'I'm scared, Ned,' said Perse. 'I don't want to die. I'm fading away. You saw how fast it took Alric. Come on, let's let them go.'

'Screed'll kill us.'

'Screed ain't here.'

'She's going to come back, though!'

'Well, then we'll tell her they escaped. Or, better still, we don't wait for her, we just go. Leave all this behind.'

Perse turned to Alex. 'Can you really stop it?'

Alex nodded. 'I think so. But you *have* to let us go quickly.'

The two guards looked at each other one last time and then, with trembling fingers, Ned untied Lorca's sack.

Ned pulled Alex towards him until they were face to face, and Alex could see tears in his eyes.

'One last thing. I think we're going to die, me and ol' Perse here.'

'Don't say that!' Perse said.

'We are, Perse!' Ned protested. And then more gently, repeated, 'We are.' He turned back to Alex. 'So, you have to promise you'll remember us. You never forget us, right? And maybe tell people about brave Ned and his best friend, Perse, and how they let you go, despite the danger they faced.'

Alex nodded solemnly.

Ned sighed and pointed. 'The Nest is that way. And listen – the only way to sneak in is from underneath. There's a rope that hangs down, for bringing in supplies and stuff. Climb up that – you'll be in. Now, go on then. Get goin'.'

'Thank you,' said Alex. 'I won't forget you. I promise.'

With a final wave, the guards walked off, their arms around each other's shoulders, almost completely transparent.

Alex peered into Lorca's sack. 'Lorca? You awake?'

Suddenly, Lorca sprang out with a fierce yell.

'Ha! I'm free! Nobody can keep Lorca Stonearm trapped for long!' She turned to Alex, who raised an eyebrow at her. 'I wasn't sleeping! I was just resting my eyes. It was so warm in the sack . . .'

Alex smiled at Lorca. 'Come on, sleepyhead. Let's get going. We don't have long.'

'I think he might have really done himself a mischief this time, you know?'

'Shh! He's waking up.'

Axel opened his eyes.

'Oooh!' he said, a dopey grin on his face. 'I feel a little bit oozy-snoozy.'

'You all right, you daft so-and-so?' Sienna asked.

'I feel all dizzy-wizzy.' Axel gave a little giggle. 'But I did it. I used my mighty brain to open the door.'

'But why *headbutt* it?' Irving asked. 'Why didn't you at least try kicking it?'

'Because my mind was moving so fast, my body started working all by itself,' Axel said. Then his hands shot to his head, his face filled with horror. 'My hair! Is it damaged?'

'Looks like somebody's back to normal,' Sienna grinned. 'Your hair is positively *heroic.*'

A moment later, the three were out of the basement. Axel fell to his knees.

'The sweet smell of freedom! I never thought I would breathe such beautiful air again.'

'Come on, get up, it's just the school corridor,' Sienna said. 'We don't have long to get to the tournament.'

'Yes! But first I must find Nathan and his gang. When I get my hands on Aëthelmrir, they shall pay a bloody price for humiliating me,' roared Axel.

'Oi!' snapped Sienna. 'No bloody prices are going to be paid round here. Remember – violence is not the answer.'

'Yeah, come on,' Irving said. 'Honestly, those guys are just idiots. And the thing with bullies is, sometimes the best revenge is to ignore them. And I should know,' he added quietly.

'Why?' Axel gasped, eyes wide. 'Are you a bully, Irving? Shame on you!'

'What?! No, I'm the one who's been bullied!'

'Ah, that makes more sense,' said Axel. 'You are far too physically weak to be a bully. You are as intimidating as a newborn goat.'

'I don't know why I bother.' Irving sighed. 'I really don't. I try and reach out . . .'

'Irving's got a point, though, Axel. Sometimes it *is* best to ignore bullies.'

'But how can I ignore this Nathan Jones?' Axel closed his eyes and hung his head. 'He has tied me up.

He has face-blasted me. And, worst of all . . . he said my hair was stupid.'

Sienna put a hand on Axel's arm.

'Axel, listen. There are different ways to be a hero. Sometimes heroism isn't just about fists and swords. Sometimes you have to walk away. And now this is that time. You have to fight the bigger battle. Your Impossible Quest. You have to defeat the father to save the world, remember? Win that money and save Alex's grandma's home. And save our Alex. So forget Nathan. Walk away. Use your brain. One day Nathan will get what he deserves. Just not today, yeah?'

Axel gave an almost imperceptible nod.

'Sweet, clever Sienna,' he said. 'You have all the makings of a wise old hag.'

'You *what*?'

Irving roared laughing. 'I quite agree, Axel. Now, shall we go defeat Alex's father?'

Axel gave a firmer nod and then a wide grin, which Sienna returned.

'Right –' she looked at her watch – 'we have precisely twenty-four minutes before registration for the tournament finishes. We need to get going NOW!'

'Thank you, Master Uber,' Axel said, waving off the taxi driver twenty-three minutes later. 'You drove with great speed and skill.'

Axel, Sienna and Irving were standing outside the town hall – a great Victorian building, blackened by pollution, gargoyles guarding each of its corners. Hanging above the door was a sign saying *National Chess Tournament*.

'Hurry up,' Sienna said, looking at her watch. 'One minute to go!'

They rushed inside.

'I wish to register for the deadly mind-combat,' Axel declared to the bald man behind reception. He blinked disbelievingly at Axel. 'Hurry, my hairless friend, I have an Impossible Quest to complete!'

'He means he wants to register for the tournament,' explained Sienna.

'You're too late,' the man said flatly, looking back down at his computer.

'Give over.' Sienna looked at her watch. 'We've still got thirty seconds.'

'Your watch is slow,' the man said. 'Now, if you wouldn't mind . . .' He gave a dismissive wave towards the door.

Irving stepped up to the desk. 'You're Stuart Blister, aren't you?'

The man glared at Irving. 'Who's asking?'

'I'm a member of the local Under Fifteen's Chess Club. You were European Junior Quarter-finalist in 2019. I saw you destroy the Icelandic champion Konungur Drottningsonn. You were an inspiration to me.'

'Really?' The man swallowed, his eyes welling up.

Irving nodded. 'You're the reason I love playing chess.'

'Thank you,' Stuart Blister croaked. 'Thank you.' He looked at Axel. 'OK, quickly. Sign here. The entrance is that way.'

Axel signed the form and they scuttled away from the desk as quickly as possible.

'That was lucky,' Sienna said. 'You knowing who he was.'

'Not really.' Irving shrugged. 'I've never heard of him. But he had a name badge on, so I googled him.'

Axel slapped Irving on the back and roared with laughter. 'Brilliant work, my grumpy friend. Looks like I have taught you to finally use your brain. But what in the gods' names is *googling*? Some type of mind control spell? And who is my first enemy in the tournament?'

'OK,' said Sienna. 'There are three rounds you need to get through first. If you do, you'll meet Mr Abiss in the final. The first one starts in three minutes, so you need to get a wriggle on, yeah?'

'Yes,' Axel said. 'And what is it I am wriggling exactly?'

'Just get going, you big muppet. Hall B, seat A12! Go, go, go!'

The first match was over in thirteen minutes. A tiny Bulgarian man was checkmated by Axel in swift fashion. Next match, a stern woman with flattened hair and permanently pursed lips was taken out by a surprise counter-attack. The third was against a devilishly handsome Russian named Alexei Bronsky. He approached the table, signing autographs for the adoring fans who surrounded him, pulled off his sunglasses to wink at Axel and gave him the finger-guns.

'Great gods above!' exclaimed Axel in a whisper. 'Look at his hair! It's . . . *magnificent*. I will never beat Bronsky.'

'Axel,' replied Sienna. 'He looks like a wally. You can beat him, no bother.'

Despite Sienna's confidence, the game was hard-fought. It lasted an hour and went down to the final few pieces.

'You know,' Bronsky whispered as Axel mulled his next move. 'You have excellent hair.'

'Thank you.'

'One day it might even be as luxurious as mine.'

Axel growled in fury and looked like he was going to jump across the board at the Russian.

'Don't let him get to you,' Sienna whispered. 'He's just trying to psych you out. Remember it's war and you need to keep your head.'

Axel glared at Bronsky, then returned his attention to the board, clearing his mind.

Ten moves later, he had checkmated the Russian.

Axel had made it to the final.

It started at 9 p.m. sharp.

'It's the best out of three,' Irving said. 'So don't panic when – sorry, I mean *if* – you lose the first game.'

'Thank you for your vote of confidence, Irving,' Axel said, his voice wobbling. 'I am beginning to fear I might have met my match. See how quickly Mr Abiss dispatched his enemies! Perhaps this quest is *too* impossible. If I lose, perhaps I shall never get home. And nor will Alex.'

'Look, Axel –' Sienna put a hand on Axel's arm – 'I told you. Just do your best. That's all you can do. And don't let him get inside your head. Now get going, you big lug! You can't be late for the final.'

Mr Abiss didn't even look up when Axel arrived at the table, just stared at the board, fingers steepled, utterly focused.

At precisely 8:59, Axel sat down. Neither said a word, waiting for the clock to tick over to nine.

The crowd went silent.

Finally, a buzzer broke the hushed quiet – the game was on.

Axel, who was playing white, moved a pawn forward.

Alex's dad finally looked up. He gave Axel a tight smile.

'I hope you are ready to lose. Then this will be the last time I have to see your disappointing face.'

'I hope *you* are prepared to lose,' Axel countered. 'The game *and* a lot of your money.'

Mr Abiss sneered and moved his own pawn.

'Well, let us see who the biggest loser is then.'

Twenty-one moves later, Axel stared at the board in disbelief.

Alex's father hadn't just outplayed him, he had *annihilated* him, barely losing a piece.

Axel had lost.

A sudden wave of misery nearly knocked Alex off his feet.

'Are you OK?' Lorca asked, putting out a hand to steady him.

Alex nodded, but he could feel gut-churning anxiety creeping through his body like Gloam's flies.

They were walking along the coast, beneath great vertiginous cliffs, vast slabs that jutted out over the jagged rocks and crashing sea.

'Well, not long now,' Lorca said. 'Till we get there,' she added quickly.

'Mmm,' was all Alex could reply.

The truth was, he was too nervous to speak. Too sick at the thought of what was to come. What could he do against the Father of Flies? And even if he did defeat him, somehow, then still ahead of him was the impossible decision. Alex was no closer to knowing what he would do, and the question rolled around his head again and again and again: save Aërth or go home?

There was no answer. No path back to happiness. No hope.

'So, what's the plan then?' Lorca asked. 'How are you going to get the Book back from Gloam?'

'You mean how are *we* going to get the Book back?' returned Alex.

Lorca looked away, a world of sadness suddenly in her eyes.

'That's the thing. And I'm ashamed to say it, what with me being your protector and all, but you see, I'm not sure I'm going to make it.'

'What do you mean?' Alex turned to Lorca, silently begging her not to give him the answer he was dreading most of all.

'It's happening too fast . . .'

Lorca pulled her sleeves back. Both her arms were pale, already almost see-through.

The White Death had spread.

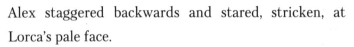

CHAPTER TWENTY-ONE

THE QUEEN'S SACRIFICE

Alex staggered backwards and stared, stricken, at Lorca's pale face.

'Just one of those things,' she said with a brave smile.

'I can't lose you,' Alex said in a tiny voice. 'Not you as well.'

'You won't lose me. Don't worry.' Lorca gave him a light punch on the shoulder. 'It'll be OK.'

'How can you say that? It won't be OK. Nothing's going to be OK.'

'It will! If we can get there quick enough, then –'

'It won't be!' Alex sniffed. 'Remember what the Finding Engine said: if I save Aërth, I can never leave here. I'll never see Gran again.'

Alex waited for Lorca to scream at him for being selfish for even thinking about himself when her whole world hung in the balance, but she said nothing. She simply reached over and gave him a hug. Then held him by the shoulders and looked him in the eyes. She seemed different to Alex. Older, perhaps.

'To live one life is hard enough,' she said. 'But to worry about two must be impossible. So believe me when I say this: whatever decision you make will be the right one, OK?'

Alex nodded dumbly, his heart breaking in two.

'So –' Lorca clapped her hands – 'we have to move quickly now, right?'

Alex nodded again.

'Let's get going, then!'

Lorca started marching, and Alex couldn't help but admire his friend's bravery, even as his heart broke. They walked on until, imperceptibly, Lorca started to flag. Alex took the lead, trying to set a manageable pace, but soon found he was having to slow down more and more.

'Let me carry that.' Alex grabbed the sack she was carrying, and strained, pulling it on to his back. 'What on earth have you got in here? Tell me it's not another dead badger!'

Lorca looked at the ground. 'It was just in case we got hungry.'

'Oh, Lorca, I was wondering what that smell was.'

Once Alex had deposited the dead badger, retching the whole time, they set off again.

The final stage of their journey was utterly devoid of life. The only sound that broke the aching silence was the lonely wind whipping in from the sea. There were no shrill cries of seabirds, no chirping or buzzing of insects, no bleating from timid sheep or lowing of curious cattle in the distance to accompany them. Occasionally they stumbled upon a disappearing body – a spectral leg or the faintest ghost of a face, staring blankly, sinking into the wet earth – but not a single living human.

And then, in the distance, they saw it, clinging on to the side of the vast Black Cliffs like a grey, tumorous growth. The Nest.

The beach below was deserted.

'Why is there nobody guarding it?' asked Alex. 'Shouldn't there be an army or something?'

'Everybody's gone, Alex,' Lorca replied weakly. 'The White Death has taken them all.'

They walked along the pebbled beach, the sea lapping at their feet, until the pebbles turned into boulders, the boulders in turn giving way to angular, dagger-sharp rocks towering over them.

Finally, as twilight settled in and the first stars pricked the cerulean sky, they reached the Nest. Their journey was complete. Skulking in a corner of the foul palace above their heads was the architect of their misery – Felonious Gloam, the Father of Flies.

As Ned had promised, a long rope hung from the underside of the Nest, the only visible entrance to the castle. Deciding to have a short rest before attempting the climb, they set up camp, cowering underneath the bulging castle, and soon a thick fog came rolling in from the sea.

Alex gathered what dry driftwood he could find and started a fire next to Lorca. He hardly dared look at her; even in the glow of the firelight her face was the colour of melting mountain snow. He could nearly see through her arms and legs.

Alex knew he would never sleep. His mind was awhirl, a jumble of fear and sadness and uncertainty. Is this what it felt like to be a hero? Alex had never felt less like one. But Lorca? Lorca, who thought nothing of her imminent fading from the world, and still gave everything to help and protect him? Now *she* was a true hero. Brave, ferocious Fetlock too.

'You OK?' Lorca whispered.

Alex shook his head. 'I'm afraid. I'm always afraid.'

'My mum used to say that fear means you're alive, and that's a beautiful thing,' said Lorca. And then she added quietly, 'I wonder if she's even still alive now.'

Lorca quickly fell asleep, but Alex lay there, watching the fire slowly die.

When the sound came, every muscle in his body froze.

He edged his hand towards his sword, his heart pounding.

Somebody was creeping towards them.

Lorca had woken too, her eyes twinkling in the dark.

Tarka Screed came charging first for Lorca, trying to run her through while she slept. Lorca rolled out of the way and jumped up, brandishing her sword. Alex was on his feet then, pointing his own sword.

'Children –' Screed laughed – 'put down your weapons. You are helpless.'

With a flash of steel, Lorca swung at Screed, but she parried the blow.

Screed also had the White Death, Alex could see now, but it didn't seem to be affecting her strength. Lorca, though, was clearly exhausted and could hardly lift her sword. Alex nervously edged towards Screed, his sword swishing in short arcs.

He got too close, though, and Screed found her moment. With a deft flick, she knocked Alex's weapon clean out of his hand, sending it tumbling through the air. He dived after it, but Screed, with one sharp blow from the hilt of her sword to the back of Alex's head, sent him tumbling to the ground, and tumbling into unconsciousness.

Back in the hall, Axel staggered away from the chessboard.

'One-nil!' gloated Mr Abiss, clapping his hands.

Axel tried shaking his head, but he still felt dizzy. He lurched towards Sienna and Irving.

'Is . . . is this how *losing* feels? It's like I have been struck a mighty blow by a warhammer.'

'That might possibly also be because you destroyed a door with your head a few hours ago,' Irving said flatly.

Sienna glared at Irving, then turned back to Axel. 'Try not to let it get to you.' Sienna gave him a light punch on the shoulder. 'It'll be OK.'

'How can you say that?' Axel asked, distraught. 'If I lose, the quest is over. I will never get home. Gran will lose her home. And your friend Alex will never return.'

'Well, you'd best make sure you win then, hadn't you? Now, you only lost the first game. You've got two more. And, whatever happens, we'll be here for you, OK?' Sienna smiled and gave Axel a hug.

'That's right. Totally,' Irving said, standing next to them awkwardly.

Sienna pulled him in so all three were hugging.

'Thank you,' Axel croaked. 'Alex is very lucky to count you as his friends.'

Sienna looked Axel in the eyes. 'You're our friend too, Axel. A great friend. And I'm sure wherever Alex is, he knows we're all thinking of him.'

'I miss my friends,' Axel said, downcast.

'You have friends?' Irving gasped.

'Yes, many friends!' Axel replied, looking affronted. 'Well, adoring fans, really.'

'Well, focus on beating Mr Abiss and you can get home to them,' Irving replied. 'I mean, have you seen the stupid look on his face?'

Axel had; a smug smirk that made his blood boil. Alex's father looked supremely confident. Perhaps too confident . . .

Axel thought back to what Gran had taught him about weaknesses, and he knew what to do.

'Now, go get him,' Sienna said. 'For Alex.'

Axel nodded. 'For Alex.'

The lights dimmed and the second game started.

Straight away, Mr Abiss went on the attack with a brutal opening that had Axel pinned back.

After half an hour, while Axel was pondering his next move, Alex's father yawned and studied his nails. 'Can we just get this over with?'

Axel smiled and moved a pawn. 'As you wish.'

Mr Abiss swept Axel's pawn away.

'Ooh, nice move.'

'I know.'

'You know, *Dad*, you're doing quite well.'

'Are you trying to distract me?' Mr Abiss snapped. 'Because it won't work – hang on, what do you mean *quite* well?'

'No, I mean *really* well. It's just . . .'

'Just what?' Alex's father spat.

'Well, *some* people are saying that, since you are playing against a child, you should maybe be doing a teensy bit better.'

'What are you talking about? Who said that?'

Axel flapped his hand dismissively. 'Oh, you don't want to know. It's nonsense.'

'Who's been talking? What have they been saying?' Mr Abiss was getting redder and redder in the face.

'Well . . . after the first game, I heard Stuart Blister saying that if you were as good a player as you think you are, you'd be able to beat me in twenty moves. But what does *he* know?'

'How dare he? I'll show him,' Mr Abiss muttered furiously. 'Hurry up!' he snapped at Axel. 'It's your move.'

'Yes, my sixteenth. Only four moves left to twenty.'

'Just get on with it!'

Over the next few minutes, Axel watched as his opponent's game fell apart in front of his eyes. Mr Abiss was so fixated on finishing the game quickly, he completely missed Axel's plan. Before he spotted what was going on, Axel had captured one of his castles. From there, he was on the ropes and a few moves later it was all over.

With a face of thunder, Mr Abiss tipped over his king and resigned.

Axel jumped up and whooped, a rush of excitement coursing through his veins.

It was one game all, with one left to play.

A sudden rush of excitement dragged Alex back to consciousness, his heart thundering.

The moon was fighting its way through the fog, bathing the world in icy silver, and, against it, two pale wraiths were battling, sword clashing against sword, their forms almost totally translucent. It took a moment for Alex to realize who they were. Screed was pushing Lorca back, hitting her with blow after blow, but Lorca was defending herself valiantly, parrying the ferocious attack.

Alex tried to get to his feet, but his legs gave way. He grabbed his sword and dragged himself along the beach towards his friend.

Lorca saw him and screamed, 'Stay back!'

The loss of concentration, a mere moment, was plenty enough for Screed. She forced Lorca back, until she tripped and fell. Screed brought her weapon down and Lorca rolled, but not quickly enough. The sword caught her shoulder and she let out a howl of pain.

Screed lifted her sword above Lorca's chest, but instead of running her opponent through, Screed simply stared down at Lorca with unreadable eyes.

'Help me,' Screed whispered, her face contorted in terror.

And then she vanished.

The White Death had taken her completely.

Alex rushed over to Lorca, and they fell into each other's arms.

'That was all a bit heroic of me, wasn't it?' Lorca wheezed.

'It was,' Alex smiled, tears shimmering. 'It really was.'

A nervous hush rippled across the hall as the buzzer for the third game sounded.

Axel took his seat opposite Mr Abiss.

'You won't distract me this time,' he sneered.

'I won't need to.' Axel eyeballed his opponent. 'It is my destiny to beat you.'

And so, the final game began.

It started slowly, both players cautious, reluctant to advance too fast and leave themselves exposed. Gradually, though, the edgy opening gave way to a brutal tactical midgame battle, with no player really making headway until a deft fork left Axel a pawn down, and then, after another attack, a further pawn and a bishop. With a sense of growing alarm, Axel realized he was on the way to defeat.

He could not lose courage, though. The balance of power had tipped away from him, but now was not the time to give up. Now was the time for bravery. For extraordinary action. For a hero.

Axel made his move.

He could see the greed in Mr Abiss's eyes, that he couldn't quite believe his luck. He moved without a second's thought and the crowd gasped.

Axel had lost his queen.

'Alex –' Lorca gasped suddenly, a look of horror spreading across her ashen face – 'I –'

She collapsed backwards on the rocky ground. She was fainter now, her body and her breath. Alex could see the beach pebbles clearly beneath her.

'I can go no further,' she said, her eyes closing.

Alex had no voice to reply. He knew what was coming.

Lorca's ghostly hands suddenly gripped Alex's arms, her eyes wide open. 'Alex . . .' Lorca whispered. 'Did I protect you well?'

'Oh, yes,' sobbed Alex. 'You did.'

'So, I succeeded in my quest?'

'Yes, of course you did. We made it to the Nest and I couldn't have done it without you.'

'Good.' Lorca gave a sad sigh. 'Then go. Face Felonious Gloam, Alex Always. Write your tale.' Lorca closed her eyes. 'And I shall sleep.'

Alex knew she was right. There was nothing else

he could do for her. He leaned forward and placed a gentle kiss on her forehead. 'Good night, Lorca,' he whispered.

And then she was gone.

Tears dripping, Alex looked up at the rope that hung umbilical-like from the bottom of the Nest, just as Ned and Perse had promised. A climb of easily a hundred metres, straight up.

It's time, Alex thought with grim determination. He started climbing.

The higher he climbed, though, the stronger the wind became. On the ground, it had been no more than a stiff breeze, but now, halfway up the rope, it whipped round him, buffeting him, and it was all he could do to stop himself from being blown against the black cliff face.

Up he climbed, his arms aching and his hands red raw, knowing that if he fell it would be to certain death on the rocks below. The wind came again, fiercer, as if from nowhere, battering Alex, and rain too, soaking him as he swung far above the ground. He knew this was no ordinary storm but something unnatural sent by Gloam, sent to kill him. He clung on for dear life, his arms screaming in pain, his hands slipping on the wet rope.

Finally, as the roaring of the wind stole the sound of his sobbing, exhaustion took him. Just a few metres above was the entrance to the Nest, but it might as well have been a world away.

With growing terror, Alex knew that the storm would take him. He could hold on no longer.

CHAPTER TWENTY-TWO

A MEMORY GIVEN

Sienna and Irving watched in horror as Mr Abiss swooped in for Axel's queen. They knew this was a blow that would be almost impossible to recover from.

Alex's father, meanwhile, was not able to hide *his* feelings – he was practically bouncing in his seat with excitement. The murmuring among the crowd was that the match was as good as done; Axel had been a fierce competitor but in the end Alex's father had just been too good.

The only person who didn't look like he believed the match was over was Axel. He was arrow-focused on the board.

'Losing your queen so easily?' Mr Abiss sneered. 'A final failure, boy. You have disappointed me for the last time.'

'That's the problem with you,' Axel replied. 'You underestimate what's right in front of you. Like your own son.'

Axel moved his knight, forking Alex's father's king and castle.

Mr Abiss's eyes widened in shock and his brow broke into deep furrows as he studied the position. He moved his king and Axel took the castle, quickly following it up by taking a pawn, and then a knight. Suddenly the game was starting to look very different. Mr Abiss began to dab at his face with a grimy handkerchief.

Sienna grabbed Irving's arm tightly. 'It was a sacrifice! Axel lost his queen deliberately.'

Irving's eyes boggled. 'It was bloomin' genius, that's what it was.'

'Sometimes,' Axel whispered over the table to Mr Abiss, 'you don't realize what you have until it is taken from you.'

Axel slid his bishop to the other side of the board, pinning his opponent's queen. Mr Abiss gasped. There was nothing he could do.

For his next move, with a hint of a smile, Axel took it.

Alex's father's head fell in his hands.

The game was now wide open.

A new ripple ran through the crowd: was the impossible about to happen?

And inside Sienna's and Irving's hearts, faint hope began to grow.

As he dangled in despair, a hundred metres above the dagger-like rocks, Alex suddenly felt something blooming inside him – a tiny flower of hope. He still did not know how he would defeat Felonius Gloam, but, by the gods, he would face him!

Using every last ounce of energy, Alex pulled himself up the final few metres of rope and collapsed through the narrow wooden trapdoor at the top.

He was inside the Nest.

It was more like a tomb than a castle, Alex thought; cold, dead and silent. Each room was shaped in a rough hexagon, like a honeycomb hewn from stone, shaped over centuries by creatures other than man. The Nest reminded Alex of the stories he had read of abandoned ships like the *Mary Celeste*; there was still wine in glasses, blood-red and half-drunk, food on brass plates, candle-stubs still sending flickering shadows across the stone walls. But there was not one person alive. He could feel the lives that had departed, though, in the dents on chair seats and lip-marks on glasses.

Alex walked through the echoing, lifeless palace, room after room, as if in an endless dream, with only the sound of his footsteps on the flagstones for company. He eventually found a great, winding stone staircase, each step worn down by the countless footsteps of those who were no more. He started climbing, every step bringing him closer to death, closer to life, closer to home – he knew not what.

Finally he reached the top, the peak of the Nest: a circular platform with a balcony overlooking the grey sea far below. And standing by the low stone wall, hands behind his back, was the author of all Alex's misery. The cause of so many deaths, including his friends'.

Felonious Gloam.

There was something uncanny about the waxen face staring back at him, something horribly unnatural, but it was Gloam, black eyes wide in shock, who seemed more horrified.

'You!' he thundered. 'What are you doing here?'

'I'm here to stop you!' Alex replied, forcing bravery into his voice that didn't come from his heart.

Gloam's mouth twisted into a sneer.

'Axel, my poor, weak boy, we both know that will never happen.'

'I'm not Axel. My name is Alex Always, and I am here to take the Book of Lifetales from you.'

'Of course, the Narrator's last hope! And yet . . .' Gloam's face wrinkled with uncertainty. 'You look so much like my son.'

Alex blinked. That could only mean one thing. Felonious Gloam was Axel's father. *That* was the father he had to defeat to save the world.

Gloam gave a cold laugh. 'You may have Axel's face, but he has none of your courage. Would he have had the bravery to challenge me as you have done, to come through so much hardship, with such foolhardy hope? He was too afraid of his destiny. My son was always such a disappointment.'

Alex heard the echo of his own father in Gloam's words and stood a little taller.

'Maybe,' he said, his chin jutting out. 'Or maybe you underestimated him.'

And then Alex, his heart pounding in his mouth, pulled out his sword and took a step towards Gloam.

'Come,' said Gloam, unmoving. 'Put away your blade. Join me! Become the first witness to what once was and all that shall be! To all that I shall create. You can tell all of my mercy and majesty! Stand by my side as a prince and help me build my new world. Be the son I should have had, not the weakling I was given.'

'You know,' Alex said, his eyes narrow. 'Sometimes you don't realize what you have, even when it is right under your nose.'

'So sentimental.' Gloam sighed. 'Pathetic. Perhaps you are more like Axel than I thought.'

'And perhaps that might be no bad thing,' Alex growled, pointing his sword directly at Gloam. He caught his reflection in the shining steel. He hadn't seen it in such a long time and he was shocked – his journey had changed him, shaped him; he was more muscular, and stronger in the face, stronger in the heart. Perhaps he *was* more like Axel than he had thought. Perhaps he could write his tale after all. Perhaps he could be a hero.

He took a step towards Gloam. 'Give me the Book, Gloam.'

Gloam laughed, mirthless and cruel. He stepped towards Alex and held his hands open.

'Enough of this! We are the last two people alive on this miserable Aërth. What would be the point in us fighting?'

Alex edged backwards, his heart pounding.

'What do you mean *the last two people alive*?'

'It is only we two now. The White Death has done its job.'

'Everybody else is dead?' Alex said, his head swimming.

Gloam nodded. 'We are all that remain. The last two stories left in this world.'

'No!' cried Alex. 'It can't be!'

'It can. And it is.' From inside his cloak, Gloam pulled out a leather-bound book – the Book of Lifetales. 'But together we shall use this to build the world anew.'

Sudden realization blossomed on Gloam's face. 'Together ... That's it. Of course! That was why the Narrator brought you here – not just to defeat me but to take *his* place! You have the same power he did. You are a narrator yourself.'

Gloam licked his lips, his cold, black eyes gleaming. 'You know, I could teach you how to bring your friends back. The girl and the dog. They would live again.'

'No!' cried Alex, although the fire of temptation began to crackle in his soul.

'Join me! I thought I could master the Book but I can only destroy, I cannot create. Without you, this planet will be a dead husk. Together we will create a new world. A perfect world. And you shall tell the story of all that I have done, all the misery and pain I have cured.'

'Never!' screamed Alex, grief for all that he had lost mixing with a volcano of anger. 'Give me the Book!'

'Well, then. If that is how it is to be —' Gloam gave a tired shrug, then drew a sword from the scabbard round his waist — 'come and take it. But know this. With the Book, I have enough power to cross dimensions. When you are dead, I shall not stay in this emptiness alone. Not when there are so many worlds to conquer . . .'

And then Gloam attacked.

Alex felt fear gripping his heart, but this time he did not freeze. No. He roared, and, sword aloft, he charged to meet Gloam.

Gloam sidestepped nimbly and swiped at Alex, slashing his arm. Alex howled, clutching the wound, but Gloam was attacking again, sending him sprawling. Alex fell on to his back, the wind knocked out of him, and his sword went flying. Gloam thrust his own sword, but Alex ducked out of the blade's way and it missed his face by centimetres. Gloam slashed again, but Alex rolled out of the way and was back on his feet immediately.

But Gloam was between Alex and his sword.

'It is over,' Gloam said. 'But take heart. Yours will be the last death in this world. Unless you prefer to swear fealty to me? Kneel, boy, and I shall let you live.'

Alex remembered a time, long ago and worlds away, when he had knelt before Nathan Jones in the sweaty school changing room, his heart pounding with shame. And he remembered the promise he had made to himself.

Today was the day he would keep it.

'Kneel!' Gloam crowed.

Alex stood a little taller and when he spoke there was a quiet confidence in his voice. 'No.'

Gloam shrugged. 'Then prepare to die.'

And he brought his sword crashing down.

Axel attacked, taking piece after piece, forcing Mr Abiss further and further back on the board, until finally he had him cornered.

Alex ducked Gloam's killing blow and, just as Lorca had taught him, rolled under the blade to his own sword. He jumped up, clasping it in his hand.

With a swift strike, he brought his sword down, Gloam only just managing to parry. Alex, his eyes

flashing with fury, rained down blow after clashing blow, driving Gloam further and further back until he was cornered, pressed against the low balcony wall, clutching the Book of Lifetales to his chest. There was nowhere for Gloam to go, just the raging sea below him.

Axel pushed his castle forward. He looked up and saw the despair in Alex's father's eyes.

'Checkmate.'

Alex pushed forward, hacking and slicing, forcing Gloam back. And then Gloam stumbled, tripping over the wall behind him, his arms wheeling desperately. Alex saw the despair in Gloam's eyes, knowing he was finished. He dived forward and swiped the Book of Lifetales out of his hand just as the Father of Flies fell backwards over the wall and down to the dagger-like rocks that waited for him far, far below.

Axel stood up and shook the hand of Mr Abiss, who looked dazed and defeated. He raised his arms aloft.

'I have defeated the evil genius! I have saved Gran's house! My Impossible Quest is complete! I am ready to go home now!' He looked around, waited for a moment, and then shouted again. 'Hello? Gods of Fate? I would like to go back to Aërth, please!'

Alex's father gave him a withering look and shook his head.

'I can't believe I lost to this imbecile,' he muttered, grabbing his belongings. 'Now, out of my way!'

Axel grabbed him by the arm. 'I believe you are forgetting your promise?'

'Ah, you can't think I was . . . ehm . . . serious about that . . .' Mr Abiss burbled.

'The treasure, *father*.' Axel pressed his nose close to Mr Abiss's nose and prodded his chest with a firm finger. 'I shall gladly take it by force, if necessary . . .'

Mr Abiss paled slightly and gulped. Then, pulling out his chequebook, he scribbled on a cheque and slapped it down on the chessboard. 'There! Fifty thousand pounds, as agreed. Now never bother me again.'

And with that he bustled off, a hand over his face, trying to avoid the laughing crowd and all the phone cameras pointed at him.

Sienna and Irving came rushing over.

'You did it!' Sienna beamed, ruffling Axel's hair.

'I knew that barnet of yours would come good.' Then she smiled again. 'Seriously, though, Axel, that was proper amazing.'

'He had a great teacher, though, didn't he?' Irving grinned.

But Axel wasn't beaming as much as they thought he would be.

'You OK?' Sienna asked, concern shrouding her face.

Axel picked up the cheque. 'I completed my Impossible Quest. So why am I still here?'

'What d'you mean?'

'Why have I not gone home? Why have I not swapped with Alex?'

'I don't know, Axel,' Sienna replied. 'But we'll work it out.'

Alex collapsed to the floor, panting. Gloam was gone. He had done it. But there was no joy in his heart. Now he was the last living soul in a cold, dead world. He was utterly alone; just one boy with an impossible choice.

In his hands was the Book, a thick, leather-bound volume decorated with indecipherable symbols surrounding a single word: Lifetales.

He ran his finger over the word. This was it. The moment he had dreaded more than anything.

Now, finally, he had to decide.

If he chose to stay in Aërth, perhaps all the astonishing life that had once teemed upon it had a chance. Lorca and Fetlock, Couth and Kempt, the moonlings, the beautiful Chorus of the Worms – maybe he could bring them all back somehow, as the Finding Engine had promised. But then he would never see his home again – never see Sienna or Irving or, most of all, Gran. And yet, if he *did* choose to leave, he would leave behind a dead world. One that would only ever exist in his memory, and he would have to carry that knowledge until his last day.

Of course, he had no choice.

Alex plucked the All-Seeing-I from his pocket and flicked it open. Sitting on the familiar threadbare sofa was Gran. She was by herself, eating cheese puffs, licking the dust off her fingers. Alex's heart ached – it was just too much.

'Goodbye, Gran. I love you.'

Weeping, he closed the All-Seeing-I.

Once the tears had stopped, he picked up the Book of Lifetales and opened it.

It was completely blank. Not a single word was

written on any of the pages. The story of Aërth was gone.

Alex blinked. What was he supposed to do? Start a new story? But what would he write? He didn't even have a pen.

He sat on the empty balcony until the sun sat low on the horizon, its rays glimmering like jewels on the sea, staring at the blank pages.

And then he remembered the words of the Finding Engine.

```
and always remember - a memory given
is a memory taken.
```

Always remember . . .

Always, remember.

Finally, the words made sense and Alex understood what he needed to do. He had to give his memories.

He held the Book open in his hands and remembered Lorca. He held the picture of her in his mind, the feel of her in his heart. He remembered every detail – Lorca's simple, open face; Lorca staggering round her hovel with a bucket on her head; Lorca handing him his nipple protectors; Lorca, who would die for him without a thought.

And there, right in front of his eyes, words began to appear on the page. They swirled and danced, but gradually coalesced into sentences, paragraphs, chapters, and it became clear what they were.

Lorca Stonearm's lifetale. Her story.

Could that mean . . .?

Although he hardly dared let hope grow, excitement pulsed through Alex's body. He jumped up and ran all the way back down the stone stairs to the room he had first entered, with the trapdoor and the rope hanging down. Taking the Book between his teeth, he clutched the rope and started climbing, ignoring the dreadful drop that yawned below him. He slid the last few metres, the rope burning his hands, but the pain was eclipsed by his desperation to get to the bottom. Finally, his feet thudded on to the rocky beach and he ran through the sea spray down the beach to the place where Lorca had faded.

And there she was.

Sitting up, waving at him, was Lorca.

He threw himself into a diving hug, knocking her clean backwards.

She was solid. So full of life.

Alex laughed and whooped.

'I'm alive!' Lorca grinned.

'You are!' Alex beamed, wiping tears from his face. 'Look at you!'

It had worked. He had given his memory of her to get her back.

But, without knowing, a memory had been taken from him.

THE
MEMORY CHAIN

Still dazed and confused, Axel, Sienna and Irving caught the bus home from the chess tournament, Mr Abiss's cheque tucked safely into Axel's pocket.

'So, I've been thinking,' said Sienna, 'and I wonder if the reason you're still here, Axel, is that Alex still needs to do something in Aërth. If you really are cosmic twins, perhaps he has an Impossible Quest too. You can only go home when both quests are complete.'

'But when will that be?' demanded Axel. 'Alex has no hero training at all. It could take him months to complete even a puny Ticklish Quest. Meanwhile I am stuck here with maths and Nathan Jones . . .' He shuddered. 'And Mr Sunshine.'

'Alex is more resourceful than you think, Axel, he –'

Sienna broke off, doubling over as if she had been punched.

Irving put his hand on her back. 'Are you OK?'

'It's Alex,' she said, tears streaming down her face. 'Something's happened, I can feel it . . .'

'What?'

'I can't explain,' Sienna replied, distraught. 'But he's *gone*. I can't explain it but I think he's forgotten me.'

'How did you bring me back?' asked Lorca.

Alex shrugged. 'I just remembered you and the words appeared in the Book!'

'Try it again!'

Without a second's thought, Alex knew exactly who he wanted to bring back.

He closed his eyes and remembered fierce Fetlock, battling the Sons of Perdition on *Siren Song*, fighting the storm-dragon and saving Alex from the snake in the Silent Forest. But he also remembered wise Fetlock and his quiet words of encouragement and stroking his soft ears in front of a crackling fire.

'It's happening!' whooped Lorca.

And she was right: on the pages of the Book, the lifetale of Fetlock was appearing.

And then, bounding down the beach towards them, was a furry-faced, floppy-eared figure.

Lorca stood up and gasped. 'It's him!'

And then Fetlock was upon them, bouncing and jumping and yelping with excitement.

'Fetlock!' cried Alex, as the three rolled together in a ball of joy. 'Oh, Fetlock!'

But even as he hugged Fetlock close and stroked his ears, which were even softer than he remembered, Alex felt a twinge in his heart, as if he'd lost something precious.

But what could it be? After Gran, there was nothing in the world more important than friends, and Lorca and Fetlock were his two best friends, were they not?

'Oh no!' Irving gasped.

It felt like a piece of his heart had been suddenly scooped out. Inexplicable, overwhelming grief overtook him.

'I feel it as well.' He sobbed. 'Alex has forgotten me too.'

'Do you remember anything?' Alex asked Lorca.

'Remember what?'

'From before. What it was like being dead?'

Lorca shook her head. 'It's hard to describe. One minute I was there. And then I was back. It was like no time passed at all.'

Fetlock nodded in agreement. 'I don't remember what it was like before I was born. And now I don't remember what it was like to be dead. It is as if there is a curtain in the way of my memory.'

'Do you think you could bring more people back?' Lorca asked.

'Like who?'

'Everybody!'

Alex grimaced. 'I don't know about that.'

'Alex,' said Lorca seriously. 'You remembered the path through the maze above the Endless Chasm. You remembered the way to defeat the storm-dragon. You remember *everything* – it's what you do! You've spent *weeks* travelling through Aërth with us, seeing everything and everyone. I bet you haven't forgotten a thing!'

Alex felt a flutter in his stomach. Could Lorca be right? Was this why he had been chosen by the Narrator? For his memory? He closed his eyes and thought back to the start of his journey.

He remembered gristly, balding Grimbald and round-faced, eager Shrude, the first people he had met in Aërth. He remembered Lorca's mother, Chelsee, the young hag who used wrinkle cream to make herself look older. He had promised to her that he would protect Lorca and, with a swell in his heart, he knew he had kept that promise. When her lifetale appeared, Lorca whooped with delight. He remembered Rattlepike, the gloomy dire-elf, guarding the Silent Forest, and Captains Kempt and Couth, doorkeepers of the Infinite Palace. He remembered the grizzled sailor, Alas McClann. And, of course, he remembered Ned and Perse, whose tale he had promised never to forget. He thought of all these people and more – every single person and thing he had seen on his epic journey, and, as he did, an ever-growing storm of words spun into life above the Book, as their tales were told once more.

But for every memory Alex gave, one was taken.

He forgot his school.

He forgot his home.

He forgot the faint fragments of his mother.

And then, finally, he lost the most precious memory of all.

Shell-shocked, Sienna and Irving leaned heavily on Axel as they staggered off the bus. But worse was to come.

As they approached Alex's flat, the door suddenly flew open and Gran appeared.

'Alex!' she cried, collapsing to the ground. 'Alex!'

The trio rushed over to her.

'Mrs A,' said Sienna. 'What's the matter?'

Gran looked up, her body wracked with sobs.

'Alex!' she cried. 'He's gone! Where is he?'

Alex sat back, laughing in delight at the lifetales refilling the Book. But to his surprise, even though he had stopped remembering, new names and lives continued appearing.

Lorca looked over his shoulder. 'Hey, that's my uncle Benny! I was just thinking about him. But you two never met. How's he in the book?'

'Other people must be remembering.' Alex gasped. 'The Book must be restoring the tale of anyone who is remembered. *Everybody's* coming back.'

And so it was. As each returning person looked into their hearts, hearts filled with love and the joy of rediscovered life, they remembered their friends and family. And as those lives were remembered, they returned. And those that returned, each remembered *their* children, their parents, their family, their neighbours. They remembered their close friends and their long-lost friends and their acquaintances and enemies. They remembered animals, the insects and the birds and every possible creature under the sun. An exploding chain of love and memories spread across the whole of Aërth until it was alive and full once again, a world full of beauty and ugliness, a world full of love and jealousy, birth and death, music and noise, pain and awe, but most of all *life*.

And the wonder of it all, the burning bright knowledge of all that life, burst inside Alex's mind as a light so blinding it eclipsed all thought. And he fell to the ground and everything was dark, and the dark was deep and it held on to him, and much time passed before he came back to the light.

Eventually, though, his eyes opened. Above him circled a pair of great birds, wings outstretched, cawing with delight.

'You're awake,' shouted Fetlock. 'Alex, it's incredible!'

Lorca ran over and hugged him. 'There's no more White Death. Everybody's alive. You saved everything, Alex!'

Alex sat up and rubbed his eyes.

'Why do you keep calling me that?'

'Alex? Cos it's your name!'

Alex furrowed his brow. 'Is it? I don't remember that at all.' He thought for a moment and then it came to him.

'My name isn't Alex. It's Axel.'

Fetlock and Lorca looked at each other, then at Alex. 'You aren't Axel,' said Fetlock. 'Do you not remember who you are?'

Alex shook his head.

'You're Alex. Alex Always,' Lorca reminded him gently. 'Try and remember.'

Alex looked at them both, baffled.

'I don't remember anything.'

And then Fetlock had an idea. 'Alex, look in your pocket.'

Alex did. He pulled out what looked like an ordinary compact mirror.

He had never seen it before.

'What is it?' he asked.

'Open it,' Fetlock said.

And so, for the last time, Alex opened the All-Seeing-I.

Carefully, Sienna and Axel half-walked, half-carried Gran back into the flat. They sat her on the sofa and Irving threw a duvet across her lap. Then they all slumped to the floor by her feet.

Axel groaned. 'My heroic brain does not know what

to do. I have completed my quest, yet still I am stuck here. And still Alex is stuck there.'

Gran closed her eyes and let out a long sigh.

'Are you unwell?' Axel asked urgently.

Gran opened her eyes and looked sadly at Axel. 'You really aren't my Alex, are you?'

Axel shook his head mournfully. 'No, I am not.'

Tears started slowly trickling down Gran's face. 'And you don't know when he's coming back?'

Axel shook his head, a lump in his throat.

Gran nodded. 'I didn't want to believe it, but then I felt him forget me. I felt it in my heart. But I hope Alex knows somehow, wherever he is, that I love him so, so much, and that it's time for him to come home.'

As he watched, a wave of love so powerful that it crossed universes washed through him, blossoming into a thousand memories.

'Gran!' he cried. 'I remember! I remember you and Sienna and Irving and Mum. And even Nathan Jones! I remember it all. I remember home. My home.'

As Alex watched, in another world three hearts exploded with happiness.

'Do you feel that?' Irving exclaimed 'It's Alex! He's back. He's OK, isn't he?'

Sienna simply smiled, with tears in her eyes.

'He's OK – and I think he's coming home.'

Alex turned to Fetlock and Lorca.

'I think it's time.'

'Time for what?' asked Lorca. 'Dinner? I bet you wish you hadn't chucked away that badger now.'

Alex did not reply but simply picked up the Book of Lifetales and looked at his friends, two worlds of sadness in his eyes.

Finally, Lorca understood.

'No!'

'I'm sorry,' said Alex. 'Brave Lorca. Dear, sweet Fetlock. My wonderful friends. I think this is goodbye.'

'Is it really?' Lorca asked, tears streaming down her face. Fetlock gave a tiny whimper, his tail low.

Alex simply nodded.

'Then go,' Fetlock said. 'Go with our love. And remember us if you can.'

Alex's face broke into the saddest smile. 'Oh, how could I *ever* forget you? I promise.'

The three shared one last, lingering hug and then Alex opened the Book.

In another world, Axel looked up sharply.

'Do you feel it?'

Gran nodded in reply. 'He's coming home now, isn't he?'

Axel nodded. 'I think so. He must have succeeded in his Impossible Quest, just as I did in mine.'

Gran's face crinkled into a wide smile. 'You did, love. You did.'

Axel turned to his friends and saw they were crying. Then he realized he was too.

'Goodbye, sweet Sienna,' he said, raising a hand in farewell. 'Goodbye, dear grumpy Irving.'

And then he closed his eyes.

Alex closed his eyes and, in his mind, he wrote a start to his tale and an ending to Axel's. And as the words appeared on the pages of the Book, they became real and the universe turned in on itself.

Alex felt himself being pulled away to a place where time and space became meaningless, and there, across a void both impossibly wide and impossibly narrow, he saw Axel, and Axel saw him. Two separate lives and two separate worlds, but together they had shared the same story, and together they now were at the centre of all things.

Alex smiled and raised his hand.

Axel smiled and raised his.

And then there was a flash of light so bright Alex had to close his eyes.

Before he opened them again, he knew.

He was home.

ACKNOWLEDGEMENT
FORM P-611

Please answer the following questions to see if you are entitled to gratitude from the author.

Question 1

Have you ever:

    a) edited or agented the author?

    b) beta-read for the author?

    c) publicized or marketed for the author?

    d) illustrated for the author?

    e) written positive reviews in the media or online?

    f) sent nice letters or flowers to the author?

    g) bought his books for yourself or somebody else?

If you have answered 'yes' to any of the above, congratulations! The author thanks you profusely and you may now ask a favour from him (only one favour per household*).

* The author reserves the right to refuse the favour, depending on how weird it is.

If you answered 'no' to all options in Question 1, sadly you have not earned any thanks from the author. That's a shame. Please now proceed to Question 2.

Question 2

Have you ever:

a) hindered the writing of the author's books in any way?

b) besmirched his good name, either online or in print?

c) chosen to purchase another author's books instead of his?

d) secretly wished for the author's downfall in any way, shape or form?

If you have answered 'yes' to any of the above, then . . . oh dear. Oh dear, oh dear. You have earned one Badge of Shame and Disgrace, and furthermore you owe the author one favour of his choosing*.

---

* You are not allowed to reserve the right to refuse said favour, which is unfortunate because this author's favours can be *very* weird.

Sam Copeland is an author, which has come as something of a surprise to him. He is from Manchester and now lives in London with two smelly cats, three smelly children and one relatively clean-smelling wife.

He is the author of the bestselling Charlie Changes Into a Chicken series (the first book of which was shortlisted for the Waterstones Children's Book Prize), *Uma and the Answer to Absolutely Everything* and *Greta and the Ghost Hunters*. With Jenny Pearson, he has also written *Tuchus & Topps Investigate: The Underpants of Chaos* and *Tuchus & Topps Investigate: The Attack of the Robot Librarians*.

Despite legal threats, he refuses to stop writing.

DON'T MISS ALEX AND
AXEL'S NEXT ADVENTURE

ALEX
VS
AXEL

THE THIEF OF TIME

COMING IN 2025